Praise for *The Hourglass Door*

"I never imagined the adventure I'd find when I opened *The Hourglass Door*. Abby and Dante's world is intoxicating and I didn't want to leave. . . . Mangum's book flowed smoothly and effortlessly and led me through a tale I'll not soon forget."
—www.teensreadtoo.com, 5-star rating, Gold Star Award

"Surprising and intriguing, *The Hourglass Door* is addictive from the very first page to the last."
—YA Book Queen

2009 Book of the Year Award for Young Adult Fiction (*The Hourglass Door*)
—*ForeWord Reviews*

"I found myself swept downriver with Mangum's Abigail Beatrice Edmunds, or as she prefers, Abby."
—www.soullessmachine.com

"With the release of *The Golden Spiral*, Mangum is firmly securing her place in the world of young adult fantasy literature."
—*Deseret News*

THE
FORGOTTEN
LOCKET

Also by Lisa Mangum

The Hourglass Door
The Golden Spiral

THE
FORGOTTEN
LOCKET

A Novel by

LISA MANGUM

SHADOW
MOUNTAIN

Library of Congress Cataloging-in-Publication Data

Mangum, Lisa.
    The forgotten locket / Lisa Mangum.
        p. cm.
    Sequel to: The golden spiral.
    Summary: Abby travels back in time to attempt to save Dante and defeat the wicked designs of Zo.
    ISBN 978-1-60908-049-5 (hardbound : alk. paper)
    [1. Time travel—Fiction.   2. Good and evil—Fiction.]   I. Title.
    PZ7.M31266537Fo 2011
    [Fic]—dc22   2011001698

Printed in the United States of America
Worzalla Publishing Co., Stevens Point, WI

10   9   8   7   6   5   4   3   2   1

For Tracy
Vapor Trails—track 1

PROLOGUE

It is the end of all he knows. He is surrounded by a vast, flat plain. Unbroken and unending. There is nothing ahead of him but emptiness, nothing behind him but pain.

He knows he is the first to arrive in this unspeakable place. Yet he still looks from horizon to horizon, straining to see someone—anyone. But he is alone.

He is on his knees, his hands buried up to his wrists in what feels like sand but isn't really. He doesn't want to look at his wrists; they are still weeping blood from the chains, both from the actual metal cuffs so recently removed and from the newly branded black marks that have taken their place.

The churning in his belly rages like the sea. The air tastes metallic and stale. He doesn't want to draw that alien air into his lungs. He wants to savor the taste of home for as long as he can. Even if it is as fleeting as a sigh.

He has only just arrived and already he is filled with regret. How will he last a month in this place? How, when it already feels like he has been here a year—a lifetime?

A tremor travels up his arms, rolls over his back, and

lodges in his legs, turning his knees to jelly. It is good he is already down; he is not sure he could survive another fall.

He closes his eyes. Faces swim up through the darkness. His father. His mother. His brother. It is for them that he has done this. That he agreed to do this. He chooses to focus on the faces of his family. It is better than focusing on the other faces that hover in his memory. The faces of the dead. So many. More than he thought there would be.

Another face crowds into his thoughts. A narrow, lean face with eyes dark and cruel. A grin splits the face like a blade. Long fingers offer up a single envelope containing life and death, a promise and a threat.

The man who had worn that face had indeed been an angel—an angel of destruction.

Hate sits on his tongue like a thistle, spiked and bitter.

He swallows it down, grateful for the sharp edge that lingers behind his heart. It's easy to hold on to pain. He welcomes it. It helps him resist the crushing pressure that weighs on him.

He is finally forced to breathe, and the last summer-sweet gasp of his past life vanishes like a wish, like a dewdrop at dawn, like a falling star at midnight. He feels his heart beating in his chest, but it doesn't mean anything. It is only muscle memory now, a habit his body doesn't know it can quit.

He opens his eyes. The faint, flat light betrays no hint of time. It could be twilight; it could be dawn. It could be now; it could be never.

It doesn't matter, though. Nothing matters anymore.

He almost laughs. Almost. Almost.

What has he done? What has he become?

He looks again into the distance, as though he can see what waits for him in the future, but all he can see is emptiness.

No, not quite. There is a sparkle on the edge of his vision. A glimmer of something that doesn't belong here any more than he does. Deep in his inner ear he can hear a chime, a bell. A snatch of music in a rising tide. He almost recognizes it. But there is something strange about the tone. A dissonance that makes him think of dark shadows and jagged edges, of teeth about to bite.

He manages to stand. If this is the end, he wants to face it like a man.

The glimmer of light widens, lengthens, takes on shape and dimension. A whiteness cuts through the flat gray of the world. Light fills a tall, narrow space. It is a doorway into forever.

He squints and turns away, but the light pours over him, coaxing him to open his eyes.

Does he dare?

He remembers standing before the other door—the towering black door that separated him and his fate. He remembers the choice: life or death. He thought he had chosen correctly. But perhaps not. Perhaps he was wrong. Perhaps—

The light intensifies until he can no longer bear the darkness behind his eyes.

He looks. The door of light opens, and he sees what waits for him beyond.

And then he falls to his knees, grateful that this moment has the possibility of lasting forever.

Standing before him is an angel clothed in light, her hands on the edges of the door as though poised for flight. The shadows hovering behind her ripple like wings.

She steps through the door and glances around. Surprise flickers on her face. But not fear. Did she expect to be here? Is that possible? Has she come to save him?

She is the one bright spot in an otherwise dark world.

She is breathtaking.

She is his lady of light.

❊

When she steps forward, the darkness seems to part around her. The heavy air shivers with the sound of chimes.

And then the doorway closes behind her. The light is extinguished. They are alone in this strange space.

She looks at him and an almost-smile crosses her face.

He opens his mouth, though he knows he has no words to speak. No words to explain what has happened. No answers. He has nothing to offer except more questions.

To his surprise, she crosses the intervening space, heading directly for him. When she reaches him, she throws her arms around his shoulders.

He doesn't know her, but he welcomes the embrace, suddenly realizing how hungry he is for contact. How fearful he is of being lost and alone. Of being forgotten.

Her hair is damp; her skin is clean and cold. She smells like the sea—all distant horizons and salty tears.

"Leo!" she says. "I can't believe it. You're here; I'm here." Her laugh is almost a cry. "I made it."

He wants to turn around, to see if there is someone else behind him, but her focus is fixed on him and he stays still.

Then she covers her mouth with her hand and surprise flits across her face. "Oh," she says. A mouse-squeak of sound. She bites her lip. "I mean, Orlando. Your name is Orlando." The squeak turns into a laugh. "You look so young. But of course you are. This is the beginning. This is the moment we meet and the start of everything we know. I can't believe it," she says again with wonder. "This is the beginning of *everything.*"

Her accent is odd. She is not speaking Italian, but he can understand her perfectly. There is a hesitation in her speech, as though the words she says are delayed reaching his ears. She doesn't seem to notice, though.

"How do you know my name?" he says. He feels he must be careful with his words, careful with his movements. He feels like glass—transparent, translucent. He does not want to break again.

Her face lights up with wonder and understanding. "I'm here to help you," she says. "If you'll let me." She smiles again, and this time there is no *almost* about it.

Questions pour from his mouth so fast they leave behind tracks of fire in his throat: "Who are you? Where did you come from? Where are we? Do you know how to take us home?"

She sits down in front of him. Her eyes reflect a faraway

memory. Her hand drifts to her neck and she touches a heart-shaped silver locket. "You passed through a door, didn't you? A black door covered with carvings and marks?"

He nods. "They said it was a time machine." The black bands around his wrists throb and itch. They weep. He forces himself not to touch them; he doesn't want to remember the darkness.

He looks instead at her hands, at her fingers that are holding a heart. Her wrists are smooth, bare of any chains at all, but she has other marks, other scars. A thin pattern of links lies on the side of her neck like the shadow of lace.

"It *was* a time machine," she says. "And it worked. And now you are outside of time. Beyond the reach of time."

"Am I . . ." He hesitates, not sure if he should ask the question, not sure which answer he wants to hear. "Am I dead?"

She takes his hand in hers. His heartbeat is suddenly in her hands. She is not afraid of his wounds. "No," she says gently. Her eyes are bright with determination. "No, you're not."

"Then where am I?"

"You are on the bank of the river of time," she says. Her smile is a little lopsided on her face. "A . . . friend explained it to me like this: Time is a river. The river bends and loops and meanders, but it always, only, flows one way—away from the past, and toward the future."

He listens, mesmerized as she speaks of the river of time and of the endlessly barren bank that runs parallel to it. She tells him the rules of his new life, of the need for balance, of how to avoid the dangers that exist for him now both in the river and on the bank.

She is patient with him, answering his questions and explaining and reexplaining until the abstract becomes concrete, until he understands. And then, when he does, when the full weight of the truth crashes down on him, she gives him hope.

"How do you know all this?" he asks. "Did you come through the door too? Are you like me? Is that why you are here?"

Her lips part; she is about to speak. Then her eyes flick up and over his shoulder.

Emotions ripple across her face, one after the other, almost too fast to identify. Almost.

Unwelcome surprise. Untapped anger. Pride and hunger. Vengeance and justice.

But also, for the first time, he sees a touch of fear in her eyes.

He starts to turn, to see what she sees, but she stops him with a touch.

"Do you trust me?" she asks.

He thinks about that question for what feels like a long time. He thinks about the last time he trusted someone, the last time someone trusted him. Does he even know how to do that anymore? Or has it been torn out of him, trapped by a slim white envelope of betrayal, burned out of him by the searing cold darkness of the black door?

He is not sure he knows the answer. He is not sure he *wants* to know the answer.

But she is waiting for him to speak. And as the reflection of fear grows in her eyes, he knows there is not much time.

If he says no, she will take flight and disappear.

His heart decides.

"Yes," he says.

She meets his eyes. "Then don't look back." She jumps to her feet, pulling him with her. Their hands lock together. They run, heading into the vast unknown.

The bank slides beneath his feet, unsteady and uneven. He doesn't know where they are going, but he keeps his eyes fixed on the girl in front of him. He doesn't want to lose sight of her.

He can hear music rising in the distance behind him. But not the silvery, shivery chimes that accompanied him through time. This music is layered, a harmony that seems to reach out to touch the deepest part of his mind, the most secret part of his heart. This music whispers, cajoles, demands. This music is dangerous.

"Don't," she gasps, and he doesn't know if she is talking to him or to the music or to whatever it was that she saw that caused her to run.

He stumbles a step trying to keep up with her. "Wait—"

"We're almost there." She increases her pace, lengthens her stride.

"Where?"

The music seems to increase in volume, dogging their every step, chasing them. He doesn't want to know what might happen if it catches them.

The girl veers to the right, and even though nothing about

the landscape has changed, he knows they have reached something different. Something special.

Skidding to a stop, he looks down. Just beyond his toes is a crack in the world. A deep chasm of light and motion. Fragments of shadow move in rhythm, coming together only to separate in a dance that has no beginning or end. Watching the ceaseless waves, he can hear the faint melody of the past, feel the delicate magic of the future rising up like mist.

He looks into the unspooling river of time, then down at his hands, at the shadows smudged across his wrists. He will never be free of the darkness. He knows that now.

The music is closer, heavy and insistent, trying to turn him inside out. The notes are sharp as claws, burrowing and searching and finding and taking. But the attack is not directed at him. The music wants the girl.

He sees her shoulders hunch under the onslaught. Her eyes fill with tears.

It is too much. He can't stand aside and let her suffer. Not if there is something he can do to help.

He touches her back, her shoulder blades. She trembles like a trapped bird. He turns her to face him. He smooths back her hair, wipes the tears from her cheeks, and covers her ears with his hands.

She wraps her fingers around the black chains on his wrists. The pain is sharp. He grits his teeth. His blood smears. He shudders as a strange sense of foreboding fills him.

She closes her eyes as a flash of pain twists her face.

He can feel a shadow growing behind him, a presence close enough to touch. He can hear someone else breathing.

He tilts his head to the side, turning to see who—or what—has been pursuing them.

She tightens her grip on his wrists. "I'm sorry," she whispers.

And then she falls backward into the river.

He has no choice but to follow.

Braced for impact, he falls into the shifting, shining water. But before he goes under, he manages to catch a glimpse of the man they left behind. A man still standing on the bank of the river, a golden beam of light in his hands and a bone-white grin across his face.

For a moment, the river encircles him, embraces him, welcomes him home.

And then all is forgotten.

CHAPTER

1

"Is this a joke?" Zo stood in front of me, all loose limbs and wide grins. "Did you really think you could escape so easily?"

I looked down at Orlando's body at my feet. His first trip to the bank and back had left him unconscious, which was both good and bad. Part of me hoped he would stay that way, at least for a little longer. I had pulled him into the river specifically so he wouldn't see Zo on the bank. But now Zo had followed us through the river and into a courtroom in sixteenth-century Italy.

And wherever Zo was, danger followed.

Zo strolled across the polished wooden floor. "I remember this place," he commented as though we were on a sightseeing tour. "The judge sat there." He pointed to a high table lined with chairs; in front of the center chair stood a golden set of scales with a small stone balanced on either side. Zo turned and pointed to a spot in front of the tall, black hourglass door, freestanding in its frame. "And I stood there."

I shivered when I saw the dark wooden door. It was still hard to believe what I had done. I had stepped through my own time machine door and walked my way back more than five hundred years to sixteenth-century Italy. I might have doubted it for an instant, but the evidence was all around me. The room where we stood was clearly not from my time or place: no electric lights, no hum from an air conditioner. The furniture looked handmade; each chair had an individual feel to it instead of the uniform look of mass-produced materials. Even the air tasted different.

I had done it. I was here. Really *here*. It felt impossible, but I knew it was true.

I wished Orlando was awake and that we were alone and that we had time to talk. I knew Orlando still had questions; so did I. Like, how had we understood each other on the bank in the first place? Orlando didn't speak English; I didn't speak sixteenth-century Italian.

Then again, maybe it was good that Orlando was unconscious. There were some things I *couldn't* explain. I had told him as much of the truth as I could while we had been on the bank—the rules, the warnings—but Orlando couldn't know the rest. Not about Zo coming through the door. Not about Dante, either. Not yet. Not until I closed the loop and protected the river from Zo's interference once and for all.

"Tony and V were over there." Zo crossed his arms thoughtfully. "You know, they shouldn't have sent all three of us through together. That was just asking for trouble."

"Why did they?" I asked.

Zo shrugged. "My guess is they were still experimenting with how the machine worked and wondered if it could handle multiple people at the same time." He looked down at Orlando on the floor. "Though clearly the machine could handle the weak and the useless."

"He was your friend," I snapped.

Zo shrugged again. "Friends come and go. Enemies, on the other hand, last forever." He did his flickering trick and was suddenly standing behind me.

His quickness was disorienting, though this time I managed to follow his travels. I hadn't been able to last time. Back when we were in the burned-out basement of the Dungeon, he and Dante were flickering too fast to track. Of course, back then, I was different. I hadn't come through the door yet. I hadn't traveled through time.

Zo's mouth was too close to my ear, his hand too tight on my arm. His breath was hot on my neck. "I have something special planned for you, sweet Abby."

"I don't want it," I managed to say. His nearness was unnerving.

"Too bad," Zo said.

And this time, when he flickered, he took me with him.

❉

I hated the bank.

Before, whenever I had traveled here I had been with someone else: Dante, Leo, even V. Or I had been safely co-cooned in a dream where Dante's voice sounded like home. Before, my trips to the bank were anomalies.

Now I had passed through the door. Now I belonged on the bank.

But I still hated it.

I hated the flatness, the emptiness. I hated how much it hurt my eyes to follow the horizon line in the distance. I hated the crushing pressure that squeezed my lungs and crushed my heart.

I remembered the first time I'd felt that overwhelming weight and how it had been Dante's kiss that had helped protect me, acclimated me to my surroundings, and taken away the pressure and the pain. But there were no kisses for me now. There was no need.

The bank was part of my life. No one needed to protect me from it anymore. No one could. If I was going to survive here, it was going to be up to me.

So as soon as we appeared on the bank, I immediately pushed away from Zo, heading toward where I could see the river cutting a path nearby. I stumbled a step or two in my haste and had just found my footing when Zo's voice rang out behind me.

"Don't move."

My body stopped cold.

"Have you forgotten the rules so soon?" Zo said. He sauntered over to where I was standing. He reached out and touched the back of my neck, and I immediately felt a zing of warmth travel down my spine. His breath lingered on my skin. "Here on the bank you have to do what I say. And I say stay."

Part of me chafed against his command, but I had no choice. I couldn't move a muscle, not to bend or blink. I could barely breathe.

"You are surprisingly hard to compel, Abby. Even that

very first time on the bank, when you crossed the bridge and opened the door for me, I found that controlling you was a bit of a challenge. And it seems like the more you learn, the stronger you are." He shook his head. "I foolishly thought the music alone would be enough to stop you. But then you ran from me, dragging Orlando with you, and now I see that stronger measures are required."

Zo circled around me as he spoke, finally coming to a stop in front of me. He wore the same clothes I'd seen him in last time: heavy black boots, dark jeans, and a long-sleeved shirt with the cuffs rolled back to display the golden chains around his wrists. His dark hair, tipped in white, was slicked away from his face. Slung over his back was a guitar, and the strap crossing his chest was embroidered with a maze of golden circles and crescents and stars.

Power emanated from him, glinting off his eyes, sparking in his smile.

I hated that smile. It was the same one he had worn when he had held a knife in his hand. When he had slashed out, cutting across Dante's eyes and making him bleed. I swore I would make Zo pay for every last drop of blood, every last tear, every last heartache that he had caused.

"How did you find me?" I wheezed, every word a stone I had to force through frozen lips. But I did it. I didn't want Zo to think he had won.

Zo laughed with honest enjoyment. "How could I not? You light up the river like fire. You always have. Did you really think Dante was the only one who could see the thread of your life?" He looked around the empty bank. "Where is your little hero, anyway? I would have thought he would come running the minute you were in danger."

"He's coming," I ground out, though it was more a hope than a certainty.

"Does he even know where you are? I suspect it's hard for Dante to see anything at the moment."

"He's coming," I insisted, shoving away the image of Dante's wounded eyes, the blood that streaked his face. "He promised."

Zo brushed aside the idea of Dante and his promises as though he were a pesky fly barely worth swatting. "You never cease to amaze me, Abby. You keep holding on—you keep fighting—long after you should know better. I admit, I thought I had seen the last of you when I left you and Dante and Leo trapped in the basement of the Dungeon with the barriers broken and the river flooding through. That evening should have been your last. But then you managed to open the door—a brilliant move, by the way, crazy, but brilliant—and I knew I would have to do something more drastic."

"I'll never stop fighting," I said, my voice a mere scratch in my throat.

"I know," Zo said sadly. "Which is why you've left me no choice." He flipped his guitar off his back and into his hands.

I tried to turn my head away, but I couldn't. With my body bound, I couldn't even cover my ears to block out Zo's music. Deep down I feared it wouldn't matter. I broke out in a cold sweat. I swallowed down a lump of panic. My heart fluttered in my chest, straining as though I had been running for an hour.

"Let's see, where should we begin?" Zo paced in front of me, his long fingers walking over the strings one by one. "I know. Let's talk about how you killed V."

The notes started slow and quiet, an alternating rhythm that sounded like rain falling or a tribal chant.

"I didn't kill him," I whispered, though my mouth felt filled with dust and my teeth tasted like bones. Guilt was a slippery emotion. I hadn't swung the knife, but I had faltered when it mattered the most.

"Really? Let's review."

A picture formed in my mind's eye, a moment from my past, recent enough to be considered my present, and yet still far into my future. Strange that such paradoxes had become my life.

Zo's music picked up speed, a shadow emerging from beneath the harmonies.

I could see that last moment frozen in place, a slice of time as still as a photograph. The blackened ruins of the Dungeon basement. The black door straight as a guillotine. Four men in the room—Zo, V, Leo, and Dante—and me. Leo and Dante were off to one side, almost out of the picture, a haze of red blood blurring across Dante's eyes. Zo and V were center stage; I stood close by as a knife descended, plunging into V's leg, the blade winking silver along the slash.

"Do you remember this, Abby?" Zo crooned softly. His words wound through the music, slipping and peeking between the notes. "Do you remember what you did to V?"

The image changed ever so slightly. Now instead of holding onto Zo's arm, I was holding onto V, trapping *him* in place.

This was wrong. I knew it in my breath and in my blood.

I let the words flow unchecked, forcing myself to remember the truth even as I spoke it. "No. *You* came to the Dungeon that night. You provoked V, insulting him and taunting him. You tricked Dante into chasing you along the river in order to weaken the barriers. And then you cut him; you hurt him." I felt tears slide from my endlessly open eyes down my cheeks at the memory of Zo's blade cutting across Dante's face, at the sound of Dante's cry. "But I trapped you. I held *you* in place so V could . . . so he could . . ."

"Kill me?" Zo suggested. "He wanted me dead. And he wanted you to do it, didn't he?"

The music was so loud in my head I could barely think. It would be so much easier to let go, to let myself drift away on the rising tide of sound. It would be so easy. It would be so wrong.

"Yes. No." I struggled to keep my thoughts organized. "He was going to kill you, but then you were behind him. *You* forced the blade into his leg. That's how he died. It wasn't me."

I could feel the memory weaken, change into something new.

There was the Dungeon. The door. Dante and Leo. V. And a knife—in *my* hand.

"It wasn't me," I gasped, struggling against the music that seemed to be growing louder the longer I listened to it. "It wasn't. I didn't do it. *I remember.*"

"Are you sure?" Zo's voice whispered in my ear even

though he was nowhere near me. "Are you so sure you can you trust your memories?"

I set my jaw and forced myself to breathe, to count my heartbeats, to find that place of stillness where it was easy for me to slide between, to find my balance. The music that enveloped me seemed to grow quieter as the world around me slowed.

I felt a crack along the edge of Zo's compulsion and seized it. I managed to turn my head and look Zo directly in the eye. "Yes," I said. "I can."

Zo raised an eyebrow, apparently unimpressed by my declaration or my movement. "What about this memory?"

The music changed between one note and the next, and so did the picture in my head.

Valerie sat on the edge of a stone fountain. The conservatory room was locked from the outside. She wore a threadbare bathrobe with a tattered hem. Her eyes were bright, but with something other than sanity. She looked thinner, hollowed out, as though the essence of her had been scooped out and tossed aside. She looked hungry for attention, desperate and alone.

It was bad enough to have seen my friend wasting away in a mental hospital. Seeing her the way Zo wanted me to see her was worse.

"You put her there, you know," Zo said conversationally. "It is your fault she lost her mind."

"No," I said again. "You took her to the bank. That's when it happened. I didn't do it. I tried to help her."

"Obviously not hard enough."

"Where is she?" I demanded. "You left the Dungeon with her that night. What did you do to her?"

"I couldn't very well bring her along on this particular trip. Don't worry; she's safe enough." His eyes narrowed. "But this isn't about her."

Zo's music twisted and Valerie was replaced with Natalie.

"What do you remember about her?" he asked with a hint of legitimate interest in his voice.

How much did he already know about Natalie? I suspected not much. I remembered the first night I'd met Zo. That cold January night when he and Tony and V had played as Zero Hour in the Dungeon. That might have been the only time Natalie had ever met Zo in person. I was glad that I had managed to keep her out of his orbit for so long. Glad that the photograph Dante and I had taken of her kept her safe and stable. I wished I could have done more, but I hadn't brought a camera with me back through time and it would be hundreds of years before such a device would even be made.

I found the crack in Zo's compulsion—the place where the music didn't quite line up—and pushed. I felt it bend, weakening to the shattering point. I could feel my freedom returning, like a limb slowly waking up from numbness. I shook my head, my body prickling with pins and needles. I pushed harder, shoving with everything in me, until it snapped under the pressure and I fell to my knees.

"My memories are my own," I ground out through gritted teeth. "I don't have to tell you anything."

Zo smiled, but not kindly, and paced closer to me. The music cut off as he crouched down by my side. "Why are you fighting so hard? You're only making it worse for yourself." He smoothed back a curl of my hair, his fingers lingering on my cheek. They were slick with sweat and warm from the heat of the guitar strings. "Don't push me, Abby. You won't like what comes next."

I jerked away from his touch, my eyes narrowed. "Nothing I say or do is going to stop you from doing whatever it is you have planned. We both know that. So why do you keep pretending you care what happens to me? It just makes you look stupid."

Zo's body stilled. The expression on his face turned as flat as the landscape around us, but I could see the anger moving behind his eyes. The air surrounding him turned cold, thin and pointed as fractured ice.

"I wanted to do this gently, effortlessly. But now . . ." He stood up, towering over me, his eyes dark and hard as obsidian. His tone was as sharp. "I can't promise that you won't feel pain. And I can't say that it won't make me happy if you do."

He stepped back, his hand curling around the neck of the guitar like it was my throat.

The music he unleashed hit me all at once. A wall of noise and sound overwhelmed my senses, feathering my vision with black, coating my skin with a slick film.

Memories stretched in my mind, elongating into tight, spiraling threads woven with each other into a vast, colorful, living tapestry of my life. The pictures thrummed with power, each one passing through my mind in a blur.

First there were the memories Zo had summoned: V, dying in front of the black hourglass door I had asked him to build. Dante, the darkness from between the doors still cling-ing to his lean body and his eyes weeping blood. Leo, turning to protect his brother, his sad eyes watching me walk away.

The music intensified. Zo hunched over the strings, his fingers striking as fast as lightning.

Other memories: Natalie, smiling while I took a picture to save her. Valerie, handing me an invisible key, telling me stories with a heart of truth.

Sweat lined Zo's brow, a drop sliding down past his closed eyes.

Painful memories: Jason, leaning close for a kiss. Mom and Dad, dancing in the kitchen when they didn't think I was watching. Hannah, painting her toenails and singing along to a song playing in her headphones.

Conflicting memories: Jason, still in love with me when he should have been with Natalie. Jason's house occupied by a different family. My parents, divorced and bitter. Hannah, un-born and unremembered. They had been part of my life—they were still part of my life—and yet, Zo had managed to redirect the river and change them, erase them. Saving them was one of the reasons I had chosen to pass through the time machine door. I tried to hold on to my memories, tried to make them stay.

The river rushed by; I could almost hear the sound of time passing, could almost feel time slipping through my fingers like water.

The memories started to fray along the edges, unravel-ing into individual threads instead of the taut tapestry they had once formed. And as each thread snapped off, torn out of me by Zo's music, a thin tendril of darkness took its place, an emptiness that felt like a scream and sounded like a fading echo.

I knew Zo was a liar. I knew it. And yet, in this he had told me the truth.

It hurt.

A lot.

CHAPTER
2

The music was everywhere. The music was everything. The notes burrowed inside of me, wriggling and writhing and eating away at the darkest parts of me. More and more notes poured into me, gathering together into a solid mass, rising up in a wall of noise. A curtain of black covered me. I was consumed by the music.

Underneath the music, a sound rose up like words, a primal language of pain.

I heard someone scream. I felt the echo of it rattle in my throat.

Had that noise come from me?

I closed my eyes, hoping I could blot out the sight of the man with the guitar who stood before me, hoping I could escape into the darkness.

Eventually the screaming stopped, but I still heard the music.

Eventually the music stopped, but I still felt the pain.

Eventually the man left, and I was alone.

"Don't move."

The voice entered my ear like a needle. I remembered another voice, a darker voice, dripping with confidence and command. That voice had said the same thing to me, piercing deep. And when I had obeyed—when I had been *forced* to obey . . .

My mind shied away from the memory. I could feel my heart beating faster as pain sank sharp claws into me. The salt from my dried tears felt gritty on my lips and tasted bitter.

"Can you hear me? I need you to stay still."

Confused, I tried to open my eyes, but my body didn't want to cooperate. I didn't want to stay still. I had been frozen in place for what seemed like a long time, like forever. I wanted to move, to run, to fly. I wanted to leave behind this place, this empty prison that had locked me in endless pain. I pushed myself to my feet, lashing out at the darkness in my mind, at the voice by my ear, searching for something to hang on to. Something to hit. Someone to hurt.

My fist connected with something solid, the thud sending a jolt through my arm.

"No—stop. Don't." The voice was closer now, and I heard a note of frustration in his tone. Strong arms wrapped themselves around me, pinning my arms to my chest and holding me close against a body hard as rock. "Be still. Let me help you."

I shook my head. No one could help me. I had been cast

adrift in a sea of agony and there was no salvation in sight. I was lost. Trapped.

I managed to crack my eyes open a slit, wincing at the dull gray light that slipped inside.

The world around me extended into a flat horizon line. I felt like I should recognize the vast, featureless landscape, but I didn't.

The man holding me against his chest was taller than I was, and his hair was dark and cut short. His skin, a dusky shade of brown, was smooth, his body toned. His face, from the line of his jaw to the slope of his nose, was all planes and angles. A cloth bandage hid his eyes, spots of blood seeping through like tears.

A swell of apprehension rose up inside me at the sight of the blood. Had I done that?

I didn't think so. Buried beneath the bright red spots on the bandage were darker smudges of older blood. The wound wasn't fresh, but it also hadn't yet healed.

I stopped struggling. I felt like I should recognize the person holding me, but I didn't. No, that wasn't entirely true. My hand twitched, and I knew that if I pressed my palm to his cheek, it would be a perfect fit.

"You're here," I said. The words came unbidden from somewhere inside me, past the pain and confusion, slipping out like a sigh. "You came."

The tension in his face softened and his body relaxed to match mine. His arms loosened into an embrace. "Of course I came," he said. His forehead touched mine. "I promised you I would."

A line of blood appeared at the lower edge of the cloth binding his eyes.

"Your eyes—" I frowned. There was something I should remember about his eyes. Something important. Something that mattered.

He pulled away from me slightly. "I would have been here waiting for you, but I misjudged the time." He shook his head briskly, absently. "I can see you, but not much else. The river, of course. I can still see that. But everything about the river is muddled—the past, the future. It makes it hard to know where I'm supposed to be."

"Be with me," I said. My thoughts drifted as if in a dream. I couldn't stop looking at his mouth. I didn't understand most of what he was saying, but the shape of his lips was mesmerizing. Inviting. I wanted to touch them, taste them. I wanted them to tell me his name.

His arms tightened around me as the embrace melted into a caress. "Always." He exhaled the word, his breath hot on my cheek.

The world around me softened and blurred. The sensation of being in a dream was stronger than ever. I felt lighter than air. I raised myself up on my toes, sure that with that small push, I would float away into the sky.

Instead, my lips met his, and if I had wished to fly before, now I was soaring.

His hands trailed lines of light up my back and along my neck as he held me close to him. His mouth moved on mine with an intensity as fierce as the summer sun.

My fingers and toes tingled, but the rest of me melted into

something soft and ethereal. A breath wrapped around a liquid core.

"Who *are* you?" I asked dreamily when he finally released me and I could speak again. "And where have you been all my life?"

His mouth curved in a small smile. "Are you feeling all right?" he asked with a hint of confusion.

"Mmm, never better," I said, lifting up on my toes again, wanting to taste that smile in another kiss.

Instead he pulled away, moving his hands from my back to my shoulders. He held me at arm's length, and I had the feeling he was somehow studying me with his wounded eyes.

I felt a giggle bubble up inside me. "You're cute when you're serious, do you know that?" I tilted my head to the side, mirroring his position. "Can I see your face?" I asked suddenly. "All of it. I want to see your eyes." I reached up and touched the side of his blood-stained bandage.

He stepped back quickly, shaking his head. "No, don't—"

I lowered my hand, a smear of red on my fingers. "Why not? What happened to them? You're not blind, are you? I thought you said you could see me."

A tremor traveled through him. He controlled it quickly, though his body remained taut and tense.

"Let me see your eyes," I said again, a little worried. "Maybe I can help."

"How long have you been here?" he asked quietly.

I shrugged. "Does it matter?"

"How long?" he demanded in a voice close to a shout.

"I don't know!" I shouted back. "I don't even know where I am. But I know I hate it here."

A muscle twitched in his jaw. "Where is the door?" he asked.

"What door?" I glanced around, wondering if perhaps I had overlooked something, but the barren landscape held nothing but us.

He frowned, a deep line crossing his forehead.

"What is your name?" he asked, but it didn't seem like he wanted to know. It seemed more like it was a test.

"What kind of question is that?" I laughed. "It's . . ." I started. "My name is . . ." And then my mind went blank. Or rather, it went black, the darkness creeping in from the edges of my consciousness. Terror followed, slipping in behind the shadows. How could I not know my own name? A cold sweat lined my scalp, left damp trails down the back of my neck. My mind felt thick with questions, stuffed with noise and chaos.

"What is *my* name?" An edge appeared in his voice, diamond-sharp and demanding. Another test.

I shrugged again, feeling a flare of anger cut through my confusion. "You tell me. You seem to know all the answers before you even ask the questions."

He took a deep breath and his whole body sharpened into stillness. He seemed to gather the quietness around him, focusing it into a single narrow point that he aimed directly at me. "I need you to concentrate. Think back. What's the last thing you remember?"

Frowning, I shook my head. When I pushed at the block in my mind, it pushed back. And it hurt. I didn't want to remember. The block wouldn't *let* me remember. All I knew was that there was a deep emptiness in me that had somehow been filled with an even deeper darkness.

"Close your eyes if you have to," he said, his body and his voice tight with intensity. "Think. Tell me what you remember." He took the step that separated us and placed his hands on my shoulders again, holding me in place.

I didn't have to close my eyes as a memory crashed into me. Just a glimpse. A fleeting impression, gone almost before it arrived. But all at once, I felt myself start to shake. My breathing became ragged, each heavy gasp torn from my body. "A song," I managed. "There was a man playing a song. I remember the music."

Another glimpse bubbled up from behind the blackness. Dark hair. Dark eyes. An aura of confidence. Of power.

"The music took . . . everything," I moaned, covering my mouth with my hands as though I could protect something I'd already lost.

The man standing in front of me made a sound—a half-moan, half-growl—deep in his throat: "Zo." It might have been a name; I couldn't tell.

The darkness in my mind flexed and stretched as though responding to a distant call.

"Zo damaged your memories and left you here to suffer, knowing the bank would finish what he had started." His voice shook with disbelief, cracking with anger. "You can't stay here. It's not safe. You're already dangerously out of balance. We've got to get you back into the river before it's too late." The anger in his voice hardened into resolve, and when he spoke again, he was quiet and serious. "I will not lose you. I will not let him win."

Before I could say anything, he took my hand and led me a short distance away across the unmarked sands to where a river of light flowed. The light was filled with a hypnotic movement that swayed and danced. Images floated along the surface of the river—people, places—but nothing I recognized. Nothing that sparked a memory strong enough to burn through the darkness eating away at me.

He placed his hands on my shoulders and held me firmly.

"Listen to me very carefully," he said. "I'm sending you back through the river. I don't know if your memories will return when I do, but if not, I need you to remember this: When you go through the river, you'll be in a courtroom. A man named Orlando will be there. You'll know him by the marks on his wrists. He has chains, like mine." He pushed his sleeve up over his arm, revealing a band of shimmering gold. "Only his will be black. He can help you. He's a good man; you can trust him."

"How do I know I can trust *you*?" I asked.

In response, he cupped my head in his hands and kissed me hard. "Because I love you, Abigail Beatrice Edmunds. I always have. I always will."

At the touch of his lips, at the sound of his voice saying my name, the darkness inside me seemed to retreat, leaving behind a golden glimmer of light flickering like fireflies. I caught my breath in wonder.

"I will find a way to return to you what was stolen."

My head throbbed, and my lungs labored to draw in even

the smallest breath. Even though I didn't understand what was happening, I knew one thing: I could trust his kiss.

"I'm sorry this has happened to you," he said. "I will make this right. I promise."

"What are you going to do?"

A grim expression settled over his face. For the first time, I was glad I couldn't see his eyes. "I'm going hunting."

Then he pushed my shoulders and I fell back. The river closed over me without even a splash or a ripple to mark my passing.

CHAPTER
3

I opened my eyes, wincing as the flickering light from a row of candles washed across the wall in waves. I was lying on my back on a wooden floor. My entire body ached and my legs were sore. My head throbbed something fierce, and I rubbed at my temples, trying to soothe the constant pounding in my brain. Tear tracks had dried on my cheeks; my eyes felt like they had been scoured with sand. Dust filled my mouth.

Standing up, I took stock of my surroundings. The candles kept the room from being completely dark, and I could see several more unlit candles wedged into sconces on the wall; the yellowish wax had dripped down over the brass brackets like dried honey. The room was crammed with several rows of wooden benches all facing a high table that dominated one wall. Was I in a church? A schoolroom?

A whisper in my mind reminded me that I was supposed to be in a courtroom.

I looked closer. On the other side of the table sat five chairs—two on either side of a center seat on a dais. Resting in front of the thronelike chair was a set of golden scales, balanced, with a small stone in the center of each tray.

I was in a courtroom after all. Strange.

I cast my mind back over the last few hours, trying to follow that little whisper back to its source, but all I remembered was a shadow of a man. A hard kiss. And then a river of light.

Ringing in the back of my ears was a voice: a name. No, two names. *Abigail. Orlando.*

I rubbed at my forehead, feeling confused and lost. I shook my head, hoping the scattered pieces jumbled up in my brain would start to fit together somehow, but the only thing I dislodged was a heavy and hungry darkness. A darkness that didn't belong to me—didn't belong *in* me.

I studied the table in more detail. It was covered with papers, random, disorganized. The candles were burning brightly, but they hadn't been burning long; the wax around the wicks had just started to melt. It looked like someone had been here—and recently—but then was called away.

In the center of the room stood a tall, narrow doorway, a freestanding frame made of blackened wood with images carved all over the surface. A sense of wrongness seemed to emanate from it. Not even the candlelight would come close to the structure, ending instead in a hard line a foot from the door. Looking at it made me shiver.

I wondered what it was.

I heard a groan next to me, and I backed away until my legs hit the high table. I held onto the edge for support.

A man lay on the floor next to the door, one hand pressed to his forehead, his eyes closed in pain. He groaned again, and then he pushed himself up into a sitting position. He shook his head slightly, his dark hair sweeping across his face.

When he opened his blue-gray eyes and looked at me, I felt the world tilt a little to the left before it snapped back into place. There was something about him that seemed so familiar, and yet it was gone before I could catch it.

"Who are you?" I managed. My throat felt raw, like I'd been screaming for a long time.

His eyebrows lifted in surprise. He opened his mouth, but the sound of approaching footsteps stalled his words.

We both looked toward the door—not the black door in the center of the room but the main door behind the rows of benches.

A tall man entered the room, an imperial stride in his step. He wore a long, dark green coat over a pair of brown trousers. Silver stars winked from his high collar. A thick belt crisscrossed his waist, and black boots thumped on the floor. Behind him scurried a second man, smaller and shorter, with a sheaf of papers in one hand, a thick candle in the other, and a satchel over his shoulder.

"Orlando di Alessandro Casella," the tall man thundered, surprise registering on his face, followed immediately by fear, before all emotion was smoothed away. "What are you doing here?" he snapped. Without waiting for an answer, he turned to his smaller companion. "Why didn't you tell me of this, Domenico?"

"I . . . he . . ." the small man stammered. "He wasn't here before. I swear." His eyes darted to the black door in the center of the room, and his face paled even more.

The words the men spoke sounded odd to my ears. I could understand them perfectly, and yet, there was a part of me that insisted the men were speaking a different language. But how could that be?

The man sitting on the floor suddenly rocked to his heels and stood up, his body tall and straight. He held his hands loose by his sides, but I could sense the power coiled in his limbs. He was strong. And clearly not someone to cross.

I noticed his wrists were black with marks that looked like chains. The sight of those chains stirred something in me, but not fear or unease. I felt a shiver of memory brush past, leaving behind a sense of calm and confidence. Whatever was going on, I felt like I was where I was supposed to be. And with a person I was supposed to find.

I took a small step, but the table was in the way. As I bumped into it, the scales tipped over, the metal making a small clang as it hit the wood.

The attention from all three men snapped to me.

"Who are you?" the tall man demanded of me. He gestured sharply to his assistant, and the small man trotted around the room, lighting the extra candles, the flames flickering madly in his haste to illuminate the space.

"How did you get in here?" The tall man took a step in my direction, his eyes dark and angry.

Orlando shifted to block his approach, his slack hands tightening into fists.

"What is your name?" the newcomer demanded of me.

My ears rang with the sharpness of his question and underneath the noise, I heard the memory of another voice asking me the same question. Testing me.

But unlike last time, now a name hovered in my mind.

My name: Abigail. I held it to me like a treasured gift. I didn't want to tell it to these strangers, though; I didn't want to let it go. It was the one thing I could hold on to against the shifting tide of my unsteady memory.

I swallowed, forcing my body to stay still and my mouth to stay closed. My eyes met Orlando's and in his blue eyes, I saw an unexpected calmness. An invitation to trust him.

"I did what you wanted, Angelo," Orlando said to the man in the green coat, positioning his body so he stood between me and him. "I went through the machine, and I came back. It's time for you to honor your promise."

Angelo weighed Orlando with his gaze. His mouth twisted into a frown. "We're not done with you yet."

"You promised—" Orlando began.

"I know what was promised. What I *don't* know is what happened to you. How did you return here? And when? We were not scheduled to open the door until tomorrow."

Orlando flicked a glance at the black door that filled the room with its silent presence. He tugged at the blood-stained cuffs of his shirt, pulling the sleeves down over his hands, hiding his chains. "I came home another way," he said quietly. "The place where I was . . . it was not safe."

At Orlando's words, I had a moment of sensory overload: gray light, a landscape that stretched beyond the horizon, the sound of water falling like broken glass. I pressed my hand to my forehead, but the memory was gone.

"And where—exactly—were you?" Angelo strode forward to the high table, past Orlando, past the black door. He didn't seem disturbed by its ominous nature; he seemed to treat it like it was just another piece of furniture in the room. I didn't think that was wise.

As he approached me, I sidestepped away, skirting the edge of the freestanding door until I was standing close to Orlando. Though I didn't know exactly who he was, I felt like there was something that bound us together, and I knew I would rather side with him than against him.

Angelo positioned himself in the elaborate center seat with all the ceremony of a reigning king. His assistant followed in his wake, quickly setting out the paper on the table and withdrawing a pen and an inkwell from the satchel at his side. Angelo pinned Orlando with a sharp look. "You will tell me everything that happened to you from the moment you stepped through that door"—he pointed at the black frame— "until the moment I stepped through that one"—he pointed at the main door to the room.

Orlando hesitated. Then he folded his arms across his chest, the fabric of his shirt pulling tight across his back. "Why are *you* here?"

"What?" Angelo barked, looking up from a scrawl on one of the papers on the table.

"If you weren't planning to open the door until tomorrow, then how did you know I would be here now? How did you know I had returned?"

Angelo's frown deepened and a muscle jumped along his jaw. "I didn't," he said finally, and I could see what it cost him to admit that. "I was here on other business. Your appearance was . . . unexpected."

"How long was I gone?" Orlando asked, a huskiness in his voice.

"A day shy of one month."

Orlando nodded as though he had expected that answer, but I could tell that it still made him sad.

"Where did you go?" Angelo asked again. He gestured to his assistant, who dipped the pen in the ink and held it over a blank parchment.

Orlando glanced at me, his blue eyes filled with a strange light. "Beyond this life. Beyond time itself. Perhaps even to heaven and back."

Angelo's assistant sucked in his breath in a small gasp. A drop of ink fell to the paper, marring its pristine surface.

Angelo's face paled. He swallowed, and a thin line of sweat graced his upper lip. "Blasphemy," he whispered. "No man could see heaven and live . . ." His eyes rested on the black door, closed and quiet. Now he seemed willing to grant it the fear he had withheld earlier.

I suspected it might be too little, too late.

Orlando lifted one shoulder in a shrug. "You told me what the machine did—what you hoped it would do—before you sent me through. Why is it so hard to believe that it worked? That it did what it was designed to do?"

Angelo kept his gaze on the door, and I could see how his fear was slowly giving way to something else. Something that looked like cunning. Like satisfaction.

His mousy assistant coughed, and Angelo returned his attention to us, quickly masking his expression. "But we sent you alone. So I must ask again: Who is she?" Angelo stabbed a finger in my direction, and I flinched even though I was across the room. "Where did she come from? And why is she wearing men's clothes?"

I looked down at my clothes: blue jeans, T-shirt, sneakers. What was so strange about that? It was what I always wore, wasn't it? I felt a weight around my neck and brushed my fingers over a heart-shaped locket on a silver chain. When I touched it, two faces appeared in my mind, but the images were sketchy. Just fleeting impressions. Two men. Both with dark hair—but one with a fringe of white along the edge, one with a hint of a curl. Both with dark eyes—but one with black, the other gray. Two smiles—one sly, one small. Had one of these two strange shadow-men given me the locket? I couldn't remember.

Orlando didn't even glance at me; he kept his gaze locked on Angelo's face. "I did what I said I would do. I expect you to keep your promises: Protect my family; tell them I died a hero; restore my name—and my honor—in their eyes. And I will keep my promise: I'll leave here and never return."

Angelo shook his head before Orlando had finished speaking. "You have information we need—"

"You know the machine works," Orlando said. "You have your list of names. I don't have to tell you anything else."

Orlando turned to me and grasped my hand before I could do more than take a single step back. He pressed his palm flat against mine.

I felt a flash of energy when our fingers touched, and for a moment his eyes took on a brighter, more electric-blue hue.

"Do you trust me?" he asked, his voice low and private.

I heard an echo of his words, but in a different voice, a different time.

I felt off balance, as though my next step would either be on land or in the air. I would either fall or fly. And either way, my fate would be decided. Would I trust him? Could I? What did my heart say?

"Orlando!" Angelo shouted, standing up behind the table.

"Please, my lady of light."

The words sent a jolt up my spine. I knew that phrase. I *remembered* it. Tracks of fire burned hot in the blackness of my mind until I could almost see the shape of the language on his lips. Could almost see that he wasn't speaking English, but Italian.

How did I know Italian?

"Domenico, stop them," Angelo ordered.

The small man at his side startled, then took a tentative step in our direction.

Orlando held my gaze. I thought I glimpsed an infinite measure of patience in his eyes, but I knew we were running short on time. The mysteries of strange languages, black doors, and missing memories would have to wait.

I knew if I wanted answers, I would have to go with Orlando.

I nodded quickly, squeezing his hand in mine for emphasis.

His sudden grin transformed his face, stripping away the strain and worry I hadn't realized was there until it was gone.

That sudden sense of familiarity was back, stronger than before. He looked so much like someone I knew. But who?

"Then don't look back," he said and pulled me toward the main doors of the courtroom.

"Domenico!" Angelo shouted.

I heard a commotion behind me—the scrape of wood on wood as a chair fell over, the flurry of papers taking to the air—but I didn't look back.

All I could see before me was Orlando's dark hair, his broad shoulders, and his strong arm linked to mine. There was a part of me that hoped he would never let go.

We pushed through the door and into a narrow hallway. More light flickered, this time from torches. My breath surged in my throat, clotted and cloying; I felt like I might throw up. I stumbled, feeling the walls close in around me. My eyes were unfocused, blurry with double vision. I had been somewhere like this before, and recently. Somewhere dark. Somewhere I didn't want to be again.

"Wait—" I gasped, pulling on Orlando's hand to slow him down.

He turned, and I saw the same claustrophobic terror around the edges of his eyes. He wanted out of this suffocating place as much as I did.

I gathered my courage and forced my eyes to focus on the here and now.

Behind us the hallway stretched out long and thin before falling off into a staircase descending into darkness. A guard stood at attention at the top of the stairs. His eyes locked with mine and he bristled with suspicion. He took a step forward.

"Not that way," Orlando said in a hurry. "That way leads to the dungeon. No, this way." He tugged me forward.

Shouts sounded from behind us. A door slammed open, the bang as loud as a drum. I could hear the staccato rhythm of boots thumping on the wooden floor, the crispness of metal on metal. The sound made me think of a knife on bone, or a fingernail scraping over a tightened string. My mind shied away from the mental image, from the music I could almost hear, and I shook my head, trying to concentrate on staying upright and moving forward.

My feet tripped over themselves until I found a fast rhythm. Keeping pace with Orlando, I counted my steps, knowing each one was taking me closer to freedom and the promise of open sky.

Thirty-five, thirty-six, thirty-seven.

Orlando swung around a corner, stuttering to a stop. Three more guards clogged the hallway, each one with narrow eyes and a thin blade. Their intensity hit us like a wave.

"Go," Orlando barked, turning me on my heel and pushing me in front of him as we ran down another hallway.

I could barely breathe; the air tasted like smoke and filled my eyes, my nose, my mouth with ash. I squinted through the darkness through eyes that burned. Was there no end to these narrow hallways?

Sixty-nine. Seventy. Seventy-one.

Orlando grabbed my hand, pulling me to the left, then left again, then to the right, until whatever small sense of direction I had retained was gone.

We ran past seemingly endless rows of torch brackets, the light blurring in my peripheral vision into one thin, unbroken stream of fire. We passed door after door; some stayed closed.

Others swung open, disgorging guards, officers, men with swords, men with clubs.

Five hundred six. Five hundred seven.

My world dissolved into a cacophony filled with shouts to stop, to go, to turn, to wait, to go back, to go forward. I clutched Orlando's hand like a lifeline. As much as I didn't want to be stopped, caught, trapped by the guards chasing us, I didn't want to be lost forever in these twisting tunnels, either.

We ran up a flight of stairs, exchanging rough-hewn stone walls and plain wooden doors for more lush surroundings: colorful carpets and rugs on the floor, tapered candles instead of torches on the wall, even a slice of a window or two. The hallways were empty here on the upper level and, though the sound of footsteps still thundered behind us, I harbored a hope that we might make our escape after all.

I ran until my lungs ached, until my sweat burned, until my legs lost their strength and a sudden cramp locked my muscles. I stumbled and fell to my knees with a cry and—*two thousand twenty-eight, two thousand twenty-nine*—the numbers ran out of my head.

Orlando turned and, without missing a step, reached out to catch me before I fell any further. He lifted me up and then, with one arm behind my back, swung me into his arms.

He was unrelenting, his energy unfailing. I could feel his breath on my neck, the rise and fall of his chest as he carried me toward the door at the other end of the hallway.

I blinked the sweat from my eyes and clutched at the collar of Orlando's shirt.

An *open* door.

Could it be true?

Orlando arrowed his way outside, breaking free from the courthouse without breaking stride.

He headed for the spacious plaza that lay outside the courthouse, his footing swift and sure across the mosaic-patterned cobblestones. Despite the late hour, there were several other people scattered across the plaza, but they were all wrapped in heavy cloaks, heads down, intent on conserving warmth and not getting involved.

I tilted my face to the stars and gulped down a steady stream of cold, clean air. The sweat on my body tingled like snow melting and I felt a trickle of relief slide down my neck and spine.

"Hold on, my lady," Orlando said. "Just another minute . . . we'll be safe in just another minute."

I turned my face toward Orlando's chest. I hoped he was right. I hoped there would be a safe place for us at the end of this journey. But deep in the black place where my memories used to be I feared it would be a long time before I felt safe again.

The sky above was dark and clear, but the air tasted of a coming storm.

CHAPTER
4

When we reached the other side of the plaza, Orlando slipped into the shadows of an alleyway as narrow as a throat before setting me on my feet. "Can you walk?" he asked, holding tight to my forearm in case I fell. His breath plumed from his mouth and nose like steam. His eyes darted from me to the plaza behind us, searching, watching.

I gulped down huge breaths of cold air and nodded. My leg still ached, a sharp pain racing from my hip to my ankle, like someone had stretched a rubber band next to my bone and then lit it on fire. "I can make it," I said, hoping it was the truth.

"Are you sure?" he said, glancing past my shoulder. "We need to keep moving." He shifted his weight forward, his chest still heaving from his run, and I knew he was eager to take flight again.

I followed his glance. Two men were hunting through the plaza, stopping each person, checking each couple. Silver moonlight lined the edges of their bared swords. I could almost hear the time ticking away while we stood in the shadows of the alley. I knew the longer we waited, the more danger we were in. There were still people in the plaza, but not many. It would take only one person to say, yes, they had seen us run past, one person pointing in our direction, and our precarious hiding spot would be exposed.

"My lady?" He squeezed my forearm lightly, but the urgency in Orlando's voice was clear.

I nodded and took a step forward. My sore leg crumpled under my weight.

Orlando caught me, concern filling his eyes.

Goose bumps lifted on my arms. A brisk wind kicked up and my teeth chattered. My skin remembered the touch of summer's warmth and rebelled at the sudden change to winter's bite.

"I don't think I can make it," I said, feeling cold tears sting my eyes.

Orlando rubbed his hands briskly over my arms, but between the shocks I'd already endured and the cold that seemed to be turning me to snow, I couldn't stop shivering. My body felt encased in frozen air, my bones as brittle as icicles.

"I'm sorry," I managed as the tears spilled down my cheeks. "You should go. I'll be fine. I'll catch up—"

Orlando cut me off with a gesture. "No. I'm not leaving you behind."

I blinked as an image flashed behind my eyes. An alternating rhythm of red and yellow lights, the sound of fire cracking open the bones of a wooden building and sucking out the marrow with a scorching tongue.

And then the image was gone as the familiar blackness cut

across my mind like a drawn curtain, denying me entrance to my own memories.

"My lady?" Orlando said again.

I felt divided, body and soul. I shivered violently, but whether from the darkness, the exhaustion, or the winter air around me, I couldn't tell.

He stepped up next to me, encircling me with his arm and pulling me close. His body shook with exhaustion and he pressed his hand to his side as though working away a stitch in his muscles. "I know where we can go. It's there—at the end of the alley. I don't think I can carry you again; do you think you can make it that far?"

Leaning against him, I managed to limp forward one step. Then two. I bit down on my lip to keep my whimpers from turning into a scream.

Slowly, one limping, halting step at a time, we shuffled deeper into the dark alley, aiming for the vertical band of lighter gray at the other end. I tried not to think about the tight quarters, the oppressive sky looming overhead. I avoided thinking about the words *trapped, locked,* and *endless* and focused instead on the words *open, free,* and *horizon.* It seemed to work, for a time.

When we emerged from the mouth of the alley, I looked up and all the words evaporated from my head. I couldn't speak. Towering above me was the most amazing, most beautiful, most elaborate building I had ever seen. A cathedral sparkling with stained glass windows. Walls of smooth gray stones set in intricate patterns. Towers pirouetting to delicate points. A light dusting of snow feathered the edges of the structure like wings.

I couldn't look away. I didn't want to. The mere sight of it filled me with peace and happiness.

Orlando directed us toward the heavy doors; I leaned my weight on his shoulder, trying to keep as much pressure off my leg as possible.

I swallowed, too filled with emotion to speak. We were going *inside* the cathedral. My heart sped up in anticipation.

Orlando pulled open the door and a flood of warm golden light washed out over us.

We slipped inside the church, the door swinging shut behind us.

I had thought the outside of the building was breathtaking, but the interior felt magical.

The moonlight that fell through the stained glass windows diffused into a rainbow of muted colors, softening the edges of the pews and rounding the square corners of the pillars that held up the high arched ceiling. The air felt still and serene in the heart of the cathedral. Statues of saints populated the nooks and alcoves along the wall. A rack of stubby candles stood by the door, many of them lit with the prayers and wishes of the faithful. Further down the aisle, I could see the heart of the nave covered in gold.

A huge mural stretched across one whole wall, countless images of angels within its golden boundaries. From the angel with a flaming sword turning away Adam and Eve to the Angel Gabriel appearing to Mary, the mother of God, to the Archangel Michael battling the dragon as the stars fell from the skies.

"What is this place?" I asked, awed.

Orlando followed my gaze. "It's the Cathedral of the Angels." His voice was reverent, and a little wistful. "My parents were married here. I had hoped—"

His voice cut off as a man in a black robe approached us. The cowl of his robe spilled over his shoulders, revealing a face weathered and worn by age. His white hair was trimmed short, and his eyes were soft and kind. His hands were tucked into the wide sleeves of his cassock. The moonlight outlined a silver cross on his chest.

"Welcome, weary travelers. I am Father Marchello. I hope you find peace and shelter here in the house of God." The priest glided toward us on whispering, slippered feet.

Orlando shifted, his body automatically moving to shield me. "We have come seeking sanctuary, Father."

The priest hesitated, stopping a few feet from us.

"Just for the night," Orlando said quickly. "We—"

A heavy knock sounded at the front door, the sound rolling through the quiet church like thunder.

Orlando pushed me behind him until my back was against the wall and we were out of sight of the doorway. My heart raced and the breath I had managed to catch slipped away from me in a low exhale of panic.

The priest tilted his head, watching us.

The knock sounded again, louder and more insistent.

"Please," Orlando breathed.

I could feel the sweat on his skin where it touched mine, hot and cold at the same time.

Nodding imperceptibly toward us, the priest walked to the door and pulled it open.

"Good evening," he said, nodding his head in greeting.

"I'm sorry to disturb you, Father," a gruff voice said, "but two prisoners have recently escaped from the courthouse. A man and a woman. He is tall, dark hair, blue eyes. She is smaller, thin, with brown hair, and is dressed as a boy. Has anyone matching that description come to the cathedral this evening seeking help? Protection, even?"

Orlando inched back, pressing me even closer to the wall until all I could see was the broad expanse of his shoulders. I could feel the tension in his body like steel. His hand found mine and held on tight.

"God extends His hand to all men who come to the cathedral seeking help and protection," the priest said smoothly.

"These prisoners are dangerous, Father. It is important we find them as soon as possible."

"Thank you for the warning, good sir," the priest said. "If anyone comes to our door who matches that description, I will be sure to personally escort them back to the courthouse."

"I would appreciate that, Father. Thank you."

"Good night," the priest said. The door made a firm thud as it settled closed.

I peeked around Orlando's shoulder, holding my breath, straining my ears in case the guard decided to return. But the church was quiet and still.

"I'm sorry you had to lie for us, Father," Orlando said, his voice low.

"Oh, but I didn't," the priest said, a smile in his voice. "The truth is, if any such people *do* come to the door tonight, I will take them to the authorities. But seeing as how you are *already here* . . ." His voice trailed off as he shrugged. "I doubt I will have much trouble keeping my word."

I heard Orlando exhale a tightly held breath and saw his shoulders drop. He stepped forward, though his hand remained closed around mine. "We are not dangerous like he said. We are simple travelers looking for a safe place to stay. We will be gone at first light, I promise."

The priest paused, as though considering Orlando's words, then he nodded. "Rest a moment. I will bring you some blankets and, if you wish, something to eat. I believe there is something we can spare from the kitchens."

My stomach growled loudly. I winced in embarrassment.

Orlando offered me a slight smile. To the priest, he said, "Yes, thank you. We would be grateful for your hospitality."

The priest nodded again and disappeared through an archway, deeper into the hidden rooms of the church.

Orlando helped me sit on the nearest pew.

"Thanks," I chattered. My breath misted in the quiet church. It was nearly as cold inside as it was out on the plaza. I hoped the priest would be back soon with the blankets.

Orlando frowned. "Wait here a moment." He padded down the aisle toward two tall, closet-sized boxes standing side by side along the wall. He slipped into one side of the confessionals and emerged a moment later with his hands full of an earth-brown cloth. Returning to me, he unrolled it, and I saw it was a cloak. He draped it around my shoulders, and I immediately relaxed into the warmth that covered me from head to foot.

"Better?" he asked.

I nodded, wrapping my arms closer to my body in a hug. "You didn't have to do this. The priest said he'd bring blankets."

"You couldn't wait."

"What about you?" I asked.

"I'll be fine," he said.

Now it was my turn to frown. His face had already turned a wind-whipped shade of red and his lips were shadowed blue. "No, you won't. Here—" I started to shrug out of the cloak.

He sat down heavily next to me, his hand on my arm. "No. You need it more than I do."

Looking more closely at him, I could see the strain in the line of his neck, the anxiety hovering around his mouth.

"Orlando?" I tried his name on my tongue.

He turned, and his eyes softened when he looked at me. "Yes?"

"Do you think he believed you? Father Marchello, I mean. Do you think he'll let us stay the night? Or do you think he'll call the guards back?"

Orlando's gaze lifted to the angel mural on the wall. "By granting us sanctuary, he's bound by all the laws of God and man to let us stay. At least for the night. I don't know what will happen to us in the morning."

"What happened to us *tonight*?" I asked.

"What do you mean?"

"I mean, I woke up in a courtroom, but I don't really understand how I got there. Part of me feels like we just met, yet there is another part of me that feels like I've known you a long time." I laughed ruefully. "I don't think I'm even *from* here, though apparently I can speak Italian—except I don't remember ever learning it. All my memories are scattered, and it's hard to remember anything." I sighed, my shoulders slumping under the weight of my frustration and fear. "Can you tell me where we are? Do you know what's going on?"

Orlando glanced at the archway where the priest had exited, but we were alone in the church. His gaze returned to me, and when he spoke, his words were quiet but intense. "The black door in the courtroom—had you ever seen it before?"

I shook my head. "I don't think so."

Orlando frowned as though I had given the wrong answer. "Did you know it was a machine that could break through the barriers of time?"

I couldn't stop the words from bursting out. "What! Are you crazy?"

His frown deepened. "I'll take that as a no."

"A time machine?" I asked, but the rest of my words died in my mouth. Was such a thing possible? No, of course not. And yet . . .

I'd been trying to force myself to remember something— anything—about my past, but so far, when I looked inward, all I saw was that strange blackness as tall and thick as a wall, blocking me from myself. And yet . . . I felt the darkness inside me shift a little at the thought. The flutter of a veil that offered a mere glimpse at the light behind it. As impossible as the idea was, it had the shine of truth to it.

Was I brave enough to believe the truth, no matter how impossible it seemed?

"I don't know how it is that you can speak my language," Orlando said, interrupting my thoughts, "but you do, as perfectly as if you had been born here. Yet, I can assure you, you are not from this place—or this *time*." He held my gaze with a meaningful look.

I didn't want to ask the question, but I had to know. "You think I'm here because I traveled through time?"

He shrugged his acceptance of the truth. "You said you felt like we had met before. We have. I met you for the first time in a place that exists only on the other side of that black door. A place that is *accessible* only by those who have been through that black door. So how could you have been in that place unless you too had passed through that same black door?"

I leaned against the back of the pew, too stunned to speak. The veil of darkness drifted in my mind again, the gleam of truth shining a little brighter than before.

"Where was it?" I asked. "The place where we met?"

Orlando hesitated, as though debating on what my reaction might be. "You called it the bank and told me how it runs alongside the river of time."

"*I* told you that?"

He nodded. "That's why I'm worried. When you arrived on the bank, you had all the answers. Now, though, clearly something has happened to you to change that. Do you remember *anything* that happened between when we were on the bank and when we were in the courtroom?"

I pressed my hand to my forehead. I remembered pain, and the harsh notes of a song that hurt, but somehow I didn't think that was what Orlando was looking for. I shook my head, ruthlessly ignoring the beginnings of a headache.

"If that door in the courtroom is a time machine, then what year is it?" I asked.

Orlando tugged at his sleeves, revealing the pair of black chains marked around his wrists.

I swallowed. I wanted to reach out and touch the chains, but I didn't dare. It would have been too invasive, too intimate. Instead I reached for the locket around my neck, following the smooth curve of the heart with my fingertips.

He rotated his wrists outward, and where the chains met on the inside of his wrists was a blank circle with two arrows pointing to the midnight mark. Beneath the curve on one wrist were the letters MD; beneath the other were the letters MDI.

He touched the marks with cautious fingers. First one wrist, then the other. "When I left. And when I arrived." He swallowed. "You asked me what year it is. It's 1501. The first month of 1501."

Orlando looked down at his hands. "They marked me like this before I went through the door."

"Why?" I asked.

"They wanted to keep track," he said quietly, "and make me remember."

"Why don't I have them?" I asked. "If I went through the door like you say I did, then where are my marks?"

Orlando shook his head. "I don't know. I don't think you went through the same machine the same way I did." He looked down at his lap, a frown pulling at his mouth. "But they said I was the first. That's what I don't understand." He looked back up at me. "How did you travel to the bank if *I* was the first one through the door?"

I shrugged, barely able to hold on to the conversation, let alone offer an answer. Especially when I still had questions of my own. "Then where did I come from?"

He carefully took both my hands, his fingers still cold from the wind, his skin still smudged with dried blood beneath the black chains.

"I don't know," he said again. "What I do know is that you helped me when I needed it most. You knew what I did not. You gave me the truth—and hope." He paused, a bright light in his blue eyes. "And now I will do my best to return the favor. I don't know where you came from, but I promise I will do everything in my power to help you return home."

Home. The word conjured the sensation of family, of refuge, of chocolate melting on my tongue. Longing welled up deep within me, but I knew that, as much as I wanted to go home, there was something I had to do first.

If I could only remember what it was.

CHAPTER
5

Father Marchello returned with two bowls of broth in his hands and a large blanket draped over one arm. He left them on the edge of the pew, carefully straightening the folds of the blanket. "Is there anything else I can do for you?"

"No, thank you," Orlando replied. "You have done more than we could have expected. We are in your debt."

The priest bowed and silently receded into the shadows.

Orlando waited until we were alone before reaching for the bowls with trembling hands. His face was haggard and pale. His dark hair was stiff with dried sweat and his blue eyes were smudged with exhaustion. As he handed one bowl to me, his sleeve pulled back over his wrist, revealing the hard edge of the black bands marked on his body.

Our eyes met at the same time as our hands did, and I quickly accepted the food, allowing Orlando a moment to tug his sleeves down, hiding the brands.

My eyes caught on the gesture and a wave of memory slid over my eyes. Another cold night. Another hand tugging a sleeve down over a slender wrist. Another set of black chains. And then the memory was gone, lost in the shifting fog. Had

I really seen something? Or was my tired mind simply playing tricks on me? I shook my head. It hurt to try to think around the block in my memory. I had just left behind my last head-ache. I really didn't want to invite another one in.

I swallowed down a mouthful of a warm broth flavored with basil and sweet milk. I could feel the warmth travel all through me. "This is delicious." I sighed with satisfaction and quickly took another drink.

Orlando watched me with a smile. "How long has it been since you've eaten?"

"I can't remember," I said around another mouthful. "Too long."

"Here," Orlando said, pouring some of his broth into the bottom of my bowl.

"Oh, no, I couldn't—"

"I insist." He used his finger to stop the drip of the broth that had spilled over the side. "There is more than enough to share."

I cradled the warm bowl in my hands and looked up at him. "Thank you," I said, knowing that those two simple words were not capable of carrying the weight of emotion that I felt. "For the food, the cloak. And for the information. You're like some kind of hero—rescuing a damsel in distress and every-thing," I said with a half laugh, quickly brushing my hand across my eyes to prevent the tears I felt welling up from fall-ing. I wanted him to think I was brave, even though I felt small and lost and alone at the moment.

"Oh, no, my lady," he murmured. "I'm no hero." A mask of sadness covered his face, seeming to age him as I watched.

The fog in my mind shifted, an almost-memory stirring, but before I could bring it to light, he leaned forward. For a moment I thought he might touch my cheek, but instead he lifted my empty bowl from my hands and set it to the side.

"You should try to rest a little. Morning will be here soon."

I nodded, yawning. I was warm and fed and feeling at peace in a quiet and still place. Rest sounded wonderful. I lay down on the pew, curling up to cradle as much of my body heat next to my chest as possible.

Through half-closed lids, I saw Orlando quietly slip from the pew and wrap the blanket around his shoulders. He walked the few steps to the main doors of the church and stood in front of the window, watching, guarding, protecting.

Between one breath and the next, I closed my eyes and let myself drift away.

❋

The dream was as dark as midnight and as vast as the sky. Woven into the darkness was a thin mist of light, a curtain of song that swayed and chimed. The song wasn't anything fancy or grand, just a few simple notes strung together in a gentle harmony.

And then out of the blackness, out of the mist of notes, a man with a bandage across his eyes emerged.

I had seen him before, hadn't I? I couldn't quite remember.

He strode forward, a lion on the prowl. In his hands, he carried a polished golden guitar like a fresh kill. He wrapped the embroidered strap around his fist and his mouth twisted into a snarl.

"You should know better than to leave your prize possessions unattended," the blind man said. "Why, anyone could just come by and take them and break them into pieces."

For a moment, I thought he was talking to me, but then I saw, standing along the edge of shadow, someone else. A second man. But he was just a blurry outline. Just a shape in the margin of my dream.

Without warning, the blind man lifted the guitar high above his head and brought it down hard, smashing the instrument with a sound of split wood and torn strings. The neck snapped in half. The sudden violence rippled through the dream like a shock wave, silencing the music that had been playing.

The shadow man dropped to his knees, and in the quiet that descended, a roar of rage and pain tore through the dream, blowing the curtain of music to tatters.

The blind man stood tall and still, listening to the wild sound as it built to a piercing crescendo.

After an endless time, the scream finally faded away.

In the silence that followed, the blind man dropped the broken remains of the guitar at his feet, turned, and walked away. The outline of his body blurred along the edges as he vanished.

The shadow man vanished as well, leaving behind the lumps of wood and strings that had once been a guitar.

I was alone again in my dream.

The darkness reached out for me like shadows.

Slowly, the music returned, but hesitantly, the chimes only occasionally ringing.

I thought they sounded a little like a voice, like they were speaking a language I could almost understand. They sounded a little like my name. A little like . . .

"My lady?" The voice came to me on a hurried breath, a tone mostly filled with deference, but underscored with a thin thread of demand.

The shape of my dream shattered as I jerked awake and sat up quickly. I hadn't been asleep for long; the windows were still dark with night. I could feel my heart beating faster, anxious and unsettled. The fragile images from my dream were already fading. There had been two men and a guitar. And there had been music. A song I almost recognized, almost remembered.

I blinked, forcing my eyes to focus, and saw someone in a worn, black cassock standing next to me. He was young—maybe the same age as Orlando, maybe a year or two older—though his black hair was snow-white along the edges. His dark eyes held mine and the light I saw shining in their depths was bright, wild and intense. He hummed a quiet tune, something insistent, something that sounded like the same song I had heard in my dream. The music of my name.

At the touch of those notes inside of me, my heart woke up. A buzz built in my mind, a high, clear note that lifted me with it as it spiraled up through my memories, cutting through the darkness that had weighed me down.

The music was everywhere. The music was everything.

And I suddenly recognized him. I *remembered* him. Seeing

him made me smile; I couldn't help it. I loved him. I *remembered* loving him.

He returned my smile. "I'm so glad to see you." His silky voice matched the music inside of me. "I was worried that perhaps you'd forgotten me."

I shook my head, not daring to speak. Filled with a sudden rush of shy adoration, I felt like I was dreaming again, the world drifting and slowing into softness around me. It was so good to see him. I felt safe, and the lingering darkness inside my mind was comfortable instead of oppressive. I wanted to stay as close to him as I could for as long as possible.

He glanced over my shoulder, and I half turned, following his gaze. Orlando had left his post at the window and was walking slowly down the far aisle toward the nave, his head tilted back so he could look up at the sculpted pillars and the filigree work around the windows.

When he reached the front of the nave, he slid into the first pew and knelt down. He locked his hands together in prayer and closed his eyes.

I turned around. The man standing before me had gone rigid. His breathing turned quick and shallow. A line of sweat broke out across his forehead. I saw an expression of pain pass across his face, tightening the skin around his eyes, before he quickly masked it. When he turned his attention back to me, his face was smooth. His eyes were the black of a raven's wing. I could see how carefully he held himself, as if any sudden movement would break him or make him lose his tightly wound control.

A flutter of emotion filled me, a blend of fear and desire.

"I want you to trust me," he murmured, the music of his voice winding its way deeper into my mind. He reached out to brush the hair back from my face. He wore leather gloves on his hands, the material smooth and soft and strangely warm. The wide sleeves of his cassock reminded me of angel's wings, though in shadow instead of stone. "You know you can."

My doubts disappeared at his touch. Of course I could trust him. I loved him.

"Will you come with me?" he asked, low and urgent.

I nodded immediately and stood up. I would go anywhere with him; I would do anything for him.

He slipped a gloved hand beneath my elbow and drew me deeper into the shadows, leading me to the foot of a statue of an angel. The carved marble wings were curved, not quite unfurled, and the angel's head was bowed, stone tears frozen on his smooth cheek. Standing in the shadow of the angel made me feel like I was sheltered in a protective embrace.

He slid his hand from my elbow down to my fingers. A shudder passed through his whole body, but he controlled it immediately. "Will you do something for me?"

"Anything," I breathed. I leaned forward, eager to hear his request and obey.

"Say my name. I want to hear it from your lips."

My response was automatic. "Lorenzo," I said, and felt a secret thrill pass through me. "Your name is Lorenzo."

"Yes," he said. "That's exactly what I wanted to hear."

He kept his eyes on me as he gently turned my bare hand in his, lifting my wrist and breathing a kiss along my skin.

His mouth never touched me, but I shivered as though it had. I felt heat radiating from his skin with a feverish intensity.

Lorenzo released my hand and my fingers tingled, aching to return to his grasp.

Another shudder suddenly passed through him, but this time he inhaled sharply in pain. He hunched over and pressed his fist to his chest. A drop of sweat slid from his forehead down the side of his cheek.

"Are you all right?" I asked in concern. "What is it? Is there a problem?"

Lorenzo forced himself upright, though I could see the effort it took him. His smile was a fixed grimace. "Nothing I can't manage. Although, there is something you can do for me." He held up his thumb and forefinger, so close they were almost touching. "A small something."

My heart leaped at the chance. "Of course. What can I do? How can I help?" I didn't feel like I had much to offer. But I wanted to do whatever he asked. I wanted to be needed.

Lorenzo closed the distance between us with a single step. He placed his hands on my shoulders, his thumbs brushing down along my collarbone to the heart-shaped locket resting against my throat. The leather of his gloves creaked over his hands.

I held my breath at the nearness of him.

"I need you to give me your heart," he said.

"Is that all?" I said with a smile. "It's yours, you know that. It always has been." I reached up and unfastened the silver chain. I held the locket in my hand, the chain spilling through my fingers like a string of stars. As I looked at the finely engraved lines that crisscrossed the heart, the music that had been in my head turned to a sour note of warning. I hesitated. A shadow of a feeling emerged. A brief memory that the locket was important and that—like my name—I wasn't supposed to give it to anyone.

I shook my head and closed my fingers over the locket, hiding it from sight. The music returned to its familiar sweet melody. This was Lorenzo. He wouldn't ask me for it if it wasn't important. If it wouldn't help him somehow.

I reached for his hand and placed the locket in his palm. A flicker of electricity zinged through me as our fingers touched, and I looked up in surprise. Lorenzo's dark eyes seemed to be even darker and his smile even wider.

"Thank you, my sweet," he said, tucking my locket into a secret pocket of his cassock. "You have indeed given me a gift. One that means more to me than you can imagine."

"I'm glad I could make you happy," I said.

"I know." He tilted my face toward his with the tip of his finger.

I closed my eyes. A fire burned inside me and I knew only his touch could grant me relief.

His kiss was like nothing I'd felt before. A wild storm passed from him to me, filled with unexpected emotions: controlled anger, a hard confidence, a darkly sweet hint of humor. His was a kiss that demanded, that took, and gave nothing in return.

The block in my memories shuddered at the touch of his mouth on mine. The warning note returned, but now it had increased in volume and pitch. This was a warning. This kiss. This moment. This wasn't how it was supposed to be.

I opened my eyes in alarm at the same moment a voice said, "What's going on?"

Lorenzo snapped away from me, his head whipping around, his body humming with controlled tension. "Orlando. It's good to see you again. It's been a long time coming, hasn't it?"

CHAPTER
6

I pressed my lips together, still feeling the touch of Lorenzo's cold fire kiss on them. My neck felt bare; I wanted my locket back. I wrapped my hand around my wrist, hoping to stop the trembling in my fingers. How could a kiss be so wrong? But it was. The sensation of being lost in a dream started to fade, my senses sharpening and alert. Something bad had just happened.

But when I looked at Lorenzo, I feared that what was about to happen would be even worse.

"What are you doing here?" Orlando demanded, his gaze never leaving Lorenzo's face.

"What does it look like?" Lorenzo asked, folding his hands into the sleeves of his robe. "I'm kissing a pretty girl."

I flushed and looked down, confused and embarrassed.

"You're not supposed to be here." Orlando took a step forward, managing to angle his body so he was partway between me and Lorenzo.

"Neither are you."

Orlando frowned.

"Besides, is there somewhere else I'm supposed to be?"

Lorenzo took a step closer to the angel statue, lounging against the wings. The angel rocked a little on the base, unsettled by the extra weight. "Maybe someplace darker? Less sacred? Am I defiling this holy church simply by being here?"

With each mocking question Lorenzo asked, Orlando inched closer to him, his right hand locking into a fist.

"Tell me, Orlando. Why, exactly, are you surprised to see me?"

"Because—" He shot a look at me over his shoulder and then lowered his voice. "Because I thought—"

"You thought I was in prison."

The truth turned Orlando's face red, and I stifled a gasp, looking between the two men.

"And yet, you are the one standing here in chains." Lorenzo nodded to the black bands around Orlando's wrists. "After what you've done, I'm surprised they allowed you to walk free. Then again, I know more about what you've done than you think."

I looked from Lorenzo to Orlando. What had they done?

Lorenzo turned to me, his dark eyes snapping with a wild light. "How much do you know about Orlando? Because he is not who he appears to be."

"He's not?" I blinked. That strange discordant note of warning sounded in my head again, but before I could focus on it, Lorenzo continued speaking, his words clipped.

"Orlando and I have a long history together," he said. "I know he's not above lying to achieve his own purposes. I know he would hurt those closest to him if he thought it would benefit him in the end." He turned a sharp smile to Orlando.

"I know he turned in his own brother to the authorities on a charge of treason."

"That's a lie!" Orlando snapped, his face mottled with rage. "You leave my brother out of this!"

Lorenzo's smile turned into a grin. "We used to be called the Sons of Italy. But he had a problem with authority—with commitment—and was asked to leave the brotherhood." Lorenzo looked at me. "He is unstable and unreliable. He is not to be trusted."

"Who are the Sons of Italy?" I asked. The name didn't sound familiar, but so much of my memory was still blocked or shrouded in darkness.

"We were patriots. Good men who deserved better than to count Orlando di Alessandro Casella among our number."

"They were murderers and liars," Orlando countered.

"You would know," Lorenzo murmured. "Tell me, what did you exchange for your freedom, Orlando? Was it worth it? Has it made you happy?" He pushed away from the angel, closing the distance in a single long stride. "Did it finally make you feel like a hero?"

Orlando's voice erupted from his throat in a wordless roar. He charged at Lorenzo, who moved out of the way so fast that his black robe seemed only his shadow.

Lorenzo laughed, the sound reaching high into the rafters like a song. "Ah, there's the Orlando I remember. You were always the bear in battle. It's nice to see you haven't lost your edge along with everything else."

The two men circled each other, each one placing his feet carefully, unwilling to turn his back to the other.

I crept away from the action, huddling close to the angel for protection.

"Why?" Orlando spat. "Why did you do it?"

"I did what had to be done. Believe me, if you had been in my place, you would have done the same thing."

Orlando shook his head. "I thought we were friends."

"I was never your friend, Orlando. I was your leader. Your superior." Lorenzo arched an eyebrow. "I always have been; I always will be."

"I should never have listened to you." Orlando leaped forward, reaching for Lorenzo's throat.

Lorenzo dodged again, but not quite as fast as before. This time, Orlando caught the edge of his robe and knocked him off balance. He pulled him close enough to lock his hand around his upper arm.

"Did you ever tell me the truth? About anything?" Orlando tightened his grip until his knuckles turned white. "Or were the lies easier for you?"

Lorenzo twisted on his heel and broke free, dancing back a few steps. Anger lit a fire in his eyes. He shook his head slowly, sadly. "I told you what would happen if you crossed me. And I always keep my word. I thought you knew that about me, Orlando."

"I keep my word too. And I swear I won't let you hurt anyone else," Orlando said. "Ever again."

Lorenzo suddenly relaxed, an aura of confidence snapping into place around him. A ghost of a smile appeared, his teeth as white as the snow in his hair. He flicked a glance at me and when our eyes met, I suddenly felt cold.

"But you're too late, Orlando," he said. "As usual."

Then he rushed forward, heading for me and the angel statue. I pressed myself back against the wall, my hands in front of my mouth, praying I wouldn't scream. The man before me bore little resemblance to the man who had kissed me a moment ago. This man was fast and deadly. Eager for violence. Satisfied to inspire fear.

I didn't want this man anywhere near me.

Orlando reached for me, but he was too far away.

Lorenzo stopped. He wasn't coming for me after all. He grabbed the angel's wing and pulled. The stone figure toppled off the pedestal, crashing to the floor. A wingtip snapped off with a sound like breaking bone. A crack appeared along the edge of his face, cutting across his eyes. A second crack ran along the floor, as thin as a thread, but quickly branching out into an entire network like a fractured web.

Orlando and I both looked at the broken angel in stunned surprise.

"Here now!" Father Marchello's voice rang out from behind Orlando. "What do you think you're doing?"

"You can't stop me, Orlando," Lorenzo said, his boots covered with a fine layer of white stone dust. "And what's done is done." He met my eyes for a brief second. He winked at me, and then, like the shadow man from my dream, he disappeared.

I gasped. Where had he gone?

The last vestiges of the dreamlike feeling that had cocooned me disappeared as suddenly. I blinked, barely able to believe what my senses said had happened. The faint music that had seemed never-ending had been cut into silence. Sparks wavered along my peripheral vision. My fingers trembled, but then so did the rest of me.

"What's going on?" Father Marchello continued. "I heard shouting—" He stopped short, the words caught in his throat. "The angel. What happened to the angel statue?" His earlier kindness had vanished, and an ugly red flush began creeping up his neck.

"I . . . I'm sorry, Father," Orlando stammered. He looked at me, his eyebrows lifted in confusion and surprise.

"You did this?" He marched forward and grabbed Orlando by the arm, pulling him out of the dark alcove and into the light of the cathedral.

Orlando didn't resist, stumbling along behind the priest, his gaze still fixed on the spot where Lorenzo had vanished from sight.

"We grant you sanctuary, and this is how you repay us?"

I stepped through the broken fragments of the angel, careful not to disturb the dust or displace the shards of stone. I felt like crying. The angel had been so beautiful, and I had felt so safe standing in his shadow. I wanted to lift him back to his place of guardianship, but I knew I couldn't do it alone. And even if I could, he would never be the same. There were too many cracks. Too much destruction.

"Why? Why would you do such a thing?" Father Marchello demanded. "Have you no respect? No honor for our holy statues? I should call the guards and have them take you back where you belong. Not dangerous, you say? Bah!"

Orlando didn't meet the priest's angry stare. Instead he meekly bowed his head and accepted the berating in silence.

What had happened to the Orlando who had faced Lorenzo with energy and intention, with fire? Why didn't he simply say it was Lorenzo's fault?

"What do you have to say for yourself?" Father Marchello asked.

"What's done is done," Orlando said quietly, his face a mask. He looked as pale as the broken statue at our feet. And as sad. "I'm sorry, Father. Truly. I didn't mean for—"

If Orlando wasn't going to say anything, I would. It wasn't fair to let him take responsibility for something he didn't do. "It's not his fault. He didn't break the statue."

"Then who did?" Father Marchello asked, folding his arms across his chest. "Certainly not you."

"It was Lorenzo," I said. This time his name left a bad taste in my mouth.

Father Marchello frowned. "I know of no one here by that name."

"He's not here now. But he *was* here. And he's danger-ous—" As soon as I said it I knew it was true. The trembling in my fingers increased. And I had kissed him? I had given him my locket? What was wrong with me?

"Then where is he?" Father Marchello looked around at the deserted cathedral. "Did he disappear into thin air?"

Orlando shot me a look; I saw some of that old fire in his eyes, and I stayed silent.

Father Marchello pointed to the main doors. "Out. I want both of you out of my church. Now."

Orlando lifted himself to his full height. A quiet strength and dignity settled over him like a mantle. He held out his hand to me. "Will you come with me, my lady?"

A swirl of memory stirred. Orlando, his hand extended, a question on his lips. I had trusted him enough to take his hand once before. Would I trust him enough to do it again? Lorenzo's voice came back to me: *He is not to be trusted.* I pressed my lips together, feeling once more the burning touch of his mouth on mine, the sweep of darkness at the mere thought of him.

It wasn't like that with Orlando. When I was with him, I didn't feel the same danger or distrust. And with Lorenzo gone, my mind felt clearer, stronger. I knew what I had to do. What I *wanted* to do.

I put my hand in Orlando's and let him lead me out of the cathedral.

Neither one of us looked back.

�֍

Cold winter sunlight had opened up the night, spilling the morning into the plaza outside the cathedral. The day was waking up, and the plaza was already crowded with small knots of people milling about, along with a few merchants who had set up stands to display their wares. But even with Orlando walking next to me, I still felt lost and alone in a strange place. A light breeze brought with it the smell of hot food, but I wasn't hungry.

At least not for food. I wanted answers. I was starved for

stability. I felt like I had been tossed and turned on an ocean of uncertainty and there was no land in sight. I was hurt and frustrated and confused.

I wrapped my cloak tightly around me, as though the rough fabric could hold me together. I knew there was something wrong with me, a heavy block separating me from my past and my memories. No matter how hard I looked at it, examined it, or attacked it, I couldn't seem to break past it. When I tried to remember something, I ended up with a blistering headache, though, strangely, some memories and images seemed to sneak up on me when I wasn't trying.

What was hiding behind that darkness? I wondered. A history filled with family and friends?

Or was it hiding horrors? Nightmares that were best kept in the dark? Maybe it was a mercy that I couldn't remember. Maybe this was my chance to start fresh with a new life in a new place.

No. The farther down that track I thought, the more wrong it felt.

I wasn't supposed to be starting over. I was supposed to be continuing.

But doing what? Going where?

I shook my head and blew out my breath in frustration.

I glanced at Orlando, walking beside me. There was something comforting about having him nearby. I had chosen to trust him more than once; I would choose to trust him a little longer. Orlando had led me from the courthouse and saved me from Angelo's guards when he could have easily left me behind. Orlando had promised he would find a way to take me home.

I thought about the narrow black door standing in the depths of the courthouse. Did I dare reenter the building and cross through that door? If it really was a time machine, would it lead me home?

I sighed. Too many questions and not enough answers.

I stopped in my tracks as a sudden, piercing pain started at the base of my neck and radiated up through my head.

I clamped my eyes shut, rubbing at my forehead and pinching the bridge of my nose. It didn't help much. The pain snaked thin tendrils down my limbs, following the path of my veins and making my blood tingle.

"My lady? Are you all right?" Orlando asked.

At least, that was what I thought he said.

A roaring erupted in my ears, the sound of an ocean crashing on a wide expanse of beach, and my vision blurred, the world around me smearing into wide paint strokes of color. I felt lopsided and unbalanced as the seams that held me together started to unravel.

I was no stranger to pain, but this was a level beyond the muscle cramp I had endured yesterday. It wasn't even like the pain that accompanied the flicker of my returning memories or the heaviness of the block in my mind that kept them away.

My breathing quickened and my heart spun in my chest.

No, this was something different. Something worse. I had never felt this kind of unconnectedness before. A looseness that made my skin feel two sizes too big for my bones. A tightness that made my nerves feel like frayed wires, pulled taut and sparking with ungrounded power. A pressure that reached into every cell of my body and *squeezed*.

Orlando's face swam into view, but it was only lines and shapes. Two circles floating inside an oval. A line of a mouth cutting through like an arrow.

His hands grabbed my shoulders—someone else's shoulders? It was hard to tell anymore where the edges of me were. "Stay with me," he ordered.

But though I wanted to obey, tried to obey, I couldn't.

I closed my eyes and felt myself falling forward—or was it backward? My balance was gone. Directions were slippery and meaningless.

I counted the number of seconds it took me to surrender to the approaching darkness.

Fewer than I thought it would be.

❁

My body knew it was a dream long before my mind did. There was a different kind of pressure surrounding me than before. It was still uncomfortable, just this side of painful, but at least it was a pressure my body recognized.

I opened my eyes and sat up, surprisingly unsurprised to see a vast, empty plain stretching around me all the way to the horizon.

My memory roared to life. I recognized the vast wasteland around me—*the bank*. I remembered a silver thread of light, images unspooling along the length of it, light dancing off the churning waves—*the river*.

I had been here before. Or *almost* here. I wasn't fully on the bank or in the river, but had managed to drift between them, ending up on the strange dream-side of the bank.

And I wasn't here alone.

I turned in a circle and came face-to-face with another girl my age. Her black hair was ragged; so were the hems of her skirt and shirt. She crossed her arms against her chest. The light flickered oddly around her body as though she were a ghost, turning the shadows on her skin from silver to gray to gold.

Even though the edges of her appeared wispy and faint, her eyes snapped with anger, and her pale face had two bright red splotches on her cheeks.

"He's mine!" she spat. "You can't have him."

Stepping back, I blinked in confusion. My head still hurt a little from the changing pressure I'd experienced. My ears felt stuffy, the sounds reaching me on a delay.

"Who?" I asked. "Who are you talking about?"

"Don't play stupid. You're not stupid, and it will just make me madder if you play pretend with me."

"I'm not pretending," I said, holding up my hands, palms out, in an effort to calm her down. I felt like I should remember her name, but even here in my dream the bulk of the block in my memory remained intact. "I honestly don't know what you're talking about."

She laughed, a high, keening sound that circled up into the flat sky like a flock of birds. "When the Pirate King sings, and the Pirate King dreams, then we all fly away on the Pirate King's wings," she chanted.

The hairs on my arms stood up.

"And what the Pirate King knows, isn't what the Pirate King shows, and we all must follow where the Pirate King goes," she continued.

I took a step back. Dream or not, I didn't want to be any closer to this ghost-girl with the strange light in her eyes and the naked note of madness in her voice.

"I don't understand what you want from me," I said. "Who are you?"

"He kissed you. He made you his," she cried, ignoring my questions. I wondered if she could even really see me, if she was even really here. "You gave him your heart!"

My fingers automatically went to my throat, but my locket was gone. Given away by my own hand to a man I thought I knew, thought I remembered. A man this girl called the Pirate King.

"And now you belong to him," she said a little sadly, but I couldn't tell if she felt sorry for me or for herself. Tears of hurt and anger shimmered in her eyes.

A chill sense of dread circled in the air around me, close but not yet closing in.

"But I will fix it." The gleam in her eye shifted to something darker and more cunning. The outline of her body rippled like water. "I know how to fix it. I will make the River Policeman arrest him and throw him in prison. He belongs in prison. And once he is gone, everything will be all better."

She turned her gaze on me, and I realized she wasn't a ghost at all, but a real person who could somehow see me even in my dream. The dread hit me full force, covering my body and stealing my breath.

"Oh, yes, you may belong to the Pirate King now, but I will make the River Policeman mine. And then we'll see. Oh, yes. Then we will see."

CHAPTER
7

I woke up with a gasp, my heart thudding in my chest and my hands reaching for something I had already lost. The locket I wanted to find was still gone, my fingers touching only the thin, interlocking links of scars looped around my neck.

Unlike other dreams, this one was still clear and sharp in my memory. I could still see the strange girl's piercing eyes, hear her fluttering laughter. I felt I should remember who she was, but I was exhausted and my emotions were tangled up in a messy mix of anger, confusion, and impatience. I was tired of living with so many questions. I wanted answers, and I wanted them now.

I sat up and looked around at my new surroundings, surprised to see I was in a shop of some sort. A heavy cloak had been folded into a makeshift bed for me.

The morning light spilled in from two round windows. Hanging outside one of them was a sign that read *Casella Apothecary*.

I lifted my eyebrows in surprise. That was part of Orlando's name.

The sign was edged with an intricate band of squares

carved into the wood, each one joined to the next in a repeating pattern of angles. Trying to follow the carved lines with my eyes made me dizzy and I blinked several times to clear my vision.

The air tasted of something bitter and metallic, and also something sweet. Almonds, maybe. Whatever it was, the combination set me at ease. I got to my feet and, once I found my balance, I explored the shop in a little more detail.

It was smaller than I had first thought. A fire crackled in a hearth tucked away in one corner. Rows and rows of glass bottles were displayed on smooth wooden shelves lining the walls. The bottles were different colors and sizes; some had liquid in them, others contained what appeared to be small rocks or crystals. A few even appeared empty except for the smoky smudges on the inside of the glass. Each bottle was neatly labeled and organized.

I caught my breath as a memory stirred. A comfortable place. A row of glass bottles. A gleaming counter spanning the length of one wall.

Looking up, I saw Orlando behind a counter, grinding something with a mortar and pestle. A large cup rested off to the side, surrounded by an assortment of bottles and boxes, some half open. He hummed a light tune, but when he saw me, he dropped the pestle in the bowl, and his song turned into words.

"What are you doing up? Are you all right?" He came out from behind the counter, concern wrinkling his face.

"I'm fine," I said, holding out a hand to forestall his hovering.

He glanced past me toward the windows, then hurried across the room. He peeked out one window and then quickly closed the shutters.

"What happened? Did I faint?" I asked.

"Collapsed is more like it." Orlando frowned and returned to his work at the counter. "One moment you were standing beside me, and the next . . . you were gone. All of you. You vanished." His voice trembled, shadowed with amazement and a little fear. "But just for a moment. Then you came back. You were unconscious, so I picked you up and carried you here." He drew his eyebrows together. "Are you sure you are all right?"

"I'm fine," I said again, but with less conviction than before. I hurried on, before he could call my bluff. "Is this where you live?"

Orlando hesitated, then shook his head. "Not anymore. Not for a long time. This is my father's shop. I'm hoping that if the guards are still looking for us, they will have already checked here. We should be safe here. For now."

I glanced at the closed shutters and nodded. "Won't your father mind us being here?"

"Father always spends this time of year traveling to the other villages and towns to sell his wares and to gather supplies and ingredients. He shouldn't be back for a couple of days."

"Ingredients?" I asked. "Is he a cook?"

He smiled and another flash of memory burned. But strangely, it wasn't a memory of Orlando, but of someone else with the same smile, someone whose eyes made me think of shadows and storms. Not a raging winter storm filled with ice and razor-sharp wind, but a summer storm filled with blown clouds skidding across a blue sky.

"No, my father runs this apothecary. He sells medicines, poultices, and custom blends for all kinds of illnesses, aches, and ailments. You were in pain; I thought if there was anything that could help, it would be here." Though he waved in the general direction of the counter where he had been concocting some unknown potion, his blue eyes remained fixed on me, their expression hard as steel. "But clearly you're suffering from something far more serious than headaches and exhaustion."

"I . . . I had a bad dream."

Orlando looked at me in disbelief over the bridge of his nose. "My brother used to have bad dreams. This is something different. Something more. You *disappeared*. What happened?"

I blew out my breath, trying to organize my thoughts. "I don't think I have a simple answer."

"Then be complicated."

I picked at the seam of the cloak I wore. I didn't even know where to begin. I barely understood what was going on myself, let alone knew how to explain it to someone else.

"Yesterday you said that you couldn't remember your past. Is that part of it?" he prompted.

I nodded.

"So tell me what you do remember. Maybe that will help." He led me to a pair of chairs close by the fire.

I sat down and leaned into the warmth, watching the flames dance to the crackle and spit of the burning logs.

Between the flickering motion of the fire, the heat, and the rare feeling of sitting still for a moment, I was able to open my mouth and let the words spill out. I told him everything I could think of, everything I could remember. It wasn't much. And it made even less sense when I tried to string it together into some semblance of a timeline or a story.

Orlando listened to me intently, without a single interruption or pause for clarification.

When I finished, I leaned back in the chair, the sweat on my forehead not entirely from the fire's heat. Exerting that much pressure against the dark block in my mind left me feeling like I had run a hundred miles. My head throbbed in time to my heartbeat.

"Can I have something to drink?" I asked. My mouth felt sticky and dry at the same time.

Orlando took a few steps and plucked the cup from among the jetsam on the counter. He handed it to me. "This should also help with your headache."

"How did you know I have a headache?" I asked. The cup felt oddly heavy for all that it held no more than an inch of liquid.

"Because I have one too," he said.

"Sorry," I said. "I know it's a lot to take in." I sniffed at the cup, identifying a combination of rosemary and lavender. I took a sip. The liquid felt a little like oil on my tongue, but it was soft and cool sliding down my throat.

He watched me take another sip, a considering look in his eye. "May I ask you something?" He hesitated, waiting for me to nod. "How do you know Lorenzo? Do you trust him?"

My hand reached to my throat where my locket used to be. I thought hard about Orlando's questions. Yes, there was a part of me that trusted Lorenzo—or at least thought I should. But the more I examined the dark part of me that told me I wanted to be close to him, the more false it felt. It didn't feel *real*. It didn't feel like *me*. It was a paper-thin *want* rather than a solid *reality*.

I remembered Lorenzo's face when he asked me for my locket and his kiss that felt more like a bruise than a caress. I remembered the taunting sneer in his voice when he fought with Orlando. I remembered the darkness in his eyes when he broke the angel statue and left us behind to clean up the mess.

I clutched the cup in my hands until my knuckles hurt. "Do you?" I countered quietly, but curious. "He said you were both known as the Sons of Italy. He also said you should have stayed in prison. What was that all about?"

The blood ran from Orlando's face, draining the blue from his eyes and leaving them gray. He lowered himself back into his chair like an old man. His expression shuffled from anger to shame to resignation. "That part of my life is over," he said quietly, looking away. "What's done is done."

I touched his arm and made him look at me. "Lorenzo said that too. What does it mean? What have you done?"

He thinned his lips to a hard line. "It doesn't matter. But I don't trust Lorenzo, and I know you shouldn't trust him either."

"I don't," I said bluntly. "Not anymore." At my words, I felt like a great weight had been lifted from my shoulders. The darkness was still there in my mind, but perhaps not quite as dark as before.

I looked down at the cup in my hands. I drank the last drop, and while my headache disappeared along with the liquid, my heart still hurt—and so did my soul. I felt turned inside out and rubbed raw.

"So what am I supposed to do now?" I asked, not really expecting an answer. "When am I finally going to find solid ground again?"

Orlando was quiet for a time. "I'm sorry, I don't know what you want me to say. I don't know if I have the answers you need. I'm as confused about what's happening as you are. I have questions too." He touched my wrist, applying enough gentle pressure to encourage me to lift my eyes to his. "And I hurt too."

He did; I could see it in his eyes, in the creased flesh around his mouth. I could hear it in the sound of his breathing, in the space between his words.

"I feel like this is all my fault," I said. Tears slipped down my cheeks, hot and salty; the back of my throat held the lingering flavor of rosemary.

"Oh, lady," he said quietly, brushing away the tears.

His kindness only made me feel like crying harder. I felt a deep, unexplainable loneliness. The part of me that was struggling to break free from the darkness in my mind felt like there was someone else who should have been there with me. Someone who knew all the answers I didn't, who knew the real me.

"It will be all right," Orlando soothed. "*We* will be all right."

"How? When?"

"Eventually," he said.

"Oh, great. That makes me feel a lot better." I scrubbed at my face with one hand, trying to force the tears back into my eyes.

"This is not your fault. Pain like this doesn't last forever—it *can't* last forever—and when it's gone, you'll feel better. We both will."

"I'm tired of waiting," I sighed.

"So am I," he said quietly. He brushed away my final few tears and leaned back. "So maybe it's time to do something about it."

"What do you suggest?"

"I think we should play a game."

It was perhaps the last thing I expected him to say, and my tears vanished in the wake of my small laugh. "A game? What kind?"

"It's a game I used to play with my brother when he was little. He used to have bad dreams all the time, and when he woke up in the middle of the night, I would try to ease his fears."

"By playing games?"

"Sometimes. Other times I told him stories. Or I gave him riddles to solve or poems to memorize. Anything to distract him and occupy his mind."

"So what was this game?"

"We called it Impossibility. One of us would present an

impossible problem and then we would both try to come up with as many solutions to the problem as we could. The best idea won."

"And our impossible problem is . . ." I prompted.

"A girl has lost her memory. How does she get it back?" Orlando finished.

I raised my eyebrows. "And what is your solution?"

"She takes a magic potion and is instantly healed."

I lifted my cup in his direction. "Sorry, that didn't work. You lose."

"I didn't say it had to be a good solution—or even workable. The idea is to come up with *creative* solutions." He gestured toward me with an elegant wave. "Your turn."

Accepting his invitation, I folded my feet under me on the chair. "She finds a journal she kept and reads about everything she forgot."

"Not bad." Orlando smiled in approval. "But that's assuming the girl kept a journal."

"As opposed to assuming she could find a magic potion to drink, you mean?" I tilted a look in his direction. "I thought the only rule was creativity."

"It is. Go again."

I shook my head. "Not my turn."

Orlando steepled his fingers and tapped them to his lips. "What about this?—the girl finds someone who recognizes her and has *that* person tell her all about her past."

"How am I supposed to find someone who recognizes me when I don't even belong here?"

"Interesting question. We'll have to save that impossible situation for another round," Orlando said with a grin.

I laughed. "And playing this game helped your brother sleep?"

"Actually, no, not very often," Orlando said. "What did work, though, was when we'd come down to the fireplace, and I would brew up a warm drink for him to help him sleep." Orlando nodded at the empty cup still in my hands. "He was particularly fond of Father's special tea, too. Though when I made it for my brother, I always mixed in a wish."

"A wish?" I repeated. A quiet memory chimed inside, a feeling of light and the taste of pink.

Orlando nodded. "He always took his wishes very seriously. He would stop and think for a long time about exactly what he wanted to wish for. And his wording was always exact—it wasn't 'I wish for happiness,' but 'I wish for the sun to shine tomorrow so that the flowers will bloom and make Mother happy.'" He shook his head in fond memory. "He was always more concerned about other people than he was about himself."

"What kinds of things did you wish for?"

Orlando turned his attention to the fire, avoiding my gaze. "Oh, I never made a wish myself."

"Why not?"

"I don't know. Maybe it was because I didn't want to look at my life and see what was missing. Once you identify what you lack, then it's all you see anymore. Wanting something I couldn't have would only lead to unhappiness, so I tried to be content with what I had."

"That's terrible," I said. "It misses the whole point of wishing. It's not to focus on what you don't have; it's to show you what *could be*. Once you know what you want, then you know what to reach for, what to dream about. It's how you change things."

"What would you wish for, then?"

"A solution to my impossible problem," I said without hesitation.

Orlando was quiet for a long moment. "What about this solution? Maybe if we go to the bank, and look back in the river, you'll see something that will spark a memory, or even bring them all back."

I bit my lip. My only solid memory of the bank was from my recent nightmare, and I wasn't sure I wanted to go back to that barren wasteland again. What if the real thing was even worse? What if that angry girl with her cryptic warnings and threats was still there, waiting for me?

"It's a creative solution," Orlando pointed out. "Besides, it couldn't hurt."

"You don't know that," I retorted, feeling unsettled and off balance. "What if going to the bank is what is causing my memory loss?"

"What if staying in the river is making it worse?" Orlando countered. "You said that was one of the dangers of being in the river for too long—having it wash your mind clean. You also said that when we felt out of balance, we were supposed to go to the bank to find that balance again."

"I said all that?"

He nodded.

I sighed. "All right. I'll go. But promise me we'll leave at the first sign of trouble."

"There won't be any trouble," Orlando said with confidence, patting my arm.

But I wasn't so sure.

CHAPTER
8

The bank was exactly as I had left it.

The river, however, was not. I remembered it as being a single flow of light and images, of time tumbling head-long from the past toward the future. Now, though, the light was dimmer, and I could see where a grayish film coated the surface in places, making it look polluted. Worse, a few faint silver lines had branched out from the main body of the river like threads fraying off a woven rope.

I looked at Orlando, but his eyes were closed, a furrow of pain crossing his forehead.

"Orlando?" I touched his arm and his eyes opened.

"I'm sorry, what did you say?"

"Are you all right?"

He nodded. "It's just . . . I haven't been back since . . ." He shuddered and a muscle jumped in his jaw. "I had hoped I wouldn't have to come back so soon."

"Maybe it won't be so bad," I said, though we both knew I was glossing over the truth. "Once we get used to it, I mean."

"I don't think I'll ever get used to this place." He exhaled slowly, his body still tense, but less so. He rubbed his chest in the spot over his heart. "At least the pressure is gone. That's something."

Orlando looked down at the river and frowned. He studied the wild rush of time that swept past us, almost too fast for the eye to follow. Crouching down, he examined one of the thin silver offshoots that had started to peel away from the main body of the river. He twisted around to look at me over his shoulder. "Let me guess. It's not supposed to be doing this, right?"

I shook my head. "I don't think so, no."

"Do you know what's causing it?"

"I'm lucky I remember enough to notice the difference."

Orlando stood up, dusting his hands together. "I wonder how far it extends. Maybe this is an isolated instance." He looked into the distance, squinting as though that might help him see farther in the flat light of the bank.

"Somehow I don't think we'll be that lucky."

We walked together along the edge of the bank, careful to make sure our steps didn't touch either the river or the newly created streams branching off it.

It didn't take long to confirm my worst fears. Once I knew what to look for, I saw the fragments of time everywhere. Hundreds, maybe thousands, of silver threads spooled off the river. Some of them pulsed with a brighter light than others, seeming to flow faster and stronger. I watched as a thin thread was absorbed into the larger stream next to it and I shivered.

Orlando stopped and I drew up next to him. Up until then, we'd manage to keep the river on our right-hand side, following the various twists and turns like a path through a labyrinth, but now the way was blocked.

The river forked into two distinct and separate directions. The main river still ran straight forward, but a new thread had broken off and curved to the left, cutting through the bank directly in front of us. The second stream was more narrow and the flow more sluggish than the main river.

"Is this as bad as I think it is?" Orlando said quietly.

I nodded, too terrified to speak.

"So if the river has become so unstable that it is branching apart, which clearly it is"—he gestured to the evidence in front of us—"then what happens when it unravels completely?"

I closed my eyes, briefly blocking out the sight of the fraying river. The implications of Orlando's deduction were too massive, too terrible. I didn't want any of the answers I thought of to be true.

"What can we do to stop it?" Orlando asked. "We have to stop it, right?"

"I don't know if we can," I said.

Orlando pointed across the river. "What's that?"

I rose up on my toes, looking past Orlando's outstretched arm to see what had drawn his attention, and my breath caught in my throat.

There was someone else on the bank besides us. A tall figure strode forward out of the barren landscape, his steps sure-footed and swift. Dark black hair swept back from his forehead. The harsh, flat light cut sharp angles across his face and turned the bandage over his eyes into a swath of shadow, but as he drew closer, I realized it was a face I recognized.

This was the man I had met on the bank once before. This was the man I had seen in my dreams. This was the man who had given me back my name.

The breath I had been holding slipped out of my body like silk.

I took a step back, my hand clutching at Orlando's elbow for support. My whole body burned with an unexpected heat, and the feather-soft brush of warmth along my nerves gave way to the flash burn of flame inside my bones. A light flared behind my eyes, illuminating the darkness that crouched like an animal in my mind. I couldn't take my eyes off the man who stood before me. I didn't want to.

He was part sunshine, part shadow. He was bright as a diamond.

I heard a strangled groan escape from Orlando, and out of the corner of my eye, I saw him head toward the figure, his movements uncoordinated and hurried.

"No, don't—" I started, but that was as far as I got.

Orlando's attention was completely focused on the newcomer and he heedlessly stepped forward—directly into the thin trickle of the new branch of the river. He realized his mistake immediately. He had one moment to look up at me in surprise and anguish, and then he disappeared.

I gasped. I wasn't sure where Orlando had gone. I hoped he would simply return to the apothecary shop, but I had no way of knowing.

For a moment, I considered following Orlando, but there was something about this new boy that made me stay, made me want to wait for him, made me want to hear him speak and say my name again.

The stranger continued to walk directly toward me as though he could see me even with the bandage across his eyes.

He walked right up to the edge of the narrow branch of the river and stopped in front of me, his toes so close to the flickering waves that I could see the shifting images reflected in his boots.

"I promised I would be waiting for you," he said, his voice soft and low, ragged with regret.

I shivered. I couldn't speak. At the sound of his voice, the darkness in my memories turned to light. My body remembered what my mind could not: the feel of his hair on my fingers, the smell of his skin, the taste of his lips. The feeling of flying. I *knew* him.

But unlike when I had fallen under Lorenzo's spell at the cathedral, this time my certainty wasn't based on a false memory or a wish of what someone else wanted me to feel.

This time, I *knew*.

"I promised to protect you." He took a breath, then slowly reached out his hand across the split river. Gold chains gleamed around the corded muscles of his wrists.

I drew a breath too, my heart already aching with anticipation. I reached for his hand with mine. Our fingers touched, and at that small point of contact, I felt the shiver move from me to him.

"I failed you," he said with a sorrow as vast as the ocean. "I wasn't there when you needed me most. And because of that,

Zo was able to hurt you." His fingers trembled as they slid into place against my flat palm. "I swore to you that I would make it up to you. I would make it right."

"How?" The single word encompassed all the questions I wanted to ask. It was all I could manage.

In answer, he took a step into the broken river.

I gasped, expecting him to disappear like Orlando had, but he didn't.

He took another step, and then he was across the river, closing the space between us. He stood next to me on the bank, close enough that when he breathed, the edges of his shirt brushed against mine.

I heard a rustle of chimes as delicate as a wish rise up and encircle us both.

He caught my hands in his and took a deep breath. "I know you don't remember me"—his voice trembled—"but I think I can reverse what has happened to you. I think I can help you regain your memories. Will you let me try? Will you trust me?"

I nodded instinctively, remembering the wish I'd made to Orlando and knowing in my heart that right here, right now, I had found the right answer to my impossible problem.

He pulled me into his arms, and I bit my lip. I hadn't realized how much I had felt like my life was in free fall until I was suddenly caught, cradled. Held.

Here was a safe harbor in the storm of my uncertainty. Here was a strength and a comfort I hadn't imagined existed. Here, I felt like I was finally home.

He pressed me close to him, molding his body around

mine. His voice whispered in my ear. "Then listen to me. To my voice. To the words. To the spaces between the words. Can you feel them? Can you hear them? Are you listening?"

The rhythm of his words matched the rise and fall of his chest, echoed the steady beating of his heart.

I nodded again, not daring to speak. I didn't want to interrupt the smooth flow of sound against my ear. I didn't want to start falling again.

The words he spoke washed over me in a waterfall. The relentless rhythm of his voice surrounded me and swept through me. The words melted into each other endlessly, effortlessly.

The music of his voice seemed to seep into my body. The cadence threatened to rock me to sleep even though I'd never felt more awake. I was acutely aware of everything that was happening to me, around me, inside me. Slowly, the beat of my heart, the flow of my blood, and the breath in my lungs drew into alignment, each element working perfectly with the next.

I felt cool and smooth. Weightless. Balanced.

I felt, if not exactly whole, at least closer to being healed.

Turning my face upward, I let the tears that had pooled in my eyes slide down my cheeks without bothering to wipe them away.

With a sound like an avalanche, the block in my mind cracked, crumbled, and was washed away. I took a deep breath, feeling free, body and soul.

And at the touch of his lips to mine, I *remembered*.

I felt like the river had split again, but this time, a branch had entered me, washing me clean. Wave after wave of memory welled up, an endless, bubbling spring of faces, names, events, emotions, and moments that I knew I would never forget. All those small, individual memories that made up *me*.

I remembered the birthday party when I had turned six. My family had set up a mini–bowling alley in the basement, and we had invited Jason and his family over to celebrate together. Jason had bowled a strike on his first frame and then refused to play anymore; he didn't want to ruin a perfect score.

I remembered the first time I'd tasted crème brulée: the sound of my spoon breaking through the crust of caramelized sugar, the taste of the smooth vanilla custard with a hint of passion fruit layered in.

I remembered each individual day when I first met Natalie. Valerie. Leo.

More: Reading *Heart of Darkness*. Dancing alone in my room, dressed in my pajamas and striped socks. Waiting up with Hannah to watch the ball drop on New Year's Eve. Hanging stockings on Christmas Eve. Crying when my pet turtle, Lightning, died.

I remembered lying in the grass on a sweet summer night and counting the stars.

I remembered a black door, a brass hinge, and the sound of silver chimes ringing through me. The chains that linked me with Tony, V, and Zo. The light in Valerie's eyes as she vacillated between sanity and madness. The photograph that protected Natalie.

I remembered *everything*.

I opened my eyes, feeling like a veil had been torn away. I

felt the weight of my life return to me and settle on my shoulders, on my heart. But it didn't feel like a burden to be carried. It felt like a mantle of power. This was *my* life in all its glory, the good and the bad. This was who I was. I had made the choices that had shaped me. And now that the puzzle pieces of my life, my memories, had been restored, I could go forward, making new choices that would shape my future.

Among the wild cascade of light and sound in my mind, though, there was one memory that gleamed the brightest, that felt the sharpest and clearest and cleanest.

And he was standing before me, his arms still around me, his mouth still close to mine.

His name was Dante.

He was the part of me that had been missing.

Now he was back, and we were together. Finally. Forever and always. The way we were meant to be.

I was whole. I was home.

And I was never going to let him go.

CHAPTER
9

"Abby?"

I smiled at the sound of my nickname. It felt so good to be wearing my own true name again. And to be able to share this moment with Dante was the sweetest gift I could have asked for.

I nestled into his embrace, unwilling to break away for even a moment.

"Abby?" he said again, and this time I heard the strain in his voice.

"What is it? Are you all right?"

His body trembled next to me. "I'll be fine. It's just . . . that took more out of me than I'd planned." Dante untangled himself slightly from me. He still held onto my arms, but I could tell that he wanted—needed—to sit down.

"You planned this?" I sat down on the flat ground, pulling him into place next to me. I crossed my legs under me, but I didn't let go of his hand. The small contact was not enough after being apart for so long—in body, soul, and mind—but it would have to do.

"Well, not all of it. There was always the chance you might have said no."

"Not likely."

Dante smiled, then winced. He touched the bandage at his temple with fingers that trembled.

"Your eyes," I said gently. "Are they bothering you?" With the block in my mind destroyed, I knew exactly how Dante had been injured. As much as I didn't want to remember that moment when Zo had drawn a blade across Dante's eyes, I couldn't seem to stop thinking about it.

"No more than usual." His voice was as shallow as his breathing.

I reached for the cloth, barely touching the edge. "Will you show me?"

A muscle jumped in Dante's jaw. "You don't want to see—"

"Yes," I interrupted gently, "I do. Please."

He hesitated, then gave one swift nod.

I shifted to my knees before him, my heart fluttering.

He sat as still as a statue as I quietly slipped my hands over his shoulders to the back of his neck. I touched the knot holding the bandage in place and, with shaking fingers, I slowly and carefully worked it free, trying not to pull the fabric tight against his eyes.

As soon as the knot was loose, Dante reached up and held the edges in place. "Abby—" he started. "No. Here—I'll do it."

"All right," I said. "I'm ready." I sat back on my heels, giving him the time he needed to unveil his eyes.

He took a deep breath, held it, then let it go. After a long moment, he lowered the bandage, crumpling the fabric in his hands, and turned his face to me.

I had thought I was ready for anything, but I wasn't prepared for what I saw or for the sharp stab of anguish I felt.

My throat closed up at the sight of his eyes; I couldn't look away. Dante's eyes had once been the gray of storm clouds and iced steel, but now a film covered them that was as thick and sluggish as the one that skimmed the surface of the river. A bold scar carved a path on his face, drawing a line from cheek to cheek, right across his eyes.

It was impossible that he could see anything.

I realized too late that he was waiting for me to say something. "Dante—" I started, hoping I could mask the despair in my voice.

He heard it anyway. "I'm sorry," he said and raised the bandage, poised to cover his eyes and hide them away again.

Touching his wrist, I stopped him. I could feel his heartbeat racing as he waited, tense and on edge, for me to do something, say something.

I reached out and placed my palm against his cheek—a perfect fit—and turned his face toward me. My fingers brushed the very edge of the scar that marked the length of his wound.

He flinched, but barely.

I took a deep breath. My words were steady and sure, though my heart shook with uncertainty. "V once told me that the only person who could hurt a Master of Time was another Master of Time. Tell me he was wrong. Tell me Zo's attack wasn't permanent. Tell me he . . . missed."

He knew what I wanted to hear, but he was Dante, so he gave me the truth instead. He always gave me the truth. "V was correct. A wound inflicted by a Master of Time is different from other wounds. The damage done is permanent. Zo's attack was precise, and since he gave me these wounds, they are . . . irreversible."

The hand I had pressed against his face flashed cold. A trembling started in my fingertips, rippling down through my wrist, my arm, and into my chest. "No."

But denying it wouldn't change the truth. Dante's eyes—his beautiful, clear eyes that could see into the soul of me—were gone. Blinded by Zo's blade. The scar would stay, and the gray film that covered his eyes would remain as a veil over his vision for as long as he lived. And as a Master of Time, he would live for a very long time.

"No," I said again, louder, covering my mouth with my hands.

Tears ran down from my own eyes. I almost didn't feel it when Dante reached out and brushed them away. "Ah, no, Abby. It's not worth crying about."

"But you're blind," I blurted out. "You can't see *anything!*"

"I can see you," he said quietly. His wounded eyes found mine and didn't let go.

My words died on my lips. I felt hope rise up in my chest, sharp and bright.

Dante's mouth moved in that small smile I loved. "I told you that before, remember?"

"But what about the bandage—?"

"I can *always* see you," he repeated. "Even through the

bandage. Even through the darkness. You are as clear to me now as you were the first time I saw you. Only now it's like you have a halo of light around you. I can see a little bit of whatever that light touches"—he took my hand and squeezed it gently—"but that's all."

"But why me?"

"Because you are my constant. You are my North Star. From the moment I first saw the river, I saw you in it. You are my past, my present, my future." He leaned forward, brushing my hair behind my ears. "I don't know why," he said, "and I don't want to. I don't want to find out it was a mistake. I don't want to lose what little I have left of you."

"You still have all of me," I said. "Always."

"Thank you," he said. "That means more to me than you'll ever know." He drew closer and pressed a kiss to my closed lids, one on each eye, and then a third on my forehead.

"We'll find a way to get your sight back. If we work together, I know we can do it," I said. I didn't know how to fulfill that promise, but I knew I would do whatever it took. I had to.

"I'd like that," he said. He wrapped the bandage around his head again, knotting it in place with a single, sharp tug.

"Thank you, Dante," I said. "Thank you for sharing that with me. For trusting me with it. And thank you for restoring my memories. How did you know what would work?"

"When I found you on the bank after Zo had hurt you, I promised you I would figure out a way to help you. When I realized that Zo had used his music to take away your memories, I thought it only fitting that I use my poetry to bring them back. Poetry seems to follow the same rules as music—the rhythm and cadence and counting—but it's easier for me to access and use. Besides, I've done something like it before, remember?"

Of course I remembered. I felt stuffed to the seams with memories. It was easy to sort through them and select the one I wanted. "The Poetry Slam at the Dungeon last February." I furrowed my brow. "Wait, was that the same poem? You used the one from the Poetry Slam to heal me?"

He blushed a deliciously dusky shade of red. "It was the only one I had. And it's my best one."

"It was beautiful," I said, and I meant it.

Dante tilted his head. "You understood the poem?"

"Of course I did. Why wouldn't I?"

"Because I said it in Italian."

"I—" I opened my mouth, but I didn't know what to say. "Are you sure?"

A smile quirked his lips. "Pretty sure."

"Then how . . . ?" My shoulders slumped as I thought through all the possible answers. It was a pretty short list.

"Do you remember having any problems with the language since you passed through the door?" Dante asked.

"No, none." I frowned in thought. "Well, I could tell something was different right away because I could understand everyone I talked to. It's like I'm speaking English—which feels *right*—but it sounds like I'm speaking Italian—which strangely doesn't feel *wrong*. When I mentioned it to Orlando, he said I spoke the language like a native." I tapped my finger against my lips. "Do you think it was because of the door? Did it change something about me?"

"Well, yes, it is designed to fundamentally change some-thing about you," Dante said. "But not like this. I wouldn't have thought it would affect your language."

"Maybe it happened later?" I suggested. "Once I was through the door, I mean." I immediately shook my head. "No, that can't be. I saw Orlando on the bank as soon as I came through the door, and we had a long conversation where we both understood each other. And he probably speaks twenty-first-century English as well as I speak sixteenth-century Italian."

Dante and I both thought for a moment, and then he said softly, "A gift."

I pulled my mind back from where I had been attempting unlikely answers. "What?"

"All of us who crossed over developed some kind of talent on the bank—a specific and unique gift to compensate for the loss of our relationship with time. I could see downstream to the future. Zo could enforce obedience. Tony could hear echoes of the past; V had a perfect sense of direction." Dante raised his eyebrows. "Maybe yours is a gift of language."

"Do you think so?"

"It's the best answer I have at the moment."

"Well, it would explain how I could talk to Orlando on the bank, but if the gift only works on the bank, then what about once I was back in the river? I've been around a lot of people and I've understood everybody." I thought for another moment, absently lifting my fingers to my neck, searching for a locket that was still gone.

"Your locket," Dante said suddenly, his voice unexpectedly

sharp. He reached out and moved my hand away from my throat. "Where did it go? Did you lose it?"

I swallowed and looked down at my empty hand. "No, I . . . I gave it to Zo."

"What?" Dante asked in horror. "Why?"

I remembered the sound of Zo's music crashing into me, the twist and pull as he slammed that black block into my memories. "He was in my mind, changing things, taking things from me. He made me forget." I closed my eyes, remembering the music Zo had brought with him to the cathedral. That song hadn't hurt, but it had left its mark on me all the same. "He made me think he was someone I could trust. I thought I loved him." I turned my fingers into a fist. A sour taste filled my mouth, coating my tongue with acid.

At the thought of Zo and his music, a corner of my mind turned to shadow and I swallowed hard. Had a ghostly taint of Zo's touch remained like a stain I couldn't erase? A drop of poison that had resisted the antidote of Dante's poetry?

"I'm sorry, Dante. I've wished for the locket back ever since I gave it to him."

Dante was still and quiet. A deep line furrowed his forehead, and the muscles tightened in his jaw, along his arm, and across his shoulders.

"You're worried about the fact that Zo has the locket, aren't you?" I asked quietly.

"It'll be all right," he said, but the line in his forehead didn't go away.

"Why is it so bad if he has it?"

Dante didn't say anything for a long time.

"Are you mad at me?" I ventured.

My question seemed to rouse him from his thoughts. He turned immediately to me. "No, it's not you. This is my fault. I did something without thinking it through and now it looks like I've made things worse. I should have known better."

"What did you do?"

Dante sighed. "Zo used his guitar to hurt you, so I used it to hurt *him* in return. I destroyed it right in front of him."

"You destroyed Zo's guitar?" I repeated. "I thought I had just dreamed that."

"When?" Dante asked. "When did you have that dream?"

"Last night, I guess." I smiled wryly. "Time is a little slippery these days."

Dante didn't laugh.

"Why? When did it happen?"

"After I found you on the bank and sent you back through the river, I immediately hunted down Zo. I found his guitar and broke it. I thought that would be the end of it, so I turned my attention to figuring out how to restore your memories."

"Is it bad, do you think? Me dreaming about events so close to when they actually happened?"

"I don't know—maybe."

I shivered. I had felt Zo's touch in my mind and on my body and I had no desire to repeat either one. The idea that he could somehow be in my dreams too made me feel oddly exposed.

Dante squeezed my hand with his, sweeping away his worried frown with a swift smile. "It's all right," he said. "We'll get the locket back. Everything will be fine. You'll see."

I wanted to believe him, but I wasn't sure he believed it himself.

❋

We walked back along the river, carefully avoiding the thin threads that were spooling out in new directions.

"This is the last thing I wanted to see," Dante said with a heavy sigh. "The river shouldn't be doing this. Any of this." He pointed to a silver thread that had separated from the main river, the shimmering line coiled around in a tight spiral like a spring. "And listen to it. It even sounds different. It's like there is this odd echo—I can't quite make it out." He cocked his head, listening.

I concentrated as well, hearing the familiar chimes of time and the melody of the river. But this time I could also almost hear words mixed in with the music.

"And it seems *softer* somehow," Dante continued. "Like it's blurred along the edges, or feathered, like an angel's outstretched wing."

I swallowed, remembering Lorenzo standing over the cracked statue of the angel in the cathedral, how the wings had been bent and broken in his fall. I didn't think they were connected, but I felt now like I had felt then: sad and small and helpless.

"Though this appears to be a little beyond *feathering*," he continued. "I wonder how many of these threads are spooling off the main river?" He crouched down and skimmed the flat of his hand over the surface of the river, close but not touching. "No wonder it's been harder to keep track of the time, with the river this unstable. Sometimes it feels like it's slipping away and I can't hold on to it. Other times, it feels as heavy as a stone and I can't make it move, no matter how hard I push."

"Can you fix it?"

Dante stood up and weighed his answer in the stillness between us. "Maybe. But I'll need to study the currents of the river in order to see the possibilities of how we might be able to cleanse it and stabilize it. And that means I'll need to stay on the bank—at least for a while."

"Can I stay with you?" I gestured to the barren landscape around us. "I'm already here, after all."

"I wish you could. But it's too dangerous for you to stay. You haven't found your balance yet. You haven't had time to. It took me nearly a year to find mine once I had passed through the door. You've only had a couple of days."

I frowned. I hated to ask my next question, but I had to. "And you're sure your eyes will be okay? You can still see downstream the way you used to?"

Dante nodded with a small smile. "Yes and yes. I will be fine. Besides, if we are going to restore the river—and restore your family, I haven't forgotten about them—then I need to know what's going on, and for that, I need to study the river."

"I still don't like the idea of you being here alone. I want to help."

"I know. And that's one of the things I love about you." He touched his forehead to mine. "You can help by staying with Orlando. By staying safe. And staying whole."

I didn't say anything. I knew Dante was right, but that didn't mean I had to like it.

"You did meet up with Orlando, right?"

"I've been with him ever since I arrived here—in this time, I mean. He was at the courtroom with me. And at the cathedral. He was even here—on the bank—right before you showed up."

"He was?"

I nodded, remembering that with Dante's limited sight, he hadn't been able to see his brother. "I think he recognized you, but he fell into the river before he could reach you."

A small furrow of worried thought creased Dante's forehead.

"What about Zo?" I blurted out. "He said he could find me wherever I was—the way you can."

"Let me worry about Zo. You concentrate on finding your balance." He slipped his hands around my waist and pulled me closer. "Do you trust me, Abby?"

"Always," I answered without hesitation.

"Then *trust* me," he said with a smile.

"I will."

A glimmering flicker of light in the distance caught my attention. As I turned toward the main flow of the river, I saw a series of flashes like a heat mirage that made the land ripple. I paused, squinting in hopes it would bring the strange images into focus.

"Abby? What do you see?" Dante asked. He angled his face in the direction I was looking, but I knew he couldn't see the shimmering light that had appeared on the bank. Not with his blind eyes behind his bandage. My heart seized up a little. We had to find a way to heal Dante. He couldn't live like this.

"It's a light," I said, knowing it was too general a description to be helpful. "It's across the river, and it looks like . . ." I rubbed my eyes. It couldn't be. It wasn't possible. "It looks like my mom." Terror clawed at my stomach, turning it into a seething mass of acid.

"Your mom?" Dante asked.

She stood motionless, her face turned toward me, a glittering veil of mist hanging between us.

"She can't be here," I moaned. "Why is she here? How?" I clenched my hands into fists, feeling my knuckles tighten with the strain. Then I shook my hands loose and bounced on the balls of my feet, wanting to race across the river and into my mom's arms.

Dante touched my shoulder, holding me in place. "It's not her, Abby. It can't be her."

"How can you be sure? What if she came looking for me? What if she managed to follow me?" I gasped. "And Dad! He's there too." I rose up on my toes, craning my neck for a better look. The light resolved into a third shape. "Hannah?" My voice cracked and bled away from me. My family stood on the far side of the split river. All of them. Together.

But I remained apart, separated from them by the vast expanse of time.

"Abby, no, listen to me," Dante stepped in front of me, blocking my view. He moved his hands from my shoulders to my arms. I tried to shrug him off, but he was too strong.

"Let me go—"

"They're not really here," he said, his voice loud but calm. He stepped aside again. "Look at them, Abby. Really look at them. Tell me what you see."

I took a deep breath and narrowed my eyes. It was hard to see past the emotions that sprang to life inside me, but what I saw made me catch my breath.

My mom looked pale white, ghostly and transparent. The outline of her body wavered, seeming to bleed away into nothingness as I watched. Her hair moved slowly in a breeze that wasn't blowing. Her eyes were soft; it looked like she had been crying.

The images of Dad and Hannah floated nearby, their bodies the same ghostly white and thin. I could see where they were holding hands, but their individual fingers were lost in a hazy cloud of white. Hannah's skirt ruffled around where her ankles would have been had she had any feet. The edges of her outline rippled like water.

Dante lifted my chin with his fingers, pulling my gaze back to his face.

In my heart, I knew Dante was right. My family wasn't really there. It was impossible. "How did you know? Can you see them?"

Dante shook his head. "Not now, but I saw them like that once before, when I tried to restore your family to you the first time. When Zo erased them from the river, it was like they became ghosts, cut adrift. They are just images, Abby. Shadows seen through the mist of time."

"We have to save them," I said, quiet but firm.

"We will," Dante said, equally firm. "We won't let them be lost forever."

I glanced back to my ghost family, desperate for another look, even knowing they were just fragments, just memories.

As I watched, a brighter light cut through the flat sky. The ground trembled under my feet like a minor earthquake. I hung on to Dante for balance.

Another figure materialized in the distance. A tall girl with short black hair, the ends ragged and choppy. She barreled forward, running on bare feet straight through the wisps of my family, scattering them into a tattered oblivion. Her worn bathrobe covered a dirty gray sweatshirt and loose pajama pants. Her familiar face was twisted with anger and madness.

"Valerie?" I whispered, confused.

Even though she was some distance away, she lifted her head as though she had heard me. She fixed me with an intense gaze, and then she smiled.

But it wasn't a smile of reunion or welcome.

It was the grin of revenge, with teeth extended and ready to bite.

CHAPTER
10

"I told you I would fix it!" Valerie's voice sliced through the air like a blade. "I told you so!"

I stumbled backward a few steps, tripping over Dante's feet. He caught me and helped me stand. "Abby? What is it?"

"It's Valerie," I managed. "She's here. Really here. Not like my family. She's really here. On the bank." The words fell out of my mouth in clumps of disbelief.

On instinct, Dante twisted to look in the direction of Valerie's voice, but I knew he couldn't see her. He couldn't see the cruel light in her eyes or the hot spots of color in her cheeks. Such visions were reserved for me.

Valerie ran in a straight line, never taking her focus from me. I thought for sure the river would slow her down—she would have to stop or else risk being pulled back into the flow of time—but the moment her toes reached the line where river met bank, she simply jumped, her momentum propelling her across and over the narrow track of unstable time. She landed hard and fell forward onto her knees, her arms shooting out to brace herself against the soft sand of the bank.

Crouched on all fours like an animal, she twisted her head

around to pin me with her hooded eyes. "What the Pirate King is not, is the Pirate King's lot, and we all will be bound in the Pirate King's knot." Her singsong voice rose in pitch the longer she chanted, while at the same time her body seemed to collapse in on itself, folding into a tight ball.

"How did you get here, Valerie?" Dante demanded, angling his body toward the sound of her voice and stepping in front of me.

She whipped her head up and grinned. "How does anyone go from place to place?" she said. "Through the door." Her voice was almost back to normal, but her eyes were not. "You should know that better than anyone, darling Dante."

"No," I breathed. The pressure that had been building inside me locked like a vise around my bones.

"That's not possible," Dante said, but I could feel the muscles in his back tighten with tension.

"Really? Because it seemed pretty easy for me to go down the spiral staircase into the burned basement of the Dungeon and waltz my way through the door V built for Abby."

"Leo said he would watch—"

"He couldn't watch forever." She unfolded herself from her crouch. "I wanted. I waited. I watched. It was only a matter of time." Her laugh sounded like nails clattering on metal.

"Do you know what you've done?" I said.

Valerie tilted her head. "I know exactly what I've done. Better, I know exactly what I'm *doing*."

"You can't go back, you know that, right?" I said. "It's not that easy."

"I don't want it to be easy," she said, taking a step forward. "I want it to hurt."

Everything seemed to happen at once: Valerie rushed toward me at the same time I screamed at the same time Dante moved to intercept her.

"Dante! No!" I shouted, but he caught her in his arms, wrapping her tightly against his chest and lifting her off her feet.

She struggled against him, kicking and screaming and biting, but even in her anger, Dante was stronger.

"Let me go!" Valerie clawed at Dante's arms, scratching deep, parallel lines all the way to his elbows. She reached up and ripped the bandage from Dante's head, throwing the cloth to the ground.

"Stop it, Valerie!" I took a step forward, my heart skipping a beat in terror.

"No, stay back," Dante called.

"Look out!" I shouted the second before Valerie rocked her head forward, and Dante dodged at the last moment.

I paced in a nervous circle around the two of them. I wanted to do something to help Dante, but I couldn't see an opening. They were too tightly locked together. And I didn't want to do the wrong thing at the wrong time and distract Dante. Sweat poured down the side of his face from the strain of trying to keep Valerie under control.

"I warned you," Valerie screamed at me. "You may have given him your heart, but he can't have you. I won't let him. He's mine!"

"It was a mistake!" I screamed back at her, my eyes

burning, my throat raw. "I didn't know . . . I didn't mean to do it."

"Too bad, so sad," she chanted, her black hair flying around her head like the shadow of a halo. "What's done is done," she growled, a feral look in her eye. "And he'll do what he's going to do. You can't stop him. You're his girl now and forever."

"Stop it!" I covered my ears with my hands, trying to block out her voice, but it was no use. Her words latched onto my mind, taking hold and not letting go. I fell to my knees. It couldn't be true; I didn't want it to be true.

"Move back, Abby," Dante ordered.

"You're late, you're late, for a very important date. And you're late, Abby. Everlastingly too late."

"Go!" Dante snapped, turning toward me. Hard lines cut through the angles of his bones, turning his face to a mask of intensity and purpose. A power and a stillness gathered around him, honed like a weapon ready to be used.

I crawled backward, trying to stay as far away from Dante and Valerie as possible without also falling into the river.

"Abby!" Dante called out. "When I tell you to, I want you to count to a hundred. Concentrate, and count. Can you do that?"

"Yes!" I called back.

"Good. Then do it—start counting! Now!" He closed his eyes and tightened his grip on Valerie.

"One. Two. Three." I bent my mind, my will, my heart to counting one number after another. I focused on each number, visualizing what it would look like, what it would sound like, what it would feel like on my tongue before I spoke. "Four. Five."

I kept my gaze locked on Dante.

He took a deep breath and then leaned as close as he could to Valerie's ear. He opened his mouth and spoke to her.

I couldn't hear what he said, but I kept counting, loudly and rhythmically. "Twelve. Thirteen."

The bank rumbled again beneath me, but quietly. More of a shudder than a shake.

I kept counting. "Twenty-five. Twenty-six."

Dante's mouth moved constantly, pouring words into her ears, and slowly, oh so slowly, Valerie stopped struggling.

"Thirty-nine. Forty."

A sharp snap echoed through the sky like lightning, but without the flash. The river hissed and spat behind me.

Dante lowered Valerie to the ground, holding her up when her knees wobbled. His breathing quickened, his chest heaving with strain. Yet, at the same time, Valerie's breathing eased, slowing into a calm rhythm that somehow matched my endless counting.

"Fifty-six. Fifty-seven."

Valerie closed her eyes. Her cheeks still burned hot pink, but the smile that spread across on her face was peaceful instead of predatory.

Dante gently lowered Valerie to the ground, cradling her in his arms, covering her with a blanket of words.

She sighed and curled up on her side as though asleep in her bed at home instead of in a barren wasteland outside of time.

"Seventy-nine. Eighty."

Dante dropped to his knees next to her, bracing himself with his straight arms against his thighs. He bowed his head, sweat running past his eyes like tears, dripping off his nose and chin. His shoulders shook with the deep breaths he pulled into his body.

"Eighty-eight." I couldn't take it anymore. "Dante!" I called. I moved to stand up, but he flung his hand out to me. His gray eyes seemed black against his unnaturally pale skin.

"Finish it!" he ordered.

"Eighty-ni . . . nine." The words stumbled out of my mouth. "Ninety." I wanted to go faster—I was so close to the end—but when I tried to speed up the rhythm I had already established, Dante turned those black eyes toward me and I had to stop and swallow and keep the pace he needed.

"Ninety-nine. One hundred."

As soon as the last number left my lips, I scrambled to my feet and ran across the distance separating us.

I crashed to my knees next to Dante and wrapped my arms around him in a bone-crushing hug. "Are you all right?"

I felt Dante instantly relax in my arms as he locked his hands behind my back. He pressed his face into the curve of my neck. "Thank you," he murmured, his voice hoarse and raw.

"What for? What did I do?"

"You trusted me," he said.

"Of course I did. You said you needed my help." I pulled back and touched his face and his scratched-up arms with my fingertips. "I'm not sure how my counting helped, though. What did you do?"

Dante shuddered one last time, the wounds on his arms already healing.

"I used a poem to help calm the storm in Valerie's mind."

"You did? Is she better?" Hope flowered in my chest and I looked down at my friend, sleeping, her face smooth and childlike.

Dante hesitated, then shook his head. "I wasn't able to go that deep inside her mind. She fought me every step of the way as it was."

"Is that why you had me count?"

He nodded. "Hearing you count helped me keep to the rhythm I needed in order to channel the power of the poem the way I wanted to."

I reached out and almost brushed Valerie's leg, but I didn't dare touch her. I didn't want to wake her up. "It looked like it took a lot of power."

"It did," Dante said, his words clipped. He wasn't angry, though, just exhausted. "More than I thought it would. Zo's always been strong, and his power over her has lasted a long time; it was hard to break down the walls."

"But you're stronger than he is, right?"

"I hope so," he said quietly. "Today I was. But I don't know how long the effects of the poem will last. A lot of it will depend on Valerie herself. If she wants to get better, I think I can help her. If she wants to stay with Zo . . ." He rubbed his arm across his forehead, wiping away the sweat, but leaving behind a streak of blood.

I shivered at the sight of the stark red line. It was too close to my memory of when Dante's wound was fresh.

"What poem did you use?" I asked, hoping for a distraction from my past. "Was it the same one that you used to help me?"

Dante shook his head. "That poem only works for you. I knew Valerie had a different problem, so she needed a different poem. I had to create one for her on the spot."

"Why wouldn't the other poem work?"

He hesitated, and when he spoke, his voice was unexpectedly shy. "Because that one was yours; I wrote it for you."

My mouth softened to an "Oh," which was as far as I got before Dante leaned in and kissed me.

His lips found mine, at once soft and strong. He ran his palms over my shoulders, one hand sliding up to brace my neck, the other sliding lower to touch the small of my back. I felt the slightest flex of his muscles, and he pulled me close to his chest.

I melted into the curve of his arms, my mind alight with all that I had lost and all that I had found.

I kissed him back, tasting his sweat and blood and desire. His mouth burned with unspoken poetry.

I curled my fingers into the fabric of his shirt, holding him as close to me as I was to him. My heart beat in double time, a quick rhythm that made me think of a song, of dancing, of wings snapping open, catching that first thermal wind and soaring to uncharted heights.

Lost in the moment, I didn't notice exactly when he loosened his hold and pulled away. I drew in a deep breath, feeling the cool air counterbalance the fire in my chest. I could still feel the heat pouring off of him.

He touched his forehead to mine. "I'm sorry," he said, though he didn't sound sorry at all. He ran his fingers down the side of my arm until they came to rest in the bend of my elbow. My pulse fluttered. "I've missed you so much."

"It hasn't been that long, has it?" I blinked, trying to bring my vision back into focus. Dante's kisses had a way of changing how I saw the world.

"Long enough. It feels like it's been forever." His hand dropped from my elbow to my hip.

"You would know," I said with a smile. "Tell me, what *does* forever feel like?"

I hadn't meant for him to answer me. Mostly I'd asked it to give me a moment to catch my breath and calm my racing heart. But Dante's face grew thoughtful.

"It feels a little like this." He half gestured to the barren bank that encompassed us.

"Really?" I couldn't keep the disappointment from my voice. "I don't want forever to be like this. I thought that going through the door a second time made things better for you. You know, so you could stay in the river and you *didn't* have to be on the bank."

"No, that's not what I meant." He tilted his face upward toward the endless expanse of sky, his eyes looking at nothing. "I meant that forever feels . . . untouched. Open, all the way to the horizon. But it's not empty like the bank. Not at all." His voice, already soft, took on a reverence I hadn't heard before. "Forever is stuffed full of . . . possibility. Potential. A blank canvas waiting for me to paint something, or draw something. To make. To change. Forever is where creation happens."

A shiver ran through me, and my breath quickened at his words. "That's beautiful," I murmured. "I wish I could feel that too. I want to be where you are."

"You are," Dante said, sounding surprised by the hint of melancholy in my voice. "You're here with me. We'll always be together."

I swept the bank with my gaze and bit down hard on my lip. How would it be to look out over such a wild expanse and see, not emptiness, but *everything*? I would never know. At least, not unless we found a way for me to go back through the door like Dante had. Not unless I became a Master of Time too. But in all my recent trips to the bank, neither a bridge nor a door had appeared for me. My future extended only as far as the thin boundary where the bank met the river. This place was my future—all the way to the horizon of my life.

I tried to shake off my bleak thoughts. We still had a lot of work to do—stopping Zo, saving my family, cleansing the river—and now there was Valerie to worry about as well. With her here, we would have to rethink our plans.

Valerie. I sighed. I wondered how she would react when she realized the extent of what she'd done. I had walked through the door with my eyes open; she had run through the darkness blindly, driven by rage.

"Abby?" Dante asked gently, touching my hand. "We need to go back. It's time."

I nodded, feeling the sharp edge of pain cut through my thoughts. I was already tired of bouncing back and forth between the river and the bank. How had Dante done it for more than a year? Or Leo, with half a millennium of experience? The weight of that thought was more than I could bear.

I picked up Dante's tattered bandage and handed it to him.

Looking at Valerie, I said to Dante, "We have to take her with us back through the river—you know that, right? We can't leave her here."

"I know," he said without hesitation, knotting the cloth around his eyes once more.

"Will you be able to keep her calm?"

Now he hesitated. "I'll do my best."

I nodded wearily. It was all I could ask for. But when it came to Dante, his best was better than anyone else's.

CHAPTER
11

The sunlight was blazing white after the flat gray of the bank. I blinked away my light-blindness, my eyes watering as my vision cleared. The pressure from the bank that had been building inside me snapped and slithered away. I wondered how long my sense of freedom would last this time.

We were standing outside the apothecary shop, which struck me as a little odd since Orlando and I had originally left for the bank from inside the shop. Then I thought about how unstable the river was; were things already changing? I hoped not. Of course, one change I didn't mind was that this time Dante was next to me, holding Valerie in his arms. She stirred a little in her sleep, readjusting her position and nestling her face closer to the curve of Dante's neck. I felt a deep sense of relief that she hadn't woken up during our return trip through the river.

"We're here," I said softly to Dante. "We should take her inside. The door should still be unlocked. Let me help." I pushed the door open, holding it so Dante could slip past me into the shop.

I helped Dante set Valerie down on the makeshift bed in the corner. She mumbled a little in her sleep but didn't wake.

I glanced around the shop, expecting to see Orlando, but the room was empty except for the three of us.

Empty? Where was Orlando? He should be around here somewhere.

"Wait here," I said to Dante, touching his arm.

Stepping back outside, I let the door swing shut behind me and turned in a tight circle outside the shop, studying every inch, every alley, every building around me.

A slight movement in the shadow of the building across the way caught my attention. I hurried over with quick steps.

"Orlando?"

He flinched away from me, his face pale. "Impossible," he whispered.

I glanced over my shoulder, but we were alone. Dante was still inside with Valerie. "No. No, it's all right. It's me. I'm back."

He swallowed hard. "You . . ." He drew a hand over his face. "It's impossible," he said again.

Too much about this situation—about my new life—was impossible. I touched Orlando's arm. "It's all right," I said again, trying to make myself believe it too.

I wasn't sure he heard me. His attention hovered past my shoulder and when he gently pushed me to the side, I turned, already knowing what he was looking at—or, in this case, whom.

Dante closed the door to the apothecary shop behind him, standing for a moment in a patch of sunlight. He removed his bandage, letting the strip of fabric dangle from his fingertips. He tilted his face up, his eyes closed to catch the warmth of the sun.

"Dante?" Orlando reached out his hand partway and then changed his mind, rubbing at his eyes with the edge of his wrist. He stepped out of the shadows, his stride uneven as he stumbled forward.

At the sound of his name, Dante spun on his heel, immediately balling up the bandage in his fist and hiding his hands behind his back. His eyes found mine and a strange mix of panic and relief flickered across his face. If I hadn't been watching, I would have missed it.

"What are you doing here?" Orlando asked in confusion, drawing closer to his brother. "Why aren't you with da Vinci? Is something wrong?"

I trailed after Orlando, wondering if I should say something. I even opened my mouth, but I didn't know what to say. In my other life—my life before I crossed through the door—Dante and I had talked about many things, but never about what to do when we faced overlapping timelines. Here, in this time, there was only one of me and only one of Orlando. But there were two Dantes: the one standing before us with the scar across his eyes and the gold chains across his skin, and the one crouching in a dark corner of a dungeon cell, unmarked, untested, and already counting down to the end of the world.

I knew instinctively that it was important to keep the two Dantes separate, to keep their timelines pure and parallel. But what about this? Dante and Orlando were face-to-face, with too many of the wrong questions waiting to be answered.

"Hello, Orlando," Dante said, his voice husky. His eyes never left his brother's face, though I knew he could only see Orlando in his memory. "I've been given leave to come home for a time."

I drew alongside Orlando, who spared a moment to glance at me, a question in his eyes. "But I saw him on the bank . . ." he said to me.

"It's all right," I said with quiet confidence. I seemed to be saying that a lot, but I wasn't sure I believed it myself yet. I could feel the pause in the flow of the river as time debated what to change, and how. I felt like I was standing on a bridge, holding a rock out over the edge, wondering when the rock would slip free and how big the splash would be when it did.

"What happened to your eyes?" Orlando asked Dante, a touch of horror in his voice.

Dante hesitated. "A fight I couldn't avoid. I'm all right, but my sight is . . . compromised."

"But you'll get better?" Orlando said, and it was less a worried question than a hopeful statement.

"Eventually." But Dante didn't look at me when he said it. His expression closed, making it clear that that line of conversation was over. He cleared his throat. "Have you been home? Have you spoken to Mother and Father?"

Orlando faltered, and his eyes darkened with anxiety. He shook his head. He scratched at his arm, then, glancing down, quickly stopped. "If . . . when you speak to them . . . don't tell them about me. Please?"

My heart hurt to hear the sadness in his voice.

Dante swallowed and I saw his body start to tremble. The muscles in his arms tightened as he gripped his wrists behind his back, trying to stay in control. "Why not? Don't you want them to know that you're safe? That you're well?"

"Of course I do," Orlando said automatically. "It's . . . it's complicated. It's best if they don't know where I am." He ran his hand through his hair in a gesture so familiar to me, my mouth went dry. I'd seen Dante do it himself a thousand times before.

I looked between them both. They shared so much—the same hair and face and mannerisms, the same family. Now they shared the same secret, though Orlando didn't know that yet. And, I realized with a rising sense of panic, he *couldn't* know.

"You shouldn't know where I am either," Orlando said to Dante suddenly. "It's not safe."

That was the truth. Orlando had told me the story of how he hadn't seen Dante at all between leaving him at da Vinci's studio and finding him on the bank all those years later. My heart stuttered. Maybe it was already too late. Maybe this meeting had already changed things.

The rock was slipping free; the river was flexing.

I touched Orlando's arm with a quick hand. "Wait here." I closed the short distance between me and Dante, grabbing his arm and pulling him around the corner of the building.

"I'm sorry. I'd hoped he would be here when we returned, but I didn't think . . . What should we do? How can we fix this?" I said fast and low; I didn't want Orlando to hear me.

LISA MANGUM

Dante drew in a deep breath. He reached his hands
around to grasp mine, their touch cool and steady. He pressed
his bandage into my hands and, after a quick squeeze, he
let me go. Then very slowly, very deliberately, he folded his
sleeves back, revealing the chains he had kept hidden. First
one, then the other.

"Dante," I hissed. "What are you doing?"

"What needs to be done," he said quietly, his eyes cloud-
ing over.

"No. It's too dangerous. For him. For everyone." I glanced
around the corner to see Orlando slumped against the wall,
stripping thorns from the stalks of the rosebushes growing
next to the sign. He kept glancing up, anxious for our return,
wary of passing strangers and the possibility of being identified
as a fugitive.

My heart sank under the weight of all the new questions I
was sure he was dying to ask.

The river shivered and shifted, bending around this unexpected encounter.

"Why did you come back here, Abby?" Dante asked.

"What? You know why."

"*I* know. But do you?"

I exhaled in frustration. "Of course *I* know why. I came
back to close the loop, to stand in front of the dungeon doorway before you—the other you—traveled through the door.
I'm here to protect the river and get it back on track. And keep
it on track."

Dante nodded. "And?"

134

"And if I can do that, then I can save my family as well. Restore them to the time and place where they belong."

He relaxed. "Exactly," he breathed. "That's all I want to do too."

"But how will telling Orlando the truth—about his past, his future, about *everything*—help restore my family?"

His eyes met mine, and I thought I saw a storm of light pass through them like lightning behind a cloud. "Because it can also restore *my* family."

Understanding flooded through me. "Oh, Dante." The words barely had shape or tone, just a sigh of empathy and love.

"I lost him once. I don't want to lose him again."

I slipped my hand back into Dante's, our fingers automatically folding together.

"He's my brother. How can I keep this secret from him? If I can help him, prepare him for what is coming . . ." Dante shrugged eloquently. "He would do it for me. He *did* do it for me."

"But what about the river?" I asked. "What will happen now?"

"I don't know. But the river is designed to accommodate change—it *is* change. And what did we come here for if not to change things? Fix things? Set things right?" He squeezed my hand in his. "I have to do it now. Once the door closes behind me—the other me—it'll be too late. Whatever we have changed—or not changed—will be locked into place."

He was right, and we both knew it. The rock was falling

and there was no way to call it back. No way of telling how far the ripples would spread.

"Will you help me save my family?" he asked me.

"Of course I will."

"Thank you." He brushed the back of his fingers against my cheek. "We should probably go back inside the shop."

"Is that a good idea?" I asked. "I mean, Valerie is in there, isn't she?"

Dante hesitated. "I don't want to leave her alone for too long. It'll be better if we're all together—less dangerous for everyone. And if she needs help when she wakes up, I'll be there." He paused, swallowing hard. "Will you help me?"

"Yes." I could feel the nervous energy crackling off him. I pressed his bandage back into his hand, but instead of covering his eyes with it, he shoved it into his pocket.

"Are you sure?" I asked, surprised.

He nodded, and I gave his hand a quick squeeze before leading him around the corner of the shop.

Orlando looked up as we approached, his eyebrows lifting at the sight of me holding hands with Dante.

"We need to talk," I said. "All of us."

"What's going on?" Orlando asked me in a low voice. "How do you know my brother? He's not even supposed to be here. Are your memories back? How . . . ?" He exhaled slowly, his mouth flattening into a thin line. "I don't understand."

"I know how you feel," I said with a faint smile. "There's a lot to understand, and all of it a little strange. And yes, my memories are back. Thanks to Dante. Come inside and we'll answer all your questions. We'll talk about everything."

I could see his uncertainty battling with hope across his face. But in the end, I knew he would come. I knew hope would win. Dante was his brother, and Orlando always came through for his brother.

We entered the shop together, and I immediately looked at Valerie. She was still asleep and quiet. I hoped she would stay that way.

I helped Dante sit in the chair next to the window, then stepped back, close enough to help if he needed me, but far enough away to not intrude on the conversation.

Orlando sat down in the opposite chair. Tension hummed from his body. "Dante? What's going on?"

Dante was silent for a long moment. Then he carefully pulled his folded sleeves even higher up his arms. The golden chains around his wrists were bright in the sunlight that fell through the window. He simply held out his arms . . . and waited.

Orlando sucked in a breath, his eyes flashing to me.

I half shrugged. "It's okay," I said, hoping that those small words would be enough to set him at ease.

Orlando waited another moment, then returned his attention to Dante. "How did you get those?" he demanded.

"The same way you did."

Orlando cut him off with a sharp gesture and an even sharper word. "No."

Dante nodded slowly, his eyes sad but determined. "They came for me in the middle of the night. I was at da Vinci's studio."

"No." Orlando's voice rose in volume.

"They took me. They imprisoned me. They tried me, judged me. Sentenced me." Dante's voice was relentless.

"It's not possible." Orlando's lips barely moved. His face had paled to a shade beyond snow.

"They marked me." Dante clenched his fists, the veins standing up beneath the golden chains.

Orlando shook his head, his eyes locked on his brother's hands.

"They stood me before the black hourglass door. And they sent me through."

"No," Orlando said for the third time, but this time it was only a whisper. A sigh. More of a wish than a denial. "Not you. They didn't . . . they couldn't have . . ."

Dante nodded. "I found myself on the bank."

Both brothers turned toward me. They looked so much alike that I felt my heart skip a beat.

Dante reached out and gripped Orlando's hand with his, drawing his attention and holding it steady. "*You* found me on the bank."

Orlando swallowed. "When?"

Dante turned his right wrist over, revealing the letters etched into his flesh: MMIX.

Orlando closed his eyes. "That far? They sent you forward that far?" A muscle quivered in his jaw. "How did you survive it?"

Dante turned back to me, his gray eyes unreadable behind the scar. "I had help," he said simply.

I caught my breath, feeling the air burn in my lungs. I closed the space between us in two quick steps and knelt by his side. I joined my hand to Dante's on Orlando's arm. At my touch, Orlando opened his eyes.

"I know this is hard to hear," I said, "but it's the truth. I promise."

Orlando nodded, but his gaze was unfocused, distant. "It's my fault. He said he'd do it. He warned me. I didn't believe him. It's my fault," he repeated.

Dante and I exchanged a glance. We both knew the man to whom Orlando was referring: Zo. He had coerced Orlando's obedience by threatening to implicate Dante as one of the Sons of Italy. And when Orlando had turned in Zo to the authorities, Zo had turned in Dante as well.

"No," Dante said firmly. "It's not your fault. And I understand—now. Everything is all right."

"How can you say that?" Orlando demanded. "I ruined your life."

"You *saved* my life." Dante wrapped his arm around my shoulder and pulled me closer to his side. "You made it possible for me to *find* my life."

Orlando looked from Dante to me, and his eyes wouldn't let me go. A spasm of pain traveled along his jaw. He clenched down on his teeth with a sound like cracking ice. "So, I wasn't dreaming just now when I saw you on the bank?"

"No. I've been through the door and back. It's how I was able to come here. How I could come home," Dante said.

Orlando was silent for a long moment. "And your marks? They are gold because you're from . . . from the future?"

Dante nodded and gave me a little squeeze. "We *both* are."

"It's where we met," I said.

Orlando looked at me, the pain in his face touched with shadow. "That's how you knew," he said quietly. "What to tell me. How to help me on the bank. Because you've been here before."

"Not exactly," I said. "I haven't been *here* before. Not in 1501. I know what I know because of you, Orlando." I reached out to touch his knee, but I stopped short; he seemed unusually fragile and I didn't want to add any more pressure. "Because when you find Dante on the bank all those years from now, you will teach him what you know. And he, in turn, will teach me. So I, in turn, could teach you."

Orlando squeezed his eyes shut and dropped his head in his hands. "It makes my head hurt to think of it." When he looked up, his eyes were bloodshot. He rubbed restlessly at the marks on his wrists. "I'll never be free of it, will I? None of us will. We'll be trapped in this endless spiral of past and future forever. Doomed to pay for our mistakes for an eternity."

"No!" I said with more force than I'd intended. "That's not true. We can still change things. We can still choose." I reached for Dante's hand without looking and gripped it tight. "We're here to close the circle—lock it so it is *safe*. So it is *protected*. And once we do, we can leave the past behind and move forward. It is possible, Orlando. I promise."

He drew in a deep, shuddering breath. As he exhaled, he took my free hand, linking the three of us through a common touch, a common goal. "You've asked me to do a difficult thing, but . . . I will choose to believe you."

The moment of time that had been in flux snapped back into its flow, running fast toward the future. The ripples were spreading; I shivered as a shroud of unexpected possibilities seemed to fall over all of us.

"I wouldn't ask you to do it if I didn't think you could," I said quietly.

"Thank you," Dante chimed in, his voice low and raw, and I knew his gratitude extended to both me and Orlando. The first connection back to his family was complete, though it remained to be seen how strong it would hold, how long it would last.

I wondered how soon we would be able to do the same for my family.

A woman's voice rose in song from the corner of the shop, a melody I recognized.

Letting go of Orlando's hand, I stood up and turned around, the hairs on the back of my neck already warning of danger.

Valerie sat in her rumpled nest of blankets, the soles of her bare feet pressed together and her knees angled away from her body like wings. An unnatural brightness glimmered in her eyes. She sang one phrase over and over; I recognized it as the opening line of "Into the River." And with the music came a shot of pain. Darkness filled my mind as Zo's black veil threatened to fall over my memories again.

I fell back to my knees, fighting with everything I had in me to keep the darkness at bay. To hold on to my self and my sanity.

"It's time, my children," Valerie sang, her eyes never leaving mine. "It's time, time, time. The waves are rising. The waters are running. The clock is chiming midnight." She unfolded herself from the floor, a single sinuous motion that lifted her to her feet. She extended her arm and pointed a sharp finger at me. "You've felt his mark, his mouth, his mind. And you'll never be the same again. Oh, no. He'll make sure of that."

And then she threw back her head and laughed and laughed and laughed.

CHAPTER
12

Make her stop!" I cried, curling into myself and covering my ears with my hands. "Please!"

Dante slipped from the chair and knelt by my side before the words had left my mouth. He covered my shaking hands with his strong ones and the extra pressure against my ears muted the sound of Valerie's voice until it was nothing but a rumbling murmur.

At the same time, Orlando rushed to Valerie's side and covered her mouth. Instantly he yelped and pulled his hand away. Shaking his fingers, he looked at Dante and me in shock. "She bit me!"

"Did not!" Valerie retorted, folding her arms in a pout.

Orlando ignored her. "What is she saying?" he asked us, confused. "I can't understand her."

"That's because I'm speaking English, silly. Would you rather I speak something else? Because I can," she said in perfect Italian. "What about this?" she added in French. "Or this?" she finished in Spanish. "I speak the language of what-ever story I'm in, and this story has Italian written all over it."

Orlando's eyes bulged in surprise.

Dante turned to me for an explanation, but I shrugged. I didn't know how it was possible, but then there was so much about Valerie that was strange and impossible. "She can speak the truth in a story. Why not Italian, too?" I murmured. I wondered what else she was hiding in her cracked and broken mind, what other talents or gifts might be at her call.

"Who are you?" Orlando demanded of Valerie. "What are you doing here? Where did you get these?" He grabbed her arm, holding up her tattooed wrist to examine the chains marked there.

"She did those to herself," I answered.

Orlando dropped Valerie's arm in horror. "Why?"

"It's a long story. She's my friend," I answered, though it felt strange to claim her as such when she was so very different from the person I'd grown up with. "She also came through the door like I did. But she's not well."

Valerie bared her teeth at Orlando and snapped at him again.

"Valerie," Dante said calmly, "don't bite people, please."

"I don't have to do what you say." Valerie yanked her arm away from Orlando and smoothed her hair down. "Or you," she tossed over her shoulder at Orlando before turning away.

Dante frowned. "Fine. Then the River Policeman says, 'Don't bite people, please.'"

Valerie turned back, her eyes opened wide. She bit her lip. "The River Policeman?" Her voice lost its high-edged intensity, replaced with a gentle reverence. She took a step toward Dante.

I flinched back in his arms, hating my instinctive reaction.

Valerie had once been my best friend, and now I didn't want her to come another step closer. I lowered my hands but kept them tucked under my chin, just in case. I still felt the darkness hanging over my mind like a guillotine's blade.

"I need to talk to the River Policeman," Valerie said. "I need his help."

"I can help you," Dante said. "But first I need you to sit still and be quiet for a moment. Can you do that for me?"

In answer, Valerie dropped to the floor, crossing her legs and sitting up as straight as possible. She drew an imaginary zipper across her lips, twisting her fingers at the corner of her mouth. She looked at her pinched fingers, a frown of concentration pulling her eyebrows together. Then she twisted around and held out her closed hand toward Orlando.

He looked over Valerie's head at us.

Valerie huffed a breath through her nose and wiggled her hand at Orlando.

"What does she want?" he asked.

"She wants you to take the key," I said, remembering how upset Valerie had been when I had once so casually discarded an imaginary key of my own.

"She doesn't *have* a key," he said slowly, as though he had missed an important detail.

Valerie reached even further toward Orlando, her body contorting in her effort to stay where Dante had asked her to stay, yet still move closer.

"I know. Like I said, it's a long story."

Orlando took a cautious step forward, extending his open hand toward Valerie's. A red crescent bite mark bloomed on the heel of his palm. When his hand was directly beneath Valerie's, she opened her fingers. Orlando folded his fingers into a fist as though he had caught whatever she had dropped, and Valerie relaxed, a smile lighting up her face.

Edging away from her, Orlando returned to where we sat by the fireplace.

Dante helped me to my feet and into the chair he had recently abandoned. He hovered behind me, his touch never far from my shoulder, my neck, my arm.

"So, will you tell me the story?" Orlando sat in the other chair. "I think I deserve to know what's going on. And what I've agreed to."

I took a deep breath and told Orlando the abbreviated version of who Valerie was and why she was the way she was and how she had ended up here, Dante chiming in as needed. I hadn't been kidding; even just covering the basics, it was a long story and my throat hurt by the time I was done. My heart hurt, too, as I relived the events of the past few months. Had it really only been since January? Since Dante had first come into my life and everything had changed?

Through the entire retelling of her history, Valerie leaned forward like an attentive pupil, her eyes moving in an endless circle from me to Dante to Orlando and back again.

Orlando leaned back in his chair, his fist still holding the invisible key. He turned his thoughtful gaze to Valerie, and when her focus was back on him, he held her eyes. "I'll keep it safe for you until you need it back," he said. "I promise."

Valerie nodded solemnly, crossing her finger over her heart, first one way, then the other.

"What does that mean?" he asked me in a low voice.

"She wants you to promise—cross your heart and hope to die."

Orlando looked at me oddly, but he mimicked Valerie's motion.

Dante cleared his throat and stepped around me, kneeling down in front of Valerie. "Thank you," he said. "You have been very still and very quiet, just as I asked. I'd like to help you now. What did you want to talk to the River Policeman about?"

She twitched her lips back and forth but didn't say anything.

Dante reached out and touched her knee. "It's all right. The key is safe. And the River Policeman says you can talk now without it."

She exhaled as though she'd been holding her breath the entire time. "Oh, good. I knew you could help me."

"What can I do for you?"

Instead of answering, Valerie tilted her head until it almost touched her shoulder. She waved her hand in front of Dante's face. "Can you see me?"

Dante didn't blink. "The River Policeman can see everything."

She hiccupped a breath, and suddenly tears filled her eyes, spilling down her cheeks. She pressed her hands to her chest. "Then you can see my broken heart?"

Dante nodded gently.

"It's not fair," she said, her voice small and sad. "I did everything I was supposed to. Everything he wanted. But it wasn't enough. *I* wasn't enough. In the end." She twisted the edge of the belt of her bathrobe into a knot.

"On the contrary, I think you might have been more than he could handle."

"It's been forever since I've seen him." She frowned, and the twisting motion of her hands turned to ripping. "He only comes to see me now when he needs something from me. I don't like that. I don't like that he just takes and takes. He used to give me gifts, you know. Bring me special things." Her face brightened through her tears. "He once gave me a doll. It was pink and silver and it had the letters *L* and *A* on the chest. He told me it stood for *l' amore,* which means *the love.* I loved it so much I didn't even care that the dolly didn't have a head."

I felt myself turn to stone. That had been my doll once upon a time. Zo had stolen it from me and returned the head as a horrible surprise gift. He had given the rest of the doll to Valerie as a token of his love? A shiver ran up and down my arms like tiny spiders.

"Go on," Dante said, though with a slight quiver to his voice. "What else?"

"He used to sing to me all the time, but now he hardly even talks to me. I miss hearing him sing," she sighed. She hummed a few bars of "Into the River," and I whimpered in pain. The darkness drew a little tighter inside me.

"Valerie," Dante warned.

The music stopped and she sat up even straighter. "Sorry. I'm sorry. I'll be good. I promise."

"Thank you." Dante took her hand in his. "Tell the River Policeman exactly what you want him to do."

She looked down at their joined hands and a tear slipped down her cheek. "I want him to fix my broken heart. I want him to make everything all better."

"How can he do that?"

"By arresting the Pirate King." A scowl of hate pulled at her face. "You must make him pay," she growled, squeezing Dante's hand until her knuckles were white. "Make him hurt. Make him leave *her* alone"—she jerked her head in my direction, but Dante didn't move—"and make him come back to me."

Dante lowered his head. A stillness surrounded him, spreading wide to include Valerie, Orlando, and me. When he spoke, his words seemed to echo through the small room. "I promise you, I will stop him. I will keep him away from Abby."

"Oh, good—" Valerie began.

Dante interrupted, holding up his hand. "But—"

Valerie bit down on her lip.

"But I will *not* allow him to return to you either."

"What!" Valerie shouted, recoiling back, her fingers snapping into claws.

Her anger rolled off Dante's calmness. "He is dangerous. And when I stop him, I will send him to prison. That is what a policeman does. That is my job."

"But we belong together! I belong to him—"

"No!" Dante's stillness shattered. "You belong to no one but yourself. His claim over you is broken. You must not give in to him again."

"But I miss him," Valerie said uncertainly. "The last time I saw him, he asked me to tell him a story." She rubbed at her eyes. "The stories are so loud in my head, and they don't all have happy endings anymore." She leveled a serious look at Dante. "I don't like stories that don't have happy endings."

"What story did you tell him?" I asked. "Was it a story like you used to tell to me? Maybe one about the Pirate King and the River Policeman?" I knew Valerie's stories were a strange blend of fantasy and fact, prophecies within plots, because it had been partly her stories that had helped me save Dante from certain destruction.

Valerie ignored me and directed her answer to Dante. "I wish it had been. I like those stories the best; they are exciting and adventurous and bloody. No, the last story I told him was about the Pirate King and the Flower Girl. I didn't like her story." She shook her head. "The Pirate King didn't like it either, but I can only tell the stories that want to be told." Valerie twisted her fingers together in agitation. "It's the saddest story I know."

"And you don't like sad stories," Dante said gently.

"No, I do not," she agreed regally.

"Will you tell us the story?" I asked, leaning forward.

"I'm not going to tell *you* anything," she sneered in my direction.

"Will you tell me?" Dante asked.

The look she gave him was soft and humble and happy. "Oh, yes. I'll tell you anything you want to know." She patted the floor next to her. "Come closer. This is a story that wants closeness."

Dante slid forward, but when Valerie sighed in exasperation, he moved even closer.

Jealousy nibbled at me at the sight of the two of them together. I knew it was silly to feel that way, but I still left my seat and knelt next to Dante on the floor.

Valerie glared at me and pressed her lips together.

"She stays." Dante's voice left no room for negotiation. "Now, tell the story."

Valerie shifted on her seat, her hands flitting from her lap to her knees and back again. She bowed her head and mumbled something under her breath.

"What was that?" Dante asked. "What did you say?"

She turned away, her gaze traveling over the glass bottles and sealed containers on the shelves surrounding us. Her fingers twitched and trembled.

"Do you need your dollies?" I asked quietly. "Would that help you tell the story?"

She whipped around to stare at me, hot smears of red on her face. "I don't need *your* help at all! I can tell the story all by myself."

Orlando stood up from his seat and walked to the counter, rummaging through the boxes and bottles that were still scattered on the surface until he found a small something he folded into his palm.

"What are you doing?" I asked. Dante tilted his head at the sound of Orlando's activity.

"Helping," he said. "I hope." He pulled out a square of gray fabric from a cupboard and wrapped it around a short, stout bottle filled with a dark red liquid. As he returned to the fireplace, he pulled out the cork and dropped whatever had been in his hand inside the bottle. He handed the bundle to

Valerie, who took it from him with shaking hands and wide eyes.

"What is it?" she asked, breathless.

"It's a doll made of glass. But you must be very careful with it or else it will break."

Valerie clutched it to her chest. "Oh, I will be ever so careful. I promise." She began swaying back and forth, rocking her doll like a baby, her eyes closed and a smile appearing on her lips.

"What did you put in it?" I asked Orlando in a low voice.

"A packet of dried apothecary rose petals. When mixed with the liquid inside, the scent will help calm her mind."

"I remember when you used to make that for me," Dante said quietly to his brother. "For when my dreams were unusually bad."

I nodded to Orlando, grateful for his quick thinking and for his ability to help Valerie now and Dante then.

Valerie's eyes fluttered open. "Even though the Flower Girl lived in a sad story, she wasn't always so sad," she began in a soft, rock-a-bye voice. She tucked the cloth tighter around the bottle, holding it up to her cheek. A kindness entered her face, softening it back to the familiar features I remembered. "When she was young, she was yellow and gold and light. She was as fragile as a wish made on dandelion seeds, as quiet as clouds across a summertime sunset."

I leaned against Dante's shoulder, lulled by the ebb and flow of Valerie's story. Unlike the tales she told of cunning pirates and stoic policemen, this one felt gentle. The cadence reminded me a little of how I felt when I listened to Zo's

music or Dante's poetry, but instead of summoning a dangerous darkness or a healing light, this rhythm made me think of
standing on the edge of the ocean and watching the waves roll
in.

"She was a mouse. Happy to be hidden, happy to nibble
at the edges of life. But even though she was small, her heart
was full of love, love, love.

"There was a meadow she liked to visit. A sprawling, rolling ocean of flowers and grass. She loved to dance in that
meadow. But then one day the Pirate King sailed up and said
that he would take her away from her meadow, from her flowers and her friends. The Pirate King said that it would make
him happy to make her live on his giant pirate ship. He said
that once they sailed away, she would never have to come
back home.

"But instead of making the Flower Girl happy, that news
made her sad. She didn't want to leave her family. And she
didn't like the Pirate King. She didn't like his black eyes or his
sharp teeth. She may have been a mouse, but even a mouse
can roar. The Flower Girl said no to the Pirate King." Valerie
shuddered with surprise and disbelief.

"So the Pirate King plucked the Flower Girl and cast her
aside." Valerie gently stroked the cloth wrapped around the
bottle in her lap. "He left her in the meadow that she loved,
where she withered and died, her heart pierced with a thorn
and all the petals of her soul crumbling to dust."

Valerie's voice trailed off into silence for a moment before
she finished the story.

"And after she died, the river swept her away, never to

return, just like it will sweep all of us away one day." She blinked slowly at me and Orlando, and a sad and broken smile fluttered across her lips. "Well, not *us,* of course—not anymore." She leaned toward Dante, whispering conspiratorially. "And not *you,* either. Not unless you choose to go."

"I'll not leave Abby behind," Dante said firmly. "No matter what."

"Then I can't promise you'll have a happy ending to your story either," Valerie said sadly. "You know the barriers are thinning. You know some of them are even breaking."

"Yes, but we're going to fix them—" I started.

"I already told you—you're too late. Everlastingly too late." She lowered the bottle to her lap, a little of the liquid spilling out onto her clothes. "The dreams are already escaping. Soon they will all be gone. And then nothing will be left."

"Do you still have a dream, Valerie?" Dante asked quietly. "Or has yours already escaped?"

She looked down at the glass in her lap; the red rose petals had darkened the liquid to the color of blood. "I dream of standing still. I am tired of feeling like I'm flying when I know I'm really falling. I want to rest. I want to find silence again." She ran her finger along the curved edge of the bottle, and when she looked up, her eyes were bright with an inner light. "People think edges are bad, but they are really there to keep us from falling to pieces. They don't hold us back, they hold us in. They hold us together."

I blinked back tears. This was the closest I'd seen Valerie to being back to her old self. Dante's poem and Orlando's potion had worked wonders. Maybe, with a little more time and a little more help, we could bring her all the way back to sanity.

"I know how you feel, Valerie," I said quietly, knowing it was the truth. "And I promise I'll do what I can to help your dream to come true."

"Oh, Abby, my sweet," a voice rang out from the front door of the shop. "You should know better than to make promises you can't keep."

CHAPTER
13

I jumped to my feet a second after Dante did. He automatically positioned himself between me and the figure who slouched against the door frame.

Valerie twisted around as well, the bottle in her lap crashing to the floor. When she saw Zo standing in the doorway, she cried out with joy.

"You came back for me! I knew you would!" She crawled through the shards of broken glass toward him.

When she was close enough to touch his knee, Zo looked down in disgust, closed the door behind him, and sidestepped her grasping hand. He stalked forward, his boots cracking against the floor, drawing a straight line from the door to Dante. And to me, standing behind him.

"Wait! It's me. Look at me! I'm here! I've been waiting for you." Valerie's voice rang out louder and more urgently the farther Zo walked away from her. "No, please! Don't go!"

Zo ignored her cries, his stride steady and purposeful.

Valerie collapsed into a puddle of despair in his wake, a mournful wail dribbling from her mouth around broken sobs.

Orlando shoved out of his chair by the fireplace, and

without looking, Zo flung out his hand. "Don't. I'm not here for you. This is not your fight. If you choose to walk away, I'll let you go. Otherwise . . ."

Orlando ignored Zo's unspoken threat as completely as Zo had ignored Valerie's desperate pleas. He moved forward to flank Dante, adding his protection and blocking Zo's access to me.

Zo's steps slowed, then stopped. "Ah, brave and noble Orlando, still playing the hero. It's good that you keep trying. Maybe one of these days you'll get it right."

I felt Orlando bristle, a hard edge of tension pulling his shoulders taut. "I don't know what game you're playing at, Lorenzo, but I should kill you for what you've done."

"You could try," Zo said amicably, "but you wouldn't succeed. I'm not who you think I am. Not anymore. Isn't that right, Dante?"

Orlando glanced at Dante and then at me, looking for an explanation or clarification, and I shook my head slightly. Now was not the time to explain. And being so close to Zo made the lingering drop of darkness in my mind buzz with angry energy.

"And valiant Dante," Zo continued. "You don't look much better than you did the last time I saw you. Of course, the last time I saw you, you were smashing my guitar. You shouldn't have done that, you know. I'm not really a forgive-and-forget kind of person." He nodded toward Dante's wounded eyes, and his mocking tone held bitter laughter. "Tell me, how is life in the shadows these days? Are you totally blind, or just mostly?"

"Why are you here?" Dante demanded.

"To make you pay the consequences for your actions," he said, all trace of humor gone from his voice. "And to take back what's mine."

"There's nothing here that belongs to you."

Zo turned to me. His eyes were the same feverish black they had been at the cathedral. "Is that true, Abby? My sweet, sweet Abigail." When my name passed his lips, the buzzing in my head turned from a roar to a shout.

I closed my eyes against the pain singing in my head. "Leave me alone!" I felt his pull on me like a magnet. But even as my feet itched to move in his direction, I knew that was the wrong thing to do. I knew the closer I was to him, the more I was in danger. I pressed my hands flat against Dante's back and leaned my forehead between his shoulder blades, hoping that the contact would help keep me grounded.

I tried repeating Dante's healing poem in my head, hoping the words would help protect me.

Zo laughed, but the sound was wild and unsettled. "You should know better than to leave your prize possessions un-attended, Dante. Why, anyone could just come by and take them and break them into pieces."

My blood froze; I had heard those same words before. The poem I had been clinging to crumbled like dust.

"She's not broken. And she's not yours. Her memories are restored," Dante said, his voice controlled and certain. "You no longer have a hold over her."

"Is that so?" Zo's long fingers twitched as though seeking for strings to play, for a song to command me. I knotted my hands in Dante's shirt and held on so I wouldn't fall. "Abby's memories may be back, but I'm still in her head. How does it feel, Abby?" he called over Dante's shoulder. "Do you remember how happy it made you to say that you loved me? Do you remember our kiss?"

My mouth burned, and I pressed my lips together to keep from answering.

Valerie made a strangled noise before her sobs cut into silence.

"You should go," Orlando said to Zo. His voice was quiet, but with an edge that sounded like a sword being unsheathed. "We all appreciate your flair for dramatic entrances, as well as your pathetic attempts at threats and insults, but you are not welcome here."

Zo arched an eyebrow. "Oh, I think someone here might disagree—" He gestured with a flourish toward Valerie, lumped in front of the door.

Only Valerie wasn't there anymore.

She stood directly behind Zo, an avenging angel of contained fury, and when he turned, she slashed out with her ragged fingernails, rocking his head to the side and cutting four grooves deep into his cheek.

Zo stumbled back a step, off balance and surprised. His hand flashed to his face, a snarl distorting his features.

"You took my heart," she said, her words clipped and her voice unnaturally calm. Zo's blood dripped off her fingers. "I want it back."

Zo dabbed at his wounds, barely glancing at the smears of red on his hand. He worked his jaw and shook his head a little. The entire left side of his face burned red from the force of Valerie's attack.

I watched in horror as the slashes on Zo's face closed up, leaving behind only clean skin. I swallowed hard.

He straightened to his full height and a smile tugged at his lips. He looked at Valerie with coal-black eyes. "No," he said.

Valerie wasn't the only one who blinked in surprise. I gasped. Orlando rocked onto the balls of his feet, ready to spring forward, but Dante gripped his arm and held him in place.

"You *gave* me your heart," Zo said. "And now it's mine to do with as I please. Break it. Burn it. Leave it behind." He shrugged. "But I'm certainly not going to give it back."

I saw the hurt and the rage descend over Valerie's face, pouring through her body like acid. "You can't make me be your new Flower Girl. I won't do it." She lashed out with her fist again, but Zo caught her wrist and twisted, spinning her around and forcing her arm behind her back.

Valerie yelped as her knees buckled. Her hair whipped back and forth as she struggled to maintain her balance.

Zo pulled her close to him, his arm snaking around her body and pinning her to his chest. "I never asked you to." He watched me from behind Valerie's shoulder, his eyes locked on mine with an intensity that I could feel like a physical presence. "Besides, there's someone else I want now. Someone I want more."

Valerie made a broken, desolate mewing sound. Red blotches bloomed on her face. Then her swollen eyes turned angry, and her mouth curled from anguish to pain. "I hate you so much it hurts," she growled out between tears.

Zo lowered his face, his smile growing into a grin, and nuzzled at Valerie's neck. "I love you too."

"That's enough!" Dante roared, springing forward. Mid-flight, he disappeared.

I stepped back in surprise, but there was no time for anyone else to move before Dante reappeared behind Zo.

Dante punched Zo in the back, a swift jab below the ribs that caused him to grunt in surprise and pain. He released his hold on Valerie, who crumpled to the floor, all her limbs loose and disjointed. Immediately, Dante grabbed Zo and they both flickered away, leaving behind only a patch of blurry air.

I knew Dante couldn't see Zo—not directly. But he could see the flow of the river clearly from the bank. I suspected Dante had gone there for a flicker of a moment, pinpointed where Zo was, and then positioned himself for a sudden attack.

It had been a brave and impulsive thing to do. Usually Dante was more reserved, prone to think things through before acting. But I was grateful to him for springing to Valerie's rescue when no one else could.

"Come on," I said to Orlando, darting around him. I grabbed his arm on my way past, pulling him behind me as I raced to Valerie's side in a handful of steps. "Help me move her."

The air rippled again and Dante and Zo reappeared, but only for a flicker of time. I caught a glimpse of Dante's hands locked around Zo's bicep. Zo's foot lashed out as though ready to take a step, or kick out a knee, and then they vanished again.

"Lorenzo vanished like that before at the cathedral. Does that mean he's been through the door too? He is like Dante? Is he from the future?" Orlando demanded, joining me and lifting Valerie from the floor.

I nodded. "Dante and Zo have both been through the door a second time, so they're free to travel the river at will." I hurried to the counter, checking to make sure it was high enough and sturdy enough that it could serve as a shield if necessary. "It's also how Zo was able to heal from Valerie's attack."

"Zo?" Orlando repeated, his confusion transforming into understanding. "Lorenzo."

Another flicker, but this time I saw that Zo had cocked his fist back, aiming a blow for Dante's head.

I gasped, ready to shout out a warning, but they were already gone.

The last time Dante and Zo had flickered like this had been in the blasted basement of the Dungeon, and Zo had done it specifically to weaken the barriers holding the river in place. I hoped that Dante was taking precautions to keep the barriers intact this time, but with the two of them fighting as well as flickering, and with the river so unstable, I didn't know if that was even possible. I couldn't take the risk.

"Here," I said to Orlando, pointing to the alcove where the counter curved to meet the wall. "Put her here."

Orlando knelt and gently helped Valerie sit up against the wall. "You're safe now. Everything is all right," he repeated in a constant wash of murmured reassurance.

She pulled her knees to her chest and gripped her wrists, the muscles in her arms tight as she strained to hold herself together. A blank mask covered her face, bone-white and flat. Her eyes glazed over gray, rolling in their sockets, looking without seeing. She swayed in place, picking up speed until she rocked back and forth so hard her head hit the wall.

I winced at the thud.

A flicker of activity drew my attention. I looked up in time to see Zo appear—but alone this time. He shook out his hand as though he had connected with something hard and unforgiving. He stepped toward me, a flat anger masking his face and his eyes burning. Orlando moved to intercept him, but at the same moment, Dante materialized and knocked Zo off his feet. They disappeared before they hit the ground.

"Will you stay with her?" I asked, touching Orlando's shoulder and nodding toward Valerie.

"Where are you going?" He twisted out of his crouch to his feet.

I had forgotten how tall he was, how imposing he could be.

"I have to help Dante," I said, pointing to the main floor of the shop where glimpses of Dante and Zo appeared and disappeared like shadows of birds in flight.

"How? They're too fast, and—"

"I don't know," I interrupted. "But I have to do something."

Faced with an impossible situation, my mind ran through the possibilities, looking for a creative, workable solution. It was a discouragingly short list. But there was one thing on the list that I thought I could do. It was crazy and dangerous and there was no guarantee that it would even work, but it was something I could *do*. And right now, that was what I wanted—action. Even if it was the longest shot I could take.

Before I had traveled through time, I had made three trips to the bank: once with Dante, once by myself, and once with Leo and V. Every time I had gone, I had brought some of my time with me. And every time I had returned to the river, I had brought back some of the bank's timelessness, too, which had appeared as a shell of glass around me, trapping me inside. And every time, Leo had been there to help restore the balance of time and set me free.

Now that I had passed through the door, I was bound to the bank and outside of time. But I wondered if I could still tap into that strange exchange of time and timelessness like I had before. If so, maybe I could craft a shell of time and trap Zo in it.

And if not, I hoped no one else but me would suffer the consequences.

I scanned the room, looking for the best place to stand and launch my attack. I would have to time it perfectly. But how could I let Dante know what I wanted to do? I would need his help. Or at least let him know where *not* to be.

A thud, and a grunt. Zo landed hard on the ground, Dante a half beat behind him, his boots thumping into place next to Zo's head. Zo rolled to the side, his dark hair falling into his eyes. Sweat covered his face. He was gone like a smeared shadow.

"Dante!" I called out before he jumped away. He looked

at me, but his body remained poised to vanish. "I have a plan. Can you get Zo next to the fireplace?"

Dante nodded, and then he was gone.

"How can Dante be following him—I mean, if he can't see?" Orlando asked.

"He can see the river," I said. "It's enough." I pointed to the patch of rippling air where Zo had been a moment ago. "Plus, Zo's getting sloppy."

Dante flashed into and out of view so fast—all dark hair and intensity—that the afterimage of him burned in my eyes. I would have only one chance, I knew that. And if I was wrong, if I misjudged the moment to spring the trap, Zo would go free and Dante would be caught instead.

I took a deep breath, shaking out my fingers and trying to steady my nerves. Zo and Dante seemed to be moving around a pivot point in the center of the floor. Each appearance brought them not only closer together but also one step forward around the circle. That was good. It meant that Dante had gotten my message and was moving Zo into place.

Between flashes, I darted to the center of the spiral, standing still and counting out a steady rhythm. If it worked for Zo and for Dante, I hoped it would work for me too.

"What are you doing?" Orlando called out, his frustration clear in his voice.

"What I have to," I called back.

"Can I help?"

I shook my head. "Just stay there. And whatever happens, don't come any closer." I felt bad enough putting Dante at risk without his knowledge; I didn't want to put Orlando in danger as well.

Concentrate, I told myself. *Count. Find that in-between space.*

I listened to the quick heartbeat sound of Dante's boots hitting the ground a moment before Zo's did—*thump-thump, thump-thump*. I listened to the slower rhythmic thud of Valerie's head hitting the wall as she tried to rock away her pain. I listened to the screaming rush of blood in my ears, of the air moving in and out of my lungs, and I felt more than heard a distant chime begin to play inside of me.

There it was. That was what I needed. The music of time. I held on to that shimmering chime, focusing all my will on keeping it ringing, keeping it whole and unbroken.

I had heard such music before—when I had opened the black hourglass door for the first time and again when I had walked my own path through time—but now the music was different. It was almost as though I could hear words taking shape beneath the chimes. A hidden language I remembered from a long-ago time—or a time yet to be. A language I felt I could speak. Almost.

The edges of my vision rippled with the sound waves that echoed through me. I breathed. I concentrated. I counted.

Thump-thump. Thud. Thump-thump. Thud.

The contents of the shop wavered, then bled away in a smear of color and light, only to be replaced by the vast, unwelcome expanse of the bank. I could see it; I was nearly there.

Thump-thump. Thud.

A stillness engulfed me, and I was in between.

Exactly where I wanted to be.

It felt similar to the times I'd dreamed my way to the bank, but not quite. I was mostly still *here*—in the apothecary shop—but I was also partly *there*—on the bank. I could feel keenly the sharp divide between the river and bank, a knife-point pressed to my ribs, painful but not puncturing. The pressure made it hard to breathe.

I saw the black shadow of Dante flicker into the shop, and then, out of the corner of my eye, I saw him appear in the distance along the bank. Tracking his movements there and back made my head hurt. The strange double vision made my eyes water and throb.

Zo was half a heartbeat behind Dante, and gaining. I didn't have much time left. If my plan was going to work, I had to pull the trigger. Now.

I thought back to when I'd been trapped in that glass shell of time—how it felt, how it looked. I felt a rising wave of claustrophobic panic. No. Not now. I pushed it aside, filling the resulting void with anger and action.

Pulling a deep breath into my lungs, I concentrated on finding that moment when time shifted into timelessness. Shadows of Zo and Dante blurred in my vision—first here, then there. The sounds around me turned loud and brassy, but brittle, as though they would come crashing down at the first wild shout.

Where was it? The moment—I needed to find that one moment where I could change things. Now, before it was too late. Before I lost my courage.

There. I had found it. And what filled my ears was different from the endless ringing of time or even the roar of the river. It was a quietness. An absence. A stillness that reminded me of Dante.

In that timeless moment, the stillness inside of me was balanced perfectly against the stillness outside of me. And then, rising up out of the depths of my mind, I heard again the music of time and the strange language that rippled beneath it.

Without knowing how, I spoke a delicate sound—half-word, half-chime—and at my call, a small bubble of time rose up from the river, a clear droplet made up of the moment *before*. The moment *between*.

Thump-thump. Zo. Dante.

I reached out for that bubble, holding my breath. What would happen when I touched it? Was I crazy for even thinking this was possible?

Thump-thump. Dante. Zo.

The bubble shivered at my touch, turning soft and pliable. It quivered in my hand, but it didn't disappear. It didn't break.

Thump—Zo.

I opened my eyes, focusing on the here and now, and saw the lean shape of Zo standing before me directly in the spot I'd indicated to Dante.

Thump—Dante.

Without hesitation, I pulled that moment of time free from that in-between place and hurled it at Zo. It hit him square in the chest, and he looked down in surprise. A clear substance stuck to his shirt, bending and shifting in rhythm with his breathing. He brushed at the small pearl of time with the back of his hand. But instead of flicking away, the clear spot shimmered and began to spread across his chest and over his arms. The more Zo tried to push it away, the more persistent it became, growing like ice on a lake, like mold.

I watched in amazed horror as a shield of glass appeared between us, rising up high over Zo's head and simultaneously wrapping wide around his body. The clear edges met and fused together in a seamless stretch of captured time.

Zo spun on his heel, but Dante stood behind him, blocking his escape. The muscles in his body flexed as he tried to jump away, but nothing happened. He turned back to face me, his eyes black holes of frustrated anger.

I looked past Zo to Dante and felt the beginnings of a smile curve my mouth. My impossible plan had worked.

And then Zo took a step forward, his hands reaching for my throat, and he hit the curve of the shell with a sound like a struck bell.

My entire body resonated with the impact. I stumbled back, my mouth open. Unexpected pain shot through me.

Zo cocked his head, watching me with a considering look in his eyes, the anger shadowed with wariness. He hit the shell a second time, and I fell to my knees on the hard floor.

As the pain intensified, I knew that Zo was trapped in time, just as I had hoped.

But I also knew he wasn't the only one caught in the trap.

The price of my plan had come due, and I feared it would be higher than I could pay.

CHAPTER
14

I had never felt such pain before. Not when I had nearly died in the Dungeon fire, not when Zo had redirected the river and erased my family, not even when Zo had stolen my memories and left me scarred and forgotten.

The pain started in the bottom of my feet, sharp pricks like needlepoint stitching a layer of heat onto my skin. I sucked in a hard breath and reached down to rub at my ankles and toes, but it seemed like wherever I touched, the pain spread, a hot red that swept up my legs, my hips, my chest, and down my arms.

"Abby?" Dante asked, his voice drifting to me from an ocean away. His gray eyes clouded over to white. A frown pulled at his forehead. "What's wrong?"

I shook his words away, afraid that if I opened my mouth only a cry would emerge. Or a scream.

He crossed the room in two long strides. When he reached my side, he brushed his hand against my back, but I hissed at even that light contact, and he pulled away. The frown deepened.

Heat bubbled up inside me like a blister, smooth and liquid.

"Talk to me. Tell me what's going on."

I leaned forward, my palms flat against the floor. I twisted my head away from him a moment before my body convulsed in pain and I vomited up a clear liquid. I drew in short, shallow breaths and squeezed my eyes shut as another needle threaded through my side. I felt like I'd been running for hours. Sweat beaded across my forehead, dripped down my temples. I could taste the salt on my lips.

Dante reached for me anyway, his hands searching to see something his eyes could not.

As much as I wanted to lean into him, let his cool hands touch me and soothe the fires that consumed me, I didn't dare. The pain spread through me like an infection; I didn't want to pass it along to Dante. I rocked away from him. My joints protested the movement and I had to bite down on my lip to hold back a moan. The taste of blood mixed with the salt in my mouth.

"Abby." Dante's voice held a note of command that I could not ignore.

"I . . . I don't know what's happening." I gasped as my bones felt the twist of a sudden torque. The whimper that had been building finally escaped, along with a sharp exhalation. "It hurts." It was all I could manage. My tears that fell were edged with ice, a coldness that burned worse than the blistering heat.

Through my blurred vision, I saw Zo pull back and punch

at the shell surrounding him with knuckles that were raw and red with blood.

Already on my knees, I felt my arms fold beneath me. I curled into a small ball, hoping to protect myself from additional, unspeakable agony. With that last blow, I finally understood what was happening to me. I'd constructed the prison that now held Zo, which meant that I was connected to it. I feared that Zo's attempts to break free would break me instead.

I looked up at Dante. "I'm sorry," I said, knowing it wasn't enough, but not knowing what else to say.

Dante set his mouth in a thin line and, in one quick motion, grasped my wrists and pulled me to my feet.

I let out a small yelp of surprise, but he held me in his arms and wouldn't let me go. The pain flared once, white-hot, and then the heat started lessening, dissipating in waves as suddenly as it had arrived. The agony that had swallowed me whole drifted away, leaving a cool relief in its place that felt like early-morning dew.

It was only then that I realized Dante had been whispering in my ear. He spoke the string of words so fast and low as to be almost unintelligible, but I managed to capture the echo of a few phrases:

> *I can take this pain.*
> *I can take this time.*
> *I will break this chain.*
> *I will make this mine.*

The rough poem lacked his usual grace and fluency, but the rhythm did its job. As before, when Dante's words had driven the darkness from my mind, now they drove the pain from my body. Blinking to clear my vision, I thought I saw the golden bands around his wrists glow brighter the longer he chanted his impromptu rhyme.

"I can take this pain. I can take this time," he repeated, his voice urgent and firm.

I pulled in a deep breath, grateful to feel the normal expansion of my lungs instead of the tightness that had locked me in place.

"I will break this chain. I will make this mine," he finished.

Looking over Dante's shoulder, I saw Zo smash his fist against the shell, but this time I didn't feel any pain. The bond between us had been broken.

When I didn't react to Zo's violence, he lowered his hand, his eyes turning to black slits of shadow. His body relaxed out of the intensity of attack into the casual slouch of a predator before the pounce.

The room was silent except for the constant stream of poetry flowing from Dante.

I touched my finger to his lips, stopping his words. "You did it. You broke the chain. It's gone. I'm better." The tears continued to flow, but now they were free and clean.

"What did you *do?*" Orlando asked quietly.

I turned in the curve of Dante's arms—I wasn't quite ready to leave his protection yet—and looked at Orlando.

True to his word, he hadn't come any closer to me. I could see the toll his obedience had taken, though. Deep lines of anxiety cut into his forehead and around his mouth. His eyes had darkened to a deep blue. He looked visibly older than he was, and I had a sudden memory flash of Leo standing over me as an inferno swallowed up the Dungeon. He had the same expression of worry on his face now as he did then. Or would, in all those years to come. It was getting harder to keep the past and the future in their proper places.

"She did the impossible," Dante said, a touch of wonder in his voice. "What made you think of it?" he asked me.

"Well, it's happened before. Not like this, of course," I added. "But I thought it was worth a try."

Orlando approached the shell of time, his eyes narrowed in thought.

Zo lounged against the far curve, his legs crossed at the ankles, his thumbs hooked into the belt loops of his pants.

It unnerved me to see him leaning up against what appeared to be nothing but air.

"Can he hear us, do you think?" Orlando asked.

"Of course I can." Zo flipped the hair out of his eyes with a casual toss of his head. "I'm trapped, not dead."

"Not yet." Orlando's lip curled in a sneer.

"Not ever," Zo shot back, but I saw him look at Dante with hooded eyes when he said it.

A scrabbling sound pulled my attention away from the standoff between Zo and Orlando. Valerie stood up from behind the counter, swaying on her feet. She held on to the edge of the counter with hands that visibly shook. Her ragged hair was matted by sweat, and tears streaked her face. She blinked, looking from me to Dante to Orlando before her eyes came to rest on Zo.

I braced myself for her reaction, for her to fly across the room in another attack, but Valerie simply drew in a shudder-ing breath and closed her eyes. An expression of true peace—the first I'd seen on her face in a long time—softened the tension in her forehead, her shoulders, her back. She exhaled a sigh.

"Valerie?" I called to her softly. "Are you all right? Do you need help?"

She opened her eyes and brushed at her bathrobe as though she could dislodge the ground-in dirt with a few swipes. She tied the belt around her waist. Rubbing her hands over her cheeks, she wiped away the last of her dried tears and then fluffed her hair with her fingers.

Gliding from behind the counter, she made her way across the room with slow and measured steps. She stopped in front of me and Dante and curtseyed as low and graceful as a noble-born lady.

"I must thank you, my darling River Policeman," she said, looking up at Dante with adoring eyes. "You held true to your promise. You found him and you caught him and you put him in prison, where he belongs. I am in your debt."

"You're welcome," Dante said gently. "But I had help." He tightened his arms around me. "Your thanks should extend to her as well."

Valerie immediately threw her arms around both of us. "My angels," she whispered.

I untangled myself from Dante's arms so I could embrace

Valerie in a proper hug. I wondered how long it had been since I'd been able to hug my friend like this—too long, I knew.

"Abby?" Zo's voice slithered into the stillness. "Can I have a hug too?"

I turned around and saw Zo standing with his arms open and his eyes soft and vulnerable. His pose didn't last long; a smirk cut through the façade, turning into a full-fledged grin.

The three of us joined Orlando next to the shell of time, lining up in a row in front of Zo. He lowered his arms, laughing. Orlando reached out toward the shell.

"No! Don't!" I grabbed his hand before he could make contact. "If you touch it—if any of us touch it—we'll break it open and set him free. Plus, I don't want you to get hurt."

"So does that mean you want *me* to be hurt?" Zo asked. He shook his head in mock sorrow. "I thought we were friends, Abby."

"What gave you that idea?" I snapped.

Zo arched an eyebrow. "You were so nice to me at the cathedral. You trusted me."

"I only trusted you because you made me." My skin crawled even being this close to him. I moved away from the edge of the glass, wanting to put as much space between me and Zo as possible.

He quirked his lips as though that were a minor point, as though he hadn't been the cause of my fractured memory. "Still—it was nice."

"No. It wasn't."

"You would be wise to stay quiet," Orlando snapped at Zo.

"Or what?" Zo asked. "You'll come in here and make me?"

"He won't," Dante said quietly. "But I will."

Zo swallowed down his sneer and shoved his hands into his pockets.

"You should be careful," Valerie whispered to Dante in a voice loud enough for all of us to hear. "He's not to be trusted."

"And yet you've all done it at one time or another," Zo commented. He turned his gaze to Orlando. "You believed in my vision." He moved his focus to Valerie. "You followed me willingly." Then to Dante. "You told me your secrets." And finally to me. "You gave me your heart."

My fingers touched the empty hollow of my throat where Dante's locket should have been, but wasn't.

"Looking for this?" Zo asked, withdrawing his hand from his pocket. A silver chain dangled from his fingers, a heart-shaped locket spinning in the air.

I heard Valerie gasp next to me.

Dante leaned toward me and spoke softly. "What is it? What does he have?" His voice was heavy with frustration at not being able to see.

"My locket," I choked out. "He still has my locket."

Dante's mouth thinned into an unhappy line. He shifted his weight next to me as though he wanted to rush forward, break open the shell around Zo, and take back the locket by force. But he settled back onto his heels, his arms folded across his chest and his fingers tapping his arm impatiently, anxiously.

"*Your* locket?" Zo asked, amused. He flicked the heart into his palm and then slipped it up through his fingers, making it walk across the tops of his knuckles, back and forth, back and forth. He paced the perimeter of his prison, following the curve of glass and shadow with careful, precise footsteps. "I'm surprised at you, Abby. You've worn this little bauble for months now and yet you still don't know what it is. What it means."

I narrowed my eyes, sensing a trap behind his words but unable to see the trigger that would snap it shut.

"Then again, maybe I shouldn't be surprised that Dante hasn't told you the truth about the locket. Maybe you'd like to believe that he didn't know the truth about it himself." Zo looked from me to Dante and back again, and his voice sharpened. "Though after what he did to my guitar, I doubt that possibility very much. No, he knew exactly what he was doing."

"Give it back," Dante growled. "The locket belongs to Abby."

"And now it belongs to me," Zo said, the silver heart catching the light as it continued to travel through his fingers. "That's my point. Don't worry. I'll give it back when I'm done with it." Zo pinned Dante with a hard look. "That is, if there's anything left."

"What truth?" I demanded. "What are you talking about?" I was tired of Zo's hints and thinly veiled barbs. I wanted to grab him by the shoulders and shake the words out of him, but the shell that kept him inside so effectively also kept us out.

Zo silently arched an eyebrow at Dante.

I touched Dante's arm. His muscles were in tight knots; his skin felt like stone.

"What truth?" I asked again, my voice quiet, gentle. "Dante?"

"The locket is more than just a symbol of my love," Dante said. "It's more than just a heart." He touched the scarred links along my neck. He hesitated, then whispered, "It *is* my heart."

Valerie squeaked in surprise and covered her mouth with one hand. With her other, she grabbed Orlando's arm. "Oh no, no, no," she murmured. "This is bad. Oh, so very, very bad."

Zo remained silent, his eyes unreadable through the wall of time.

I tried to pull my thoughts together. "But I've always known that. You told me that when you gave me the locket."

Dante started to shake his head before I even finished. "No, Abby, listen to me. The *locket* is my heart. When I said that my life and my heart were always in your hands, I meant it. I am linked to the locket, and so whatever happens to *it*—"

Dante didn't finish the thought, but he didn't have to. Understanding crashed over me and I turned in horror toward Zo, who held the locket in the palm of his hand. He closed his long fingers into a fist and smiled at me.

No. It couldn't be true. I wouldn't let it be true. I hadn't come so far and risked so much only to lose Dante now. I gripped his hand with mine, my thoughts spiraling away like so many loose threads. How had we ended up in this impossible situation? How had Zo managed to collect and control so much of our hearts? First Orlando, his heart broken by a loyalty betrayed; then Valerie, her obsession repaid with pain.

Zo had invaded my mind, twisting both my memories and my heart. And now Zo held Dante's life, literally, in his hands.

I couldn't look away from Zo's fist. My heart beat high and hard in my throat. I had regretted giving Zo the locket the moment it had left my hands. Now that I understood exactly what I had done, I had to do whatever I could to get it back.

Zo lounged against the shell of time, clearly enjoying my distress. "When I came to you in the cathedral, Abby, I was so mad at Dante for breaking my guitar. I was—if you'll pardon the expression—blind with rage. I wanted to make him hurt. I wanted to make him bleed. And I knew that making you mine would kill him. After all, what would be worse than seeing the woman you loved be with the man you hated? But then you gave me the locket like the obedient little girl that you are, and when I realized what I held in my hands . . ." Zo smiled in delight, a teacher whose pupil had unexpectedly provided the right answer. "I couldn't believe my luck. Imagine it. I can have you, Abby"—he held out his left hand, palm up, as though waiting for me to take it—"*and* I can destroy Dante"— he opened his right hand where the silver locket lay tangled in its chain—"at the same time."

"No," I whispered.

"A victory like this deserves an audience, don't you think? And I suspect Dante's destruction will be even more satisfying to watch than his death," Zo said, tipping his right hand and allowing the locket to clatter to the ground.

It bounced once, twice, and the moment it settled on the ground, Zo lifted his boot and slammed the edge of the heel down hard, directly onto the locket.

A sound like a shot rang out and Dante fell to his knees, his hand clutching at his chest.

I screamed and crouched down next to him, immediately wrapping my arms around him as though I could hold him together. He groaned in pain at my touch.

Orlando roared in protest, leaping toward Zo, but stopped short of contact with the shell. I had told him not to touch it, and, ever true to his word, he wouldn't, even though the effort of his restraint caused him to ball his hands into fists. I could see the hard muscles in his arms pull tight under his skin.

I brushed Dante's hair away from his face, trying to see where he had been hurt. He seemed fine, but I had seen Zo's boot hit the locket. I had heard the snap. I feared the wound was internal, somewhere I couldn't see it. Where I couldn't fix it.

Zo's maniacal laughter cut through the sound of my blood roaring through my ears.

Looking up, I saw him lift his boot again, ready to deliver the final, crushing blow.

It felt like everything around me—everything inside me— froze in horror.

And then I saw a blur of movement out of the corner of my eye. Valerie hit the shell with the flat of her hand. A web of cracks appeared beneath her palm, the thin black lines racing away from the epicenter of the blow.

Zo dropped into a crouch, looking up at Valerie in surprise.

"Valerie!" I screamed. Dante groaned in my arms, his skin clammy and cooling fast.

Orlando whipped his head around at my shout and

grabbed Valerie, wrapping his arms around her, pulling her away.

"No!" she shouted, fighting to get free. "He isn't supposed to have the River Policeman's heart! We have to get it back!"

A crackle of neon-blue energy arced off the curve of the glass, leaping across the distance to Valerie's hand. She screamed in pain, cradling her hand against her chest. A bright light surrounded her entire body, the glow bleeding over Orlando's hands. She shook like a leaf on a tree, and she would have fallen if Orlando had not been holding her up.

But it was too late. The damage was done.

The crack zigzagged vertically along the shell, branching out into multiple fragments, each break sounding like an out-of-tune chime.

Zo's small prison shattered to pieces around him.

"The locket!" Valerie called out. "Take the locket from him. Take it!"

I stood up in a half-crouch, torn between wanting to snatch the locket away from Zo and wanting to stay close by Dante's side.

Orlando spun Valerie out of his grip and jumped toward Zo, his hands spread and murderous anger in his eyes.

But his hands closed around nothing, and he stumbled to a stop, standing where Zo had been only a moment ago.

Zo had moved too, and faster than ever before. He was gone without even a ripple in the air to mark his passage. He left nothing behind, in fact, except for the echo of his laughter and a small silver locket that had been split in two.

CHAPTER
15

Orlando bent down and carefully, reverently picked up the two halves of the silver locket from the floor.

Even though Dante's skin was cold, I was the one shaking uncontrollably. Everything had happened so fast. I could barely keep the sequence of events straight, but that didn't stop me from replaying the action in my head, looking for where I could have changed something or done something different. But all I saw was the moment when Zo had broken the locket and Dante had fallen to the ground.

I had failed. And now Dante was paying the price for my weakness.

Without looking up, I held out my hand for the locket.

As Orlando placed the pieces in my palm, one of the halves broke again.

Dante shuddered once, goose bumps lifting on his arms.

Numbness settled over me. I couldn't stop looking at the four misshapen lumps of silver in my hand: a flat, heart-shaped piece with the hinge still attached, a second heart-shaped piece, rounded on top, but tapering off into nothingness, the small triangle tip of a broken heart, and a silver key that belonged to a door that no longer existed. I felt as small and jagged as the key in my hand. And as useless.

Zo had done his work thoroughly. I couldn't imagine how to even begin to mend the locket.

Orlando knelt across from me. He placed his hand on his brother's chest, his movements swift and sure. "He's still breathing," he said with relief. "And his heart feels strong."

My eyes immediately flashed to the broken locket in my hand before I realized what Orlando was really saying.

Orlando continued his report, his tone brisk and official. "It's slower than I would like, but still strong." He ran his hands over the length of Dante's body. "It doesn't feel like anything is broken. No fresh blood. At least, not that I can see." He leaned back on his heels, his hands resting on his thighs. He frowned. "Without knowing exactly what happened to him, I don't know what else I can do."

I wondered fleetingly about Orlando's efficiency in dealing with trauma, and then I remembered that he had been a soldier, had been to war. He had probably seen much worse than this.

I sat down heavily on the floor, settling Dante's head in my lap. The scar across his eyes looked terrible.

I carefully touched the fragments of the locket still in my hand. When Dante didn't react, I slowly shifted the pieces closer together, laying the broken half of the front heart on top of the back half, trying to reassemble the locket as best as I could. I slipped the key back inside, too; it seemed right that they stay together. I watched Dante for any signs of distress, but the only change seemed to be that his breathing became easier the closer the locket came to being whole again. A light pink even returned to his face.

Valerie crawled toward me on her hands and knees. "I'm sorry, sorry, sorry," she mumbled, tears streaking down her face. A faint blue glow still surrounded her right hand from where she had broken open Zo's prison. "I was trying to help. But I didn't. I made it worse, didn't I?" She peered into my open palm. "Did you get it? The locket—is this the locket? Is this all that is left?"

I couldn't speak. At the sound of her voice, my numbness disintegrated in a flash of anger so hot it made my blood crackle like fire in my veins. If Valerie hadn't broken the shell, Zo would still be here. And if Zo was still here, I was sure I could make him fix the locket. I didn't know how, but the blind rage inside me insisted that it was true.

I closed my fingers over the locket in a fist. I didn't want Valerie to be anywhere near it or even see it.

"Get her out of here," I ordered Orlando in a flat voice. "Now."

Orlando moved and gently lifted Valerie to her feet, drawing her away from my side.

The more rational part of me observed coolly that if Valerie *hadn't* broken the shell, then Zo would surely have destroyed even more of the locket than he already had. Yes, Zo was gone, but at least he had left behind the locket in his haste to get away. And with these small fragments of the locket in our possession, maybe we could do something to help Dante. At least, I hoped so.

"Oh," Valerie sobbed, covering her mouth in horror.

"Hearts are so very fragile in the Pirate King's hands. You saw what he did to mine." She moved her hands from her mouth to her chest, covering the breast pocket of her bathrobe. "And to yours." She pressed her hands to Orlando's chest. "And to the River Policeman's." Her voice sank into a strange, singsong chant. "What the Pirate King takes, is what the Pirate King breaks, and we all must suffer the Pirate King's fate." Valerie touched her forehead and looked up at Orlando with glassy eyes. "I don't feel so good. My head feels all wobbly."

Orlando tightened his grip on Valerie, holding her upright in his arms so she didn't fall.

Valerie turned toward me, her face pale and drawn. "I don't want to hurt anymore," she said with a whimper.

"Take her to the bank," I said wearily to Orlando, my anger having burned itself out. "When she touched the shell around Zo, she absorbed the time I used to create it. If she doesn't burn off the extra time, it'll make her sick."

Orlando hesitated, looking from me to Dante.

"Go," I said to Orlando quietly. "You said it yourself. There's nothing else we can do. I'll watch over him. Come back when you can."

Finally, Orlando nodded. "As you wish, my lady."

They left, and the shop fell into silence. It was just me and Dante. Alone for the moment.

"Dante?" I called softly, placing my free hand against his cheek.

He didn't answer, but I felt him relax a little at my touch.

Reassured by his reaction, I relaxed a little as well.

I wiped away the sweat from his forehead, careful not to

touch the wound across his eyes. I brushed back his hair. I placed my hand that held the locket on his chest, right above his heart. I counted the beats of his heart, until I felt confident that each one was stronger than the one before it.

"Come back to me," I whispered. "Wherever you are, whatever happened to you, come back to me. Please."

He didn't move, but his skin didn't feel quite so cold anymore.

I sighed and rubbed at my forehead. The room looked like I felt: confused and chaotic. The counter was still covered with open boxes and bottles. A few shelves had been dislodged during Zo and Dante's altercation, and the floor was scuffed with a mixed pattern of prints from their boots, Valerie's bare feet, and my sneakers. The fire still burned bright, but there were also black smudges of soot along the hearth.

Clearly the shop had seen better days. But then, hadn't we all?

I felt a huge weight of weariness lodge in my chest. What was I supposed to do now? This wasn't how I thought events would unfold at all. The plan was for me to come through the door and close the loop and save Dante. Instead, Zo had found me on the other side of the door, he'd ruined my memories and invaded my mind, and Dante—my indestructible Master of Time Dante—was wounded body and soul.

Without warning, Dante stirred in my lap, his head tilting toward me. He reached up with one hand, and I clasped it before he could touch my face. I didn't want him to feel the tears on my cheeks.

"Dante?" I felt like a light had come to life inside of me,

igniting a joy that reached deep into my soul. "Are you all right? Can you hear me? Can you talk to me?" I had more questions, but I didn't want to overwhelm him with too much too soon.

"Zo's gone, isn't he?" Dante asked. His voice was weak, but at least he was talking. He was still with me. He was going to be okay.

I nodded.

"He broke the locket, didn't he?"

I nodded again.

Dante exhaled slowly as though his ribs pained him. "I felt it. Here." He touched my hand that still rested on his chest above his heart. "It felt like a fist had reached inside me and squeezed. The pressure . . . it was worse than going through the door. Worse than my worst day on the bank." Dante grimaced. "If what Zo felt when I broke his guitar was anything like that—"

"He doesn't deserve your sympathy," I interrupted. "Or your pity."

"I have no pity for Zo," Dante said. "No, what I was going to say was that if what he felt was anything like this, then it's a wonder he survived at all."

"How *did* he survive?" I asked. "I mean, when you collapsed, I thought you were . . ." I swallowed, unwilling to say the word.

Dante was braver than I was. "Dead?" he finished. A hint of a smile crossed his face. "Not yet."

"How did this happen, Dante?" I asked quietly. The locket

felt like shards of rocks in my hand. "I don't understand. Why are you linked to the locket? What made you do it?"

Dante slowly pushed himself up on his elbows. I slipped my arm around his shoulders and helped him sit all the way up. He crossed his legs and took a deep breath. Wincing, he pressed his hand to his chest again, rubbing a small circle over his heart. He exhaled slowly.

"Dante?" I asked, worried that the color in his cheeks came from pain and not from his strength returning. "What can I do?"

He shook his head. "Give me a moment."

"You can have all the time you want," I said, trying to lighten the mood.

He laughed, but there was no trace of humor in it. He looked at me. "I'm sorry I didn't tell you about this before."

"Had you planned to tell me someday?"

He nodded.

"Then tell me now. Tell me everything."

He was still for a moment, gathering his thoughts. "The year after I came through the door was . . . difficult."

I touched his arm, moving closer. "Leo told me. He said you almost didn't make it."

"I don't think I would have made it except for two things. You"—he brushed his fingers over my wrist—"and the locket." He covered the shattered silver in my hand with his.

I looked down at our hands. Though his skin was still a little pale, I could feel the energy returning to his body the longer we touched.

Dante spoke quietly, his words slowly gaining speed and

strength as he told me the truth of the one last secret he had kept from me.

"It started the night of the Poetry Slam at the Dungeon. That was the first time I had tried to use a poem to help alleviate the pressure weighing me down—to do what Zo, Tony, and V were doing with their music."

"I remember," I said, conjuring up in my mind the memory of Dante standing on the stage, his poem rolling out over us like a wave, or a blessing. He had used the same poem to heal me on the bank and restore my memories. It was a poem I would never forget. "You were amazing. I still remember how your voice made me feel."

The night of the Poetry Slam had been the same night Valerie had won an invitation to the Valentine's dance with V, taking her first step down a path that would ultimately lead her into insanity. But that had also been the night that Leo had made me a Midnight Kiss and I had made a wish. So much had happened that night. So many small threads that were only now coming together to form a complete picture.

"The poem worked, but barely," said Dante. "And it came at a high price. After Leo closed the Dungeon, he found me collapsed by the back stairs. I was barely alive. At least, that's what he told me. I don't really remember what happened." He drew in a tight breath. "Well, that's not exactly true. I remember feeling like I was drifting between the river and the bank. Like I was being pulled in two different directions. Torn in half."

I deliberately didn't look at the broken halves of the

heart-shaped locket in my hand, though I felt the points and edges pressing into my palm.

"It felt a lot like when I was trapped in the darkness between the doors of the time machine," he finished. "Before you called me back into the light."

I squeezed his hand, trying to send all the strength I had inside of me to him.

Dante cleared his throat. "Leo helped me recover, though it took some time to find my balance again. That was when he told me about something he had learned that might help. He knew of a way to link a small part of yourself to an object in order to help stabilize the whole. That way, the object could serve as a kind of anchor, a touchstone that would be easy to find wherever you were and easy to hold on to. He said he had taught the process to the others who had been through the door and it had seemed to help them. He believed it would help me too."

"Others?" I echoed. "You mean Zo and his guitar."

Dante nodded.

"What about Tony and V? Did they have touchstones too? Did Leo?"

"If they did, I didn't know about it. It's possible they didn't feel like they needed one. Or wanted one. It was a personal choice; Leo wasn't going to force the decision on anyone. He said if I wanted to try it, having a touchstone might help me maintain my balance until I had mastered it by myself. More, he said it could help protect me from drifting like that again." Dante lifted his hand to reveal the locket in my palm. "It was an easy choice to make."

"You chose the locket," I said.

Dante shook his head. "I chose you."

The broken bits of silver suddenly felt like ice.

"I followed Leo's directions. I crafted the locket. Shaped it. Poured my heart into it. And then I gave it to you. I wanted you to be my anchor, my touchstone."

I remembered the night Dante had come to my house to give me the locket. He had placed it around my neck with a kiss and said that it held the key to his heart. I hadn't known then that the key inside the locket would open the black hourglass door or that the locket itself was part of Dante's heart. I wondered how much of what had followed would have been different if I had known the truth.

The hollow of my throat felt strangely exposed. I thought back to all the times when I had drawn comfort or strength from having the locket around my neck. Every time I had touched the shape of the heart, it had reminded me of Dante. It had linked me to Dante as surely as it had linked Dante to me.

And I had unwittingly handed over the most vulnerable part of Dante to the one person who could do him the most harm.

"Why didn't you keep it with you?" I asked, trying not to let my voice tremble. "It would have been safer that way. If you had kept it, I wouldn't have had it when Zo asked me for it. I wouldn't have given it to him, and he wouldn't have broken it—or you." I took a deep breath. "What *did* he do to you, Dante? He hurt you, but I don't know where or how, and so I don't know how to help."

"First of all, you didn't *give* it to Zo. He *stole* the locket from you in order to hurt me. It's not your fault; you're not to blame." A deep cough racked through his chest, his breath catching hard at the end. "Second of all, what he did to me was the same thing I did to him. The part of me that was tied to the locket—and the part of Zo that was tied to his guitar—is gone. Broken, and unrecoverable."

I pulled my eyebrows together in a frown. "He didn't seem very broken to me."

"The wound may be in a different place from mine, but trust me, Zo is not functioning at full strength anymore."

"But you said that damage done to a Master of Time *by* a Master of Time is permanent. That's why your eyes . . ." I shook my head, still finding it difficult to think of Dante being blind forever. "That same rule doesn't apply to this kind of wound, does it?"

"What's done is done," Dante said, looking down and away.

I forced him to face me again. "What part of you has been damaged?"

His eyes were dark and his face paled as though he saw something horrible waiting for him in the distance.

My heart froze in my chest. I suddenly didn't want to hear the answer to my question. But I had never shied away from the truth, no matter how difficult it was to bear. I had to know. How could I help Dante if I didn't know what was wrong with him?

Dante licked his lips. "Do you remember when I was trapped with Tony between doors—" He hesitated and I saw a shadow cross his face. "After the darkness took him . . . after he was . . ."

I covered his hand with mine, silently encouraging him to continue.

He cleared his throat, and his next words were steadier. "I told you that I felt like there was a sudden concentration of time. Almost like time accelerated around me."

"I remember," I said quietly.

"When the locket broke, it felt like that. Like an enormous amount of pressure had settled inside me. Here—in my heart." He touched his chest again. "But this time, it feels like there is a hole as well."

"The part of you that Zo damaged."

Dante nodded. "And all this pressure—all this accelerated time that is flowing through me—it feels like it's draining away through that little hole."

"Well, maybe, once all the pressure is gone, we'll be able to figure out a way to patch that hole," I suggested, feeling a touch of hope.

"Except Zo is responsible for the hole. Which means it can't be patched." Dante looked down again.

A sinking feeling dropped all the way to my toes. My tongue stuck to the roof of my mouth. I bit down on an inhalation, feeling like a sharp knife had cut a hole in my chest that matched the one in Dante's. Even though I was frozen in place, I felt like I was falling; I could almost hear the sound of wind rushing past my ears.

"But you're a Master of Time," I started. "You're not bound

to the bank *or* the river. Time doesn't have any kind of power over you."

"That's what I thought, too. But things have changed. I've changed. All I know is that now I can feel time slipping away when I couldn't feel it before. And I don't know what will happen to me when that time is gone."

My fist tightened around the locket. I couldn't believe we were having this conversation. It couldn't be true. Dante couldn't be dying.

"Then fix it," I said desperately. "If you fix the locket, then your heart will be healed, right? Regardless of what Zo did?" I opened my hand and held out the locket to him. "I know you can do it. You created it once; you can do it again."

Dante gently closed my fingers over the broken heart and pushed my hand back to me. "I don't think I can fix the locket. At least, not until my eyesight is back."

But we both knew that was impossible.

Tears of sorrow and loss burned my eyes, even as the bitter taste of hate filled my mouth. I hated Zo for what he had done to Dante, for all the ways he had wounded the man I loved.

Dante still held my hand. "Abby, I gave you the locket as a way to be with you even when I couldn't be with you. It was a way for me to finally be whole again and feel at peace. And if I had it to do over again, I would do the exact same thing."

"But you're not whole," I pointed out, my voice shaking. "Not anymore. There's a part of you that's missing. That's . . . dying." I choked on the word.

He didn't deny it.

His fingers trembled on my skin. "I knew what I was doing when I gave you my heart the first time. I know what I'm doing this time, too."

"But I can't fix it." My words were a whisper. My tears were endless. "I can't fix you."

Dante brushed my hair across my forehead, running his fingertips down my cheek and around my ear. He reached down and, lifting my hand in his, he kissed the tops of each of my fingers. Then he pressed my empty palm flat against his chest, right over his heart.

I could feel the exact moment when his broken pulse found a steady rhythm at my touch.

"If anyone can find a way, it will be you," he said. "You have risked everything to come to this time and this place to help me—to *save* me—and I believe in you, Abby. I know we will find a way to return home, healed and whole. Both of us."

He leaned in until our lips were almost touching. I could feel his breath move across my open mouth. "I trust you," he said simply. "I have given you my heart and my soul. I know I can trust you with my future, too." His lips were so close that they touched mine when he spoke. "We'll be together, Abby. I promise. Always," he said softly. "Always and forever."

His kiss was lightning in a storm, a heat that warmed me to the core, a brightness I could cling to as everything inside me—all my doubts and fears, all the darkness and confusion—whirled away into light.

CHAPTER
16

"Dante?"

I thought at first that I had said his name—he was all I could think about, after all—but my lips still tingled from his touch and I doubted I could have formed a single coherent word.

"Dante?" Orlando cleared his throat, once, then twice. "Abby?"

I looked around and scrambled to my feet, trying to brush my hair back into place and feeling a blush burn in my cheeks.

Orlando leaned against the counter, his arms folded and a concerned frown on his face. "Dante, are you feeling better? Are you both all right?"

I slipped the pieces of the locket into an inner pocket of the cloak I wore, glancing back at Dante as I did so to see if my jostling the pieces caused him any pain.

"I'm fine," Dante said, pushing himself to his feet and reaching for my hand. He stood straight and tall and looked so much like his regular self that I wondered for a moment if maybe we had been wrong about the dying part of his heart.

Then I felt the slightest tremble in Dante's fingers and knew that it was taking all his energy to mask the pain he was in.

I knew Orlando deserved to hear the truth about the hole in Dante's heart, but I didn't know if I had the words to explain it. I could barely wrap my mind around it myself.

"Abby and Dante were k-i-s-s-i-n-g," Valerie sang with a smile, clapping her hands together on the offbeat.

"I saw," Orlando said quietly, looking down and away.

"You're back," I said needlessly. "How was it?" As soon as I spoke, though, I winced. They'd been to the bank; I already knew how that was.

Orlando didn't answer, but Valerie's face brightened. She rushed to my side and grabbed my free hand.

"Oh, it was wonderful!"

I looked a question over her head at Orlando, who shrugged in answer.

"I feel so much better," Valerie gushed. "I've been to that place before, but it was horrible—all flat and full of nothings—but this time it was different. This time it was full of all the people from the stories in my head. I could see all the stories—all the different endings—and it was like magic watching them come and go depending on how the story traveled."

"Who did you see, Valerie?" asked Dante. "Which stories?"

"Oh, you were there, of course. The River Policeman is in a lot of stories right now. Some of them are scary—I didn't watch those—but most of them are good. There was even one about the River Policeman's locket, but I didn't see how that one ended." She squeezed my hand with hers. "Oh, and you were there, too. K-i-s-s-i-n-g."

The blush I thought I had conquered came back to life.

"You all were there. Even him." She pointed toward the door.

I spun on my heel—and gasped in disbelief.

Leo stood on the threshold of the shop, anger snapping from his blue eyes. The wind gusted through the door, wrapping the tail ends of his coat around his legs and ruffling through his silver-gray hair. "What's this? What are you doing in my shop?"

The sound of his voice seemed to resonate deep inside me.

I looked from Dante to Orlando to Leo, and the penny dropped.

They looked so much alike—all three of them—the only difference being in height and age. But they all shared the same shape of face, the same posture. They even had similar eyes; Dante's were gray, but Orlando's and Leo's were the exact same shade of blue.

"Father?" Orlando said into the stillness. "What are you doing back? I thought—"

Not Leo, then. Though he looked exactly like the man Orlando would become so many years in the future.

Dante looked to me for confirmation, and when I nodded, he swiftly pulled down his sleeves to cover his gold chains. He turned his face away. I knew Dante didn't want anyone else to see his injury, but I also knew how much he wanted to be able to see his father.

My heart skipped a beat, sharing his pain and his longing. How long had it been since I'd seen my own dad? My own family? It felt like it hadn't been that long at all, and at the same time, like it had been an impossible span of time.

Alessandro rocked back on his heels, the bag in his hand slipping free and landing on the floor with a thud. He gripped the door frame for balance. Surprise erased his anger, his whole body relaxing with happiness. Then he smiled, and I saw the echo of Dante in his face.

"Orlando?" he said, awed.

Alessandro stepped forward, and Dante stepped back in an attempt to blend into the background. Alessandro stopped, drawn by the movement. "Dante?"

I let go of Dante's hand and pulled Valerie aside so we wouldn't be in the way of the unexpected family reunion. I held a finger to my lips, hoping she would follow suit and stay quiet.

Valerie nodded and pressed both of her hands against her mouth, her eyes shining.

"Hello, Father," Dante said without looking up, his voice catching on the last syllable.

"My boys. My sons." Alessandro rushed forward, sweeping both Dante and Orlando into his arms and crushing them into an embrace. "I didn't know . . . I hadn't heard you were coming." He laughed a little. "When did you get here? Have you been home yet?" He pulled away a little, but only so he could hug them individually.

When it was Dante's turn, he glanced at me over his father's shoulder, and I saw both worry and relief on his face.

"We just arrived," Orlando said at the same time that Dante said, "No, we haven't been home."

Alessandro laughed again, a wild release of joy. "Oh, your mother will be speechless when she sees you. And I will be the hero for bringing you both home to her."

Orlando swallowed and glanced at Dante, who kept his face turned away to hide his scar.

I knew what he was thinking—what they both were—because I was wondering the same thing: Should they tell their father the truth? And if so, how much of it? And if not, then what could they possibly say?

"We can't stay—" Orlando started.

"Nonsense." Alessandro waved away the very idea. "Let me put a few things away, and we'll be off."

"This is where the story changes," Valerie whispered to me from behind her hands. "If Dante says yes, the story goes one way. If he says no . . ."

"What *should* he say?" I whispered back, wondering how I could get the information to him without drawing undue attention.

"It doesn't matter now," she said. "He's already picked."

"We'd love to see Mother," Dante said.

"And there it goes," Valerie said with a sigh. "Oh, I'm glad he said yes. It makes for a much better story."

Alessandro looked at Dante, and then looked closer. He touched his son's chin and tilted his face upward.

I could see Dante's body tense at the contact. He kept his eyes closed, but the scar was obvious. Jagged and uneven, it looked even worse against the paleness of his skin and the tightness of his face. A line of sweat broke out along his hairline.

"Who did this to you?" Alessandro demanded softly.

Dante swallowed, but didn't answer. How could he, without inviting more questions?

"Was it da Vinci?" Alessandro said, cupping Dante's face with his broad hands. He ran the pad of his thumb along the edge of the scar. "Did this happen at his studio?"

Dante winced at even that small touch. "No," he said firmly. "It wasn't him. I got into a fight."

"You? In a fight." He shook his head and frowned. "I would have expected that from your brother, but not you."

"It was unavoidable." Orlando chimed in, coming to Dante's defense. "Isn't that what you said?"

Dante nodded, deftly moving his head away from his father's touch. "It's fine, Father. I'll be fine. Let it go."

"He wouldn't tell me the details either," Orlando said with a wry smile.

Alessandro thinned his lips. "Well, I suppose a man is entitled to his secrets. Tell me this, though—did you leave him worse than he left you?"

Dante hesitated. A muscle moved in his clenched jaw, and a hardness sharpened his features and his tone. "Not yet."

I thought I had seen every emotion possible cross Dante's face during the time I'd known him, but this controlled fierceness was something new. Seeing it helped me understand where Dante's intensity came from, how Orlando's desire for justice had led him into battle. There was warrior blood in the Casella men.

"That's good to hear." Alessandro nodded in approval, his own features drawn in grim determination. He glanced at Orlando. "You will help him, if he needs it, yes?"

"Yes, Father. Always."

"Good," he said again. "Now, about this wound." He held up his index finger and passed it in front of Dante's eyes; his frown turned to a scowl. "How long ago did this happen? This fight?" he asked Dante. "I would expect scars like this to take at least a month to form, and yet . . ." He pushed back Dante's eyebrows, pulling the area around the scar taut. "There are things that suggest this wound happened mere days ago."

"Can you do something for him?" I blurted out.

All three men turned my way, and I shrank back against the wall. I'd been so careful to keep Valerie quiet, I'd forgotten my own rules. But I didn't regret asking the question. Dante needed his sight back, and if his father could help him, so much the better. More, if Alessandro could help heal Dante's eyes, maybe he could help heal the wound hidden in Dante's heart.

"And you are . . . ?" Alessandro looked me up and down.

I swallowed. I hadn't thought I would ever actually meet Dante's parents, and now that I was, I found myself unexpectedly shy and self-conscious.

"She's with me," Dante said, holding out his hand for me to take.

I stepped up beside him, our fingers automatically folding together. Out of the corner of my eye, I caught a flash of something cross Orlando's face. Disappointment? Regret? I didn't know, and it was gone before I could identify it.

Alessandro's eyebrows lifted at the sight of our joined hands. "Oh, I see," he said knowingly, that same joyous smile spreading wide. "And what is your name?"

"Abby," I said softly. "Abigail," I amended, thinking it sounded a little more appropriate to the time and place.

"And I'm Valerie," she said, popping forward and wrapping her arms around Alessandro in a hug.

Orlando pulled her away as quickly as he could. "I'm sorry, Father. Valerie is . . . impulsive sometimes. She's not well," he added in a low voice.

"Some people say I'm crazy," Valerie chimed in, her voice low to match Orlando's. "But I don't think that's a very nice thing to say, do you? I prefer to think of myself as . . . visionary."

Alessandro frowned, studying Valerie intently. "Interesting," he said, tapping his finger to his chin. "I've heard of cases like this, but I've never had the opportunity to see one for myself." He held out his hand for Valerie. She took it and he led her a few steps forward. He raised his eyebrows at the sight of the black tattoos on her wrists. "Where are you from, child?"

"Here and there and everywhere," Valerie said, curtseying as though they had been dancing. "I have been to there and back again and can tell you the tale of tomorrow."

"Fascinating," Alessandro murmured.

"So, do you think you can help Dante?" I interrupted before Valerie could say anything else.

"Abby—" Dante started, but his father looked up, startled out of his study.

"Oh, yes, yes, of course." He nodded and headed toward the counter in the back of the shop. "Come," he said, gesturing for all of us to follow. "Let me see what I can do. Orlando, would you bring me my bag, please?"

Orlando obeyed, crossing the room and picking up the black leather satchel from the floor. He swung the front door closed with a quiet click.

Alessandro slipped behind the counter, tsking at the mess strewn over the surface.

Orlando set the bag off to the side, and the four of us lined up in a row.

A memory sparked: a row of friends in front of a bar, Leo mixing up a sweet drink. There was a part of me that missed those days. The days before I knew about the river or the bank, before I had felt the weight of time sitting heavy on my heart.

Dante pulled me in front of him, wrapping his arms around me and resting his cheek against my head. I breathed in the familiar scent of his skin, feeling at home in his arms. Even with all the twists my life had taken, I didn't want to go back to those days. I wouldn't. Not without Dante.

I would find a way around the impossible problem of his broken heart. No matter what.

"What are you doing home?" Orlando asked his father. "I thought you were out traveling."

"I could ask you the same question." Alessandro pushed aside the open boxes and the mortar. He examined the bottom of the pestle and sniffed at the rosemary still clinging to the stone. "I thought you were living the soldier's life."

Orlando's jaw tightened. "I was. I mean, I am. I've been given leave to undertake a special assignment."

"One that allows you time to come home and visit your parents?" He replaced the pestle and brushed his hands together. "I'm not complaining, mind you. I just assumed that, given the recent rumors, most soldiers would want to keep a low profile."

"Why is that?" Orlando asked, his glance flicking to me. We all had reasons to keep a low profile. "What rumors?"

Alessandro looked up in surprise. "You haven't heard?"

"Oh, I know, I know." Valerie waved her hand in the air. "I know this part of the story."

Opening his bag, Alessandro withdrew a vial half filled with a clear liquid. "The Sons of Italy," he said. "The rumors are everywhere. From what I've heard, these so-called Sons of Italy were soldiers—honorable, loyal soldiers—who committed treason yet claimed they were the patriots."

My whole body tensed, a bolt of unexpected panic traveling through my nerves. I knew this part of the story too. Dante's chest hardened behind me, a deep breath turning him to stone.

I glanced at Orlando, but he appeared unruffled. Even serene.

"I've heard of them," he said, his voice steady. "What's the latest news?"

Alessandro continued to empty his bag, lining up a variety of bottles one after the other. "Word in the marketplace is that the authorities captured the last member of the conspiracy last month and have locked him in prison."

"Oh? And do the rumors include an identity for any of the conspiracy members?"

I wondered how Orlando could be so calm about the topic. The rumors were about him—him and Dante and Zo. The inside of my mouth tasted dry and swollen, and I wasn't even directly involved. I could feel the vibrations of Dante's heart beating in his chest.

"No. The authorities have been close-lipped about specific names and identities. But you know how people talk. I've heard at least a hundred different names listed as the leader of the conspiracy. I even heard *your* name." He snorted in obvious disbelief.

Tightness closed up my throat. I couldn't look at Orlando; I didn't dare.

"But you think they've captured them all?"

Alessandro nodded. "It's a good thing, too. There's enough unrest as it is. No need to add to it by arguing about who is and isn't a true patriot these days." He clucked his tongue, a sharp sound of disapproval. "I'm glad to know that you weren't involved—either one of you."

"You don't have to worry about us," Orlando said, reverent and intent. "We would never do anything to bring dishonor to you or your name."

I felt like crying. I knew exactly what Orlando had done to protect the honor of his family, to atone for the wrongs he had committed. I knew what it had cost him. What it had cost all of us.

I leaned back into Dante's arms. I hoped it wouldn't cost us even more.

Alessandro must have heard something in Orlando's tone because he slowly set down the small packet of flowers he'd extracted from his bag and looked up at his son. "I know," he said seriously. "You and Dante"—he nodded in our direction—"you are the *true* sons of Italy. And I am proud to have you both carry my name."

My breath hiccupped in my chest, and Dante tightened his arms around me.

"Hush, Abby. It's all right," he whispered in my ear.

But I could hear a hint of anguish in his own voice.

"I'm sorry," I said. "I . . . I think there's something in my eye." I dabbed at my eyes with my fingertips. "I'm all right. I'm sorry."

Alessandro became all business. "No need to apologize, young lady. And speaking of eyes"—a smile tugged at his lips—"I have not forgotten your request. Yes, I think there is something I can do for Dante."

"No, Father, you don't have to—" Dante started again.

"I insist." He closed up his bag and stored it beneath the countertop. He didn't wait for Dante to reply, but simply began gathering up a handful of supplies—the vial he had pulled from his bag, a container of some ground-up powder, a pot of green paste, a scrap of heavy fabric—and setting them out in a neat row.

I could see where Dante got his stubbornness from.

I turned in Dante's arms and touched his cheek. "Why not? Don't you want his help?"

I almost missed the shake of his head. "I don't want to disappoint him," he said under his breath. "Or you."

"How could you?"

"What if it doesn't work? It's not a regular wound; I don't think it'll heal like a regular wound."

"What if it does?"

He didn't reply.

"Please?" I asked quietly. "For me?"

Dante's expression softened and his mouth turned up in a small smile. "That's not fair."

I smiled back. "I never said it was."

Valerie reached out and brushed Dante's arm with hesitant fingers. "You should say yes. It's a better story if you say yes."

"I'd do what she says," I said. "She knows her stories."

"Dante?" Alessandro called. "Are you ready?"

"It'll be fine," I said; I had a good feeling about this. "You'll see." Then my words registered and I grinned. "I promise."

CHAPTER
17

I t's not too tight, is it?" I asked, touching the scarf knotted around Dante's head.

He reached up and made minute adjustments to the fit and placement. "No, it feels fine."

"Good. Alessandro said to keep the bandage on for at least twenty-four hours. Then we'll clean and re-dress the wound. With luck, we should start seeing some improvement right away."

"I know, Abby. I heard him too."

I leaned back against the side of the wagon, trying to find my balance as it rocked and swayed over the rocky ground. The horse kept up a steady pace, and I was glad we didn't have far to travel. The road was crowded with all kinds of people, some riding horses, most walking. The dust kicked up by so many feet turned the air hazy, and the noise of so many voices swirled around us in a small storm of words, some light as laughter, others weighed down by complaints.

Dante, Orlando, and I were wedged in the back of the wagon among the boxes and bags containing Alessandro's apothecary supplies. I was grateful for the cover; I suspected the courthouse guards were still looking for us and I knew none of us wanted to be found.

I tucked my feet beneath the hem of my cloak, leaning up against Dante's shoulder for more warmth.

Alessandro laughed, and I looked up. Valerie sat next to him, gesturing widely. Alessandro had found a spare cloak for her to wear, and when she waved her arms, the long sleeves fluttered like wings. I could hear only bits and pieces of their conversation over the creak of the wagon and the clopping of the horse.

"And the story ends when the girl realizes that there's no place like home and that she'd rather be with her family than anywhere else."

"That is a fine story, indeed."

"It's one of my favorites." Valerie sighed. "I can't wait until it comes true."

I tapped Dante's knee. "Do you think it was a good idea to let her sit up front?" I pitched my voice low. I didn't think there was much chance that anyone would overhear us, but I wanted to be careful.

"It was her choice," Orlando said from Dante's other side. "And Father doesn't seem to mind."

"And it gives us a chance to talk," Dante added, his own voice low and rumbling. "Which we need to do before we arrive at the house."

"I know," Orlando said. "Why did you even agree to go home? It's too dangerous. It was bad enough that Father came back early and caught us at his shop; we should have left before things became so complicated."

"Things are already complicated," Dante pointed out. "And it's important for us to go home—if only for a day."

"But is today really the best day?" Orlando asked, flicking a glance toward his father. "You heard what he said about the Sons of Italy. If he knew the truth—"

"You handled it fine back at the shop. He doesn't know what happened, and he doesn't have to know."

"Then why? Why risk everything with a trip home?"

Dante was quiet, his fingers idly tracing patterns on my leg that was pressed up against his. "Father said the authorities had captured the last member of the conspiracy." He turned his face to his brother. "That was me. He was talking about me and didn't even know it."

Orlando paled and Dante swallowed.

"I'm currently locked in the dungeon at the courtroom, waiting for judgment. Waiting for my turn to go through the black hourglass door."

I focused on Dante's finger, slowly realizing that he was writing my name on my leg: the round swoop of the A, the double Bs, the elegant Y, complete with a little hook on the end.

"Imagine what it must have been like for Mother and Father," he continued. "You send your oldest son to war, only to receive word that he died in battle—never knowing it was a lie."

Orlando opened his mouth, but Dante overrode him as easily as if he had seen the beginnings of his brother's protest.

"I know what they offered you in exchange for your cooperation—a hero's death and a life of exile. But even believing your son died as a hero doesn't bring him back. And there was never a funeral, never a chance to say good-bye."

Orlando looked down at his hands, locked into fists in his lap.

Dante's voice was relentless. "Imagine what happens to that sorrow, that grief, when you then learn that your second son has vanished without a trace. At best, there is no story to explain his disappearance, and you spend the rest of your life hoping for some word, some kind of answer. At worst, you are visited by the same officials who broke your heart the first time, and who have come to tell you that your second son was executed as a traitor to his country."

From where I sat, I could see Alessandro's face in profile. His strong jaw, the slope of his nose, the black-and-gray hair that held a hint of a curl. "It must have been awful for them," I murmured. "To lose both of their children at the same time like that . . ."

Orlando licked his lips, his voice a dry rattle. "I didn't think . . . I didn't know."

Dante kept tracing my name, a hint of gold peeking out from the cuff of his sleeve as he moved his hand over my leg. "When I came back, I knew I wanted to have our family to-gether again. Even if it was only for one day. Even if it's only to say good-bye. I owe them that much, at least."

We were all quiet for a moment, each of us lost in our own thoughts.

I couldn't help but think that with time bleeding out of Dante, his good-bye to his family might be a literal one. I stopped that train of thought; we would find a way to fix what was broken.

I leaned my head against Dante's shoulder, shifting as the wagon hit a particularly bumpy patch of road. The wind blew bitter cold, and I pulled my cloak tighter around my shoulders.

"Oh, yes, I know lots of stories," Valerie said to Alessandro, her cheerful voice sounding loud in the brief lull of our own conversation. "Do you want me to tell you one about a pirate?"

"I suppose your parents must be worried about you, Abby," Orlando commented. "I mean, if they know where you are."

I half laughed. "I'm more worried about my parents right now than they are about me."

"Why is that?"

"Do you remember how we saw the river fraying? Different streams branching off in different directions?"

Orlando nodded.

"Well, long story short, my parents are trapped in one of those loose threads. The river is dangerously unstable and unless we do something—and soon—my whole family will be lost in time."

"We'll find them, Abby," Dante said. "We'll bring them back."

"I hope so," I murmured, thinking back to the ghostly visions of my family I'd seen on the bank. I didn't want that to be the last image I would ever see of them. "Dad hated being lost," I said, my mind drifting back over a lifetime of memories. "But he would never ask for directions. Made my mom crazy. I remember the summer we took a family vacation to the Grand Canyon when I was thirteen. You'd think it would be easy to find. I mean, it's only a huge canyon in the middle of the desert, right? But we drove in circles for a whole day before Mom insisted that we stop and ask someone where we were supposed to go." I laughed a little at the memory. "Everyone was so mad. Mom and Dad were mad about being lost, and Hannah was mad because she'd finished her book hours before and hadn't thought to bring an extra."

"What about you?" Dante asked. "Were you mad?"

"Me?" I grinned. "I was furious. All the driving around made me sick, Hannah kept poking me every three seconds out of boredom, and Mom and Dad alternated between yelling at each other and giving each other the silent treatment. It was the best vacation we ever had."

"Wait—it was the *best* vacation?" Dante asked.

I laughed and nodded. "We finally stopped for directions at the cutest little bed-and-breakfast, and we decided to stay there for the night. It was a good thing we did because a huge storm rolled in the next day and we spent the whole weekend together, playing games and talking and laughing. We never did visit the Grand Canyon. But, yes, it was the best vacation ever."

"Sounds like it," Dante said with a smile in his voice.

"I hope you are able to find your family," Orlando said. "And if I can help—"

Alessandro pulled on the horse's reins and the wagon jolted to a stop.

Dante twisted around, his hands gripping the side of the wagon. "We're here," he said even though he couldn't see the landscape or the house. A smile lit up his entire face. "We're home."

Valerie hopped down from the wagon without any help. She bounced on her toes, whispering to herself, "There's no place like home," over and over like it was an incantation.

Orlando slid out of the back of the wagon and extended his hand to help Dante and me down. I dusted the dirt from my cloak and took my first look at where Dante had grown up.

The house was beautiful. A long walkway lined with winter-brown hedges led to a front porch of a multilevel villa framed with elegant pillars. A small flight of stairs led up to the door. Windows lined the front of the house. Terraces and gables and gardens all created a beautiful balance of symmetry and structure.

The front door opened and a woman stood in the doorway, her hand raised to shade her eyes from the light.

"Caterina, love," Alessandro called out. "Look who I have found!"

He reached out and slung his arms over his boys' shoulders, pulling them close to his sides. His grin split his face.

Caterina's body stiffened. Her hands flew to her mouth. Her eyes opened wide in surprise. Then she rushed outside, down the stairs, her arms outstretched in welcome. Her dark hair frayed out the sides of her bun. The ends of her shawl trailed behind her like wings.

"My boys," she cried, tears streaking down her face. "Oh, my boys are home!"

Caterina ushered us into the house immediately. She fussed and fluttered about her family: she touched Orlando on the arm, commenting on his obvious strength; she ruffled Dante's hair like he was still a little boy, frowning at the bandage across his eyes; she kissed Alessandro on the cheek. Through it all, she kept up a constant chatter of welcome.

Clearly, this was her domain, and she was the reigning queen.

Dante made the introductions, glossing over some of the more complicated details, and answered her expected questions with his well-rehearsed answers. Yes, he was injured. Yes, he would be fine. Yes, he was happy to be home. No, he wasn't sure how long they could stay.

I smiled, basking in the outpouring of love that filled the elegant home.

Valerie and I hung back a little, unwilling to intrude too far into the reunion without an invitation.

It wasn't long, though, before Caterina turned her formidable attention to us. She hovered and bustled around us, making sure we were warm, fed, and comfortable. The perfect hostess, she asked just the right number of questions to keep us talking, allowing us to tell the details of our story at our own pace, and not passing judgment on our words or our silence.

I tried to be careful with how much I said, but it was hard not to open up to Dante's mother and tell her everything. There was something about her personality that made me want to trust her. I could sense a strength in her that told me she could handle whatever might come her way, no matter how strange it might seem.

She didn't seem bothered by the fact that we were wearing the wrong clothes or that our answers were sometimes on the sketchy side. Her happiness at having her family home spread over us like a heavy blanket, covering and hiding any oddities that might have been out of place.

I was more than happy to surrender to her will. I felt like I had been running from one disaster to the next, and it was nice to let someone else be in charge for a while. Somehow, being under a mother's protective wing—even if she wasn't *my* mother—made me feel warm and cared for. I felt safe for the first time in a long time.

Even Valerie seemed at peace. She soaked up Caterina's calming influence, a quiet expression on her face and her behavior surprisingly docile and polite. I didn't know if it was the presence of a strong mother figure or something else, but Valerie seemed more like her old self when Caterina was around.

Eventually, Caterina announced that it was time for dinner, and by then it seemed only natural for us to join her in the back room of the house to change and freshen up.

The low murmur of men's voices followed us out, and I glanced over my shoulder. Alessandro dozed by the fireplace, but Dante and Orlando were deep in conversation. I hoped that Dante would have a chance to tell his brother about the repercussions we were facing from the broken locket. I didn't know if there was anything Orlando could do to help, but I knew that giving him all the information we had couldn't hurt.

The guest room was small, but clean and cozy. A bed filled most of the space, with a washbasin and a mirror placed on a small table. Two chairs waited by the window.

In short order, Caterina helped us wash hands, hair, and faces and settled us both into chairs.

Valerie looked at herself in the mirror and frowned. She tugged at her hair as though trying to even it out.

"Would you like me to help?" Caterina asked gently.

Valerie nodded, suddenly shy.

Caterina ran a brush through Valerie's hair, carefully working out the knots and snarls. She hummed a soft lullaby tune as she worked, her face relaxed and happy.

And why shouldn't she be? Her family was home and whole.

I used my fingers to comb through my own hair. I felt a pang of something that felt a little like envy and a lot like longing. As wonderful as it was to be safe in Dante's home, surrounded by people who treated me like family, I still wished I could be with *my* family. Thinking about the vacation we had taken had been both good and bad. It was good to think of the past, but bad because I missed Dad's laugh, the sound of Mom's voice; I even missed Hannah's moods.

But Dante had promised we would restore my family, and I trusted him.

Tucking my thoughts back into a corner of my mind, I focused my attention on Caterina.

She was what I'd always imagined when I thought of a *lady*. Regal and graceful. Her face reflected a life spent with hard work, but also still held the traces of her youthful beauty.

She had unpinned her bun, and her long black hair showed hints of gray. She was a woman who knew who she was and how she had gotten there.

"You have pretty hands," Valerie said as Caterina worked, smoothing out Valerie's hair. "I bet you've done a lot with those hands."

"Thank you," Caterina said. "And, yes, I have. I love to sew and cook and paint. Most importantly, though, I've raised two boys with them."

"What was he like?" I asked. "Dante. When he was a child, I mean."

Caterina smiled as only a mother could. "Oh, he was a curious child. He wanted to know everything about everything. And he had so much energy. He would finish a task in half the time I thought it would take." She picked up a dark ribbon from the table. "But he was also careful and precise. He could be quiet and still for hours on end if he needed to be."

"He hasn't changed much, then," I said, reflecting on how Dante had managed to find his balance between action and thought. I remembered that Leo had called Dante a dreamer. It was still the best description I could think of for him.

"I'm not surprised," Caterina said. "Dante was a boy who always knew exactly what he wanted out of life, and he was determined to get it." She tilted a look in my direction, a half question in her eyes but a certain smile on her lips.

Was she implying what I thought she was? Without meaning to, I glanced toward the door that led into the main room. I could hear Dante's voice—not his exact words—but the rhythm was familiar and instantly recognizable to me.

Dante had once told me that even when we were apart, he could always point to me; he always knew. And I realized I knew that about him as well. It was as if an invisible chain connected us, a link that let me know exactly where he was.

"There," Caterina said, tying the ribbon in Valerie's hair. "What do you think?" She handed a small mirror to Valerie and stepped back.

Valerie turned her head one way, then the other, patting the shape of her hair with the flat of her hand. "Good. Now we can go shopping."

She hopped up from her chair and made a beeline for the narrow cupboard standing in the corner. Throwing open the door, she flipped through the clothes as intently as if she were at the mall.

"Here. Let me help you," Caterina said, following in Valerie's wake. She deftly reached past Valerie's shoulder and withdrew three dresses that she then laid out on the bed.

"These are beautiful," I said. "Did you make them?"

Caterina nodded. "I find sewing relaxing. And there is a certain satisfaction in seeing something you designed and created come to life."

I smiled. I understood why Dante's love of art and his creative skill were so healthy and alive; his mother had the same fire in her.

"Oh, I like the green one," Valerie said, scooping up the heavy fabric and clutching it to her chest. She looked across the room to me. "Dress shopping with you is always an adventure."

I blinked in surprise. I hadn't thought Valerie remembered

that long-ago shopping trip we'd made with Natalie, but her eyes were steady and clear. Maybe she really was getting better. I hoped so.

Caterina nodded. "That one will look lovely on you." She turned to me. "Abigail, which one do you like?"

I looked back at the remaining dresses, but it wasn't even a choice. I stepped forward and touched the warm golden-brown dress with a gentle hand. "This is beautiful." The bodice had a white lace overlay, and the buttons down the back looked like pearls. A strip of gold ribbon lined the round neckline.

Caterina measured me with smiling eyes. "Yes, I think that one will be a perfect fit. You can change behind there." She nodded toward a folded wooden screen painted top to bottom with a beautiful landscape of flowers and a sky full of birds. "I'll help your friend."

I lifted the dress from the bed and slipped behind the partition, noticing that the artwork continued all the way around to the back. The lush greens of the landscape scene were soothing while the bright reds and yellows of the flowers popped like living blossoms. Birds darted and swooped from tree to tree, caught in midflight.

"This is a lovely screen," I said as I kicked off my shoes. Before I took my heavy cloak off, though, I carefully collected the pieces of the locket from the inside pocket. I couldn't leave the locket behind, but I didn't know where I could keep it. I couldn't wear it around my neck anymore, and Caterina's dress didn't have any pockets.

"It is, isn't it?" Caterina agreed. "Dante painted it for me before he left for his apprenticeship with da Vinci."

I paused. Of course. How had I not recognized his work immediately? He had a way of infusing life into his art. A vibrancy that lifted my spirits.

"Have you seen his work before?" Caterina asked.

I looked down at the locket in my hand. "Yes," I managed, my voice trembling. "I've seen quite a bit of it, actually."

Quickly, I ripped off a small piece of cloth from the cloak and wrapped it tightly around the locket so the broken pieces wouldn't move around. Then I slipped the packet inside my bra, close to my heart. I pulled my shirt up and over my head. Goose bumps rose up on my exposed skin; I missed the convenience of central heat.

"Abby knows all about Dante's work," Valerie chimed in. "He is very talented. And he is planning to make something special just for her."

"He is?" Caterina asked, intrigued.

I wondered the same thing. How could Dante make anything with his sight gone?

"But he doesn't know what it is yet. It's still a secret," Valerie continued.

"Oh, I see," Caterina said. "But if so, then how do you know about it?"

Valerie's voice took on a proud confidence. "I know everyone's secrets. Even the ones the Pirate King doesn't know I know."

I didn't like the sound of that. Valerie might be getting better, but she wasn't there yet. Quickly pulling on the dress,

I stepped around the screen, hoping to redirect the conversation before it went any further.

Valerie looked up at me, her mouth opening in honest surprise. "Oh, Abby," she breathed. "You look beautiful."

Caterina fairly beamed, and, to my surprise, tears welled up in her eyes. "Yes, I agree. It looks wonderful on you."

I smoothed my hands down the front of the skirt, suddenly self-conscious. The dress fit better than I'd expected, a little tight around the waist, and a little short in the sleeves and the hem—I was slightly taller than Caterina—but the fabric was lush and lovely.

Caterina walked to my side, a faraway look softening her already expressive face and bold features. She ran her fingertips down the embroidered sleeve. "I was wearing this dress when I met Alessandro for the first time. He was so young and handsome. I knew I would marry him the moment I saw him."

"Oh, I'm sorry, I didn't know—I can wear something else." I turned back to the screen, intending to change back into my clothes.

"No, no, please. It's all right."

"Are you sure?"

She nodded. "I've seen how you and Dante are together— even during this short time tonight. And a mother knows." She took my hand in hers. "Dante is a good man, and all I've ever wanted was for him to find happiness. Which is why I'm so glad that he found you. I hope he never lets you go."

CHAPTER
18

I felt a little silly wearing my sneakers underneath such a beautiful dress, but Caterina's shoes fit Valerie, not me. Besides, she needed them more than I did.

Valerie looked more like herself once she had taken off Alessandro's cloak and changed out of her hospital sweats and bathrobe and into Caterina's green dress. Though the gown hung loosely on her thin frame, the color went perfectly with her dark hair and blue eyes.

When we entered the room, my eyes immediately went to Dante. He was alone by the fireplace, holding his hands out to warm his palms against the rising heat. He lifted his head and turned toward me.

I knew he could see me, but I still wasn't prepared for his reaction.

He walked directly to me, took me in his arms, and kissed me, right there in front of his parents and Valerie.

Surprised, I didn't know what else to do but kiss him back. I could feel his lips trembling against mine, and I wondered at his sudden rush of emotion.

Valerie gasped and clapped her hands. "Oh, they make the cutest couple."

"That they do," Caterina said.

"Reminds me of us, when we were young," Alessandro said, sweeping his arm around his wife and kissing her cheek.

"Are you saying I'm not young anymore?" Caterina teased. "Perhaps now that I'm an old lady, you won't love me like you used to."

"Impossible," Alessandro declared. "I will love you forever."

Dante broke off the kiss and touched his forehead to mine. "Forever," he echoed. "Forever and always."

The door swung open and I saw Orlando come inside, his arms full of chopped wood. He stopped at the scene in front of him, but only for a moment. Then he headed for the fireplace and dropped the logs in the bin on the hearth. When he passed me and Dante, still in our embrace, he averted his eyes. His face was red, but I didn't know if it was from the cold or from chopping wood—or from something else.

"Oh, thank you, Orlando," Caterina said, untangling herself from her husband's arms.

"You're welcome, Mother," he said, a peculiar strain in his voice. "I'm happy to help."

She looked at him with thoughtful eyes. "May I speak with you for a moment?"

Orlando brushed the wood dust from his hands and obediently went to his mother's side.

"In private?" she added, drawing him behind her as she headed toward the back of the house.

I took Dante's hand and pulled him to the corner of the room.

"Why did you kiss me like that?" I demanded.

A breath escaped along with a laugh. "Do I need a reason?"

"You didn't even hesitate. And everyone saw us." I said the second part in a low voice.

"I kissed you to make sure you were real. And to make sure my eyes weren't playing tricks on me."

"Are your eyes getting better?" I asked, feeling a spark of hope.

He shook his head. "You are still all I can see." A small smile crossed his lips. "But you are enough. And you are just as beautiful today as you were the first time I saw you." Dante ran his hand down my arm. "When I saw you standing at the dungeon door, I knew what hope looked like. And when I saw you today, I knew what my future looked like. You have always brought me joy, Abby. And you always will. All the way to the end of time." He stifled a cough, turning his head to keep his pain private.

But I heard the rattle when he caught his breath, and it made me shiver. If we didn't do something, and soon, the end of Dante's time might be sooner rather than later.

He winced and pressed his hand to his chest, a grim expression on his face.

"We have to find a way to get you better," I said. "Let me go to the dungeon. You're already there, aren't you? The other you, I mean. Maybe if we close the loop early, it will help. Or give us the time we need to focus on finding a way to patch your heart." I was ready to have the loop be closed. I wanted to protect the river, save Dante and my family, and finally, *finally,* put all this behind us.

"It's not that simple."

I sighed. "Why not?"

"Seeing you in that exact moment at the dungeon was what gave me the strength to endure the rest of my time in prison. It's the key to everything. Yes, it's almost time, but missing that exact moment—by being either too early or too late—would be catastrophic. I don't dare risk it. No, events *must* unfold in the correct order and at the correct time or else the loop won't be closed—or stay closed."

A pang shot through my heart. I was so focused on simply being at the dungeon for Dante, I'd forgotten that that moment had happened in the *middle* of his imprisonment. Even after he had seen me, he had waited and suffered for days and weeks on end before he was released—only to be sent through the door into a different kind of prison.

"But I want to help," I said.

"I know. And you are. And when the time comes for you to go to the dungeon, you will help even more. Believe me."

I looked up as a sudden, terrible thought occurred to me. "But I can't go to the dungeon—at least, not directly."

"Why not?"

"When Orlando and I escaped from the courthouse, the guards came looking for us. I suspect they are *still* looking for us—for me. I can't simply walk into the courthouse, can I? What if someone recognizes me?" I bit my lip, thinking hard. "Can you take me there? Isn't it possible for you to take me to the bank and then, from there, directly to the dungeon? We could go together."

Dante thought for a moment. "Yes, that might be possible," he said slowly. "But it's a dangerous plan."

"Why? I only have to be at the dungeon long enough for you to see me, and then we could come right back." My hope was renewed. This was a good plan. A quick strike, in and out, and everything would be fixed.

"It's not me seeing you that I'm worried about. It's me seeing *me*." He shook his head at the complexity of the idea. "There are two of me in the river right now—the me in the dungeon and the me standing here—and if we were to see each other, the paradox of the two of us being in the same place at the same time could destroy the river entirely. The barriers are already so fragile, the river is already so unstable, I don't want to risk any further damage."

"There are two of Zo," I pointed out. My hope suddenly reversed to worry. "Can he use his other half to destroy the river?"

Dante frowned. "I doubt that would be his first choice."

"He's already tried several things and failed. If he thinks this is his last option . . ."

"The danger is not only to the river," Dante said. "Seeing our other self is dangerous to us personally. Zo may be many things, but he's not suicidal. He'll not risk his own life or sanity if there is any other way. And since he is already wounded, I suspect that his interest in destroying the river has been set aside in favor of his interest in saving himself."

"What if he sees his other self by accident?"

"I think that would be unlikely. I can feel the other me—
the me still in prison—like a constant buzz in the back of my
head. He is an echo I can't ignore. It seems to get louder the
closer I get to him." His smile tightened to steel. "I'm sure
Zo is feeling the same thing with his other half. Trust me.
Neither one of us will run into our other self by accident—or
on purpose."

I sighed. "I wish I were a Master of Time. Then I could
take myself to the dungeon without putting anyone else at
risk." I had said it as a half joke, but then I stopped. My smile
turned into a grin. "That's it! That's what we should do." My
words tumbled out in a rush. "I've been through the door once
already. All I'd have to do is go back through and I could be
a Master of Time too. And if Valerie and Orlando came with
me, then together the four of us could stop Zo and save the
river and help you and—" I stopped as Dante touched his finger to my lips, quelling my excitement. "What?" I asked. "It's
a good plan."

"Becoming a Master of Time might not be that easy."

"Why not? It was for you."

"Nothing about the time machine is *easy*," Dante said, a
shadow behind his words. "I could only return through the
door a second time because you summoned the other half of
the hourglass door on the bank as well as the bridge to get
there. Zo, Tony, V, Leo, me—we had all been to the bank
countless times and the door had never appeared for any of us.
It wasn't until I took you to the bank—and you brought some
of the river with you—that the door appeared."

My shoulders slumped in defeat. "And you think the same

thing will have to happen for me? Someone else will have to come to the bank—someone straight from the river like I did—in order for the other half of my door to appear?"

Dante didn't answer, but he didn't have to.

"I'm not going to be a Master of Time like you are, am I?" I asked quietly, all my earlier feelings of hope vanishing for good. "I can't be, because who will come to the bank and open the door for me? Who could I ask to risk their life or their sanity to even try?" My voice sounded impossibly small. "Who is going to save me?"

Dante wrapped his arms around me, holding me close. "I will," he said. "I will find a way. I promise."

But as I listened to his heart beating in his chest, I imagined I could hear the soft sound of time sliding away, as swiftly as sand through an hourglass.

❋

Later that evening, after we had eaten dinner and Alessandro and Caterina had retired for the night, I stood by the window with Dante, watching the moon rise in the sky. The pale light touched the gray-green winter grass, caught in the barren trees that spread their thin branches into the sky, and blanketed the villas scattered across the landscape.

Dante had once told me that what he missed most about his former life had been the quiet. Now I understood what he meant. The silence of the night was warm and comforting, like the silence of a heavy snowfall.

I only wished my thoughts were as silent or as comforting.

Dante seemed confident that we would find an answer to the problem of the broken locket, but I wasn't so sure. No matter how many different ways I looked at it, I couldn't see a solution. I reminded myself that at least Zo was suffering from the same problem, though the thought was a small comfort.

Dante sighed, and I peeked a glance at him. The moonlight highlighted the angles of his cheekbones, casting shadows beneath his bandaged eyes. He looked worn out. Worn down. I realized it had been a long time since I'd seen him look so tired.

He ran a hand through his hair and slumped against the wall next to the window.

"Are you okay?" I asked, instantly worried that perhaps his eyes were bothering him or, worse, the wound in his heart was deteriorating.

"I'll be all right," he said.

"Something on your mind?"

He shook his head. "It's strange. Being back here. So much has happened since I last stood here in my family's home—and yet, in some ways, I feel like nothing has really changed. Except me." He rubbed at his wrists absently as though he could strip away the gold chains.

I took his hand in mine to stop his restless activity. Gratitude flashed in his smile and he pulled me closer, allowing me to lean against his chest.

He sighed, his voice low and weary. "I remember *everything* about this place. This is my home. This is where I was born. I never thought I would *be* here again, experiencing it, feeling it, and there is a part of me that never wants to let it go." He drew in a deep breath. "I am so grateful for this chance to be here—even for such a short time—but I know I don't belong here anymore. As much as I want to stay with my family, I know that all this"—he gestured out the window and then at the room around us—"is gone. More than five hundred years gone." He looked away. "And knowing my family is alive and vibrant—hearing my father's voice, my mother's laugh—it almost makes it worse. I feel like I'm trespassing in someone else's dream."

"It's not a dream," I said. "We're really here."

"But for how long? As soon as we leave, the river will wash over this part of the past without even leaving behind a ripple. And everything here—my home, my family, everything—will vanish. Swallowed up as if they had never been."

I frowned and stepped back. "That's not true. They *were* here. They existed, and they matter. What we're doing here— trying to protect the river—is as much to help us and our families as it is to help everyone. Your neighbors, the priests at the cathedral, all those people who don't even know they are in danger. Yes, the river will wash them away—it will wash all of us away eventually—but until it does, we can't live our lives obsessing about the past or mourning the future. We have a responsibility to ourselves and to each other to live every moment of our lives the best we can."

Dante was quiet for a long moment.

I blushed. "I'm sorry, I shouldn't have said all that."

"No, I'm glad you did. You're right. I've been so worried about the river, about Zo, about keeping the timeline stable that I've forgotten the importance of the here and now." He brushed my hair behind my ear, his thumb sweeping across my cheek. "And being with you here and now is the best moment I could imagine."

I turned my face into his touch.

"Except every moment I spend with you is better than the one before it," he said. He pulled me back into his arms, and I nestled close against his chest, my body fitting perfectly next to his, finally feeling at peace. Feeling like I was home.

CHAPTER
19

No, I told you, the rook can only move in a straight line—" Dante tried again.

Dante had spent the last hour trying to explain to Valerie how to play chess, but she seemed to be more interested in making up stories about the war between the knights and the pawns or about how the king and queen met than learning the strategy of the game.

"That doesn't make any sense. Castles can't move." Valerie picked up the black rook. "And where is the princess? Usually castles have princesses inside."

"Abby?" Orlando's low voice startled me from where I stood by the window.

"Yes?"

"Would you mind taking a walk with me?"

"Now?" I gestured out the window. "It's a little late."

A serious expression settled over Orlando's face. "It will only take a moment." He pressed his lips together and glanced toward Dante and Valerie. "Please. It's important I speak to you in private."

"Of course," I said slowly, wondering what conversation

would be important enough to warrant a midnight walk in the winter wind. But I trusted Orlando, and if he said it was important, I believed him. "Dante?" I called out. "Orlando and I are going out for some fresh air."

"Bring me back some," Valerie called back. "Have fun, be safe, don't take any wooden nickels."

Dante stood up from the chessboard. "Is everything all right?"

I nodded.

"We'll be right back," Orlando said. "I promise."

He swept his father's coat around my shoulders and then held the door open for me as we stepped out into the chilly winter night.

The cold hit me like a fist and I exhaled a cloud of steam.

"Are you warm enough?" he asked.

Shivering, I nodded. "I will be. What about you?" Orlando had changed into a clean shirt and dark jacket, but neither one looked particularly warm. "The wind is a bit brisk," I added.

"It usually is this time of year." As if to prove his point, a cold breeze swept his words away on a puff of misty air. He gestured for me to follow him along the path toward a manicured garden that spread out behind the house. The moonlight lit the world with a pale glow, as if everything had been coated in ice. It was breathtakingly beautiful. Cold, but beautiful.

"I'm sorry you ended up here during the winter. Spring is much better. All the flowers are in bloom then, and the whole world looks fresh and green."

"It sounds lovely," I said, leaning into the wind as we

rounded the corner of the garden. A trickle of rocks turned underfoot and I was suddenly glad I had kept my sneakers.

We climbed a small hill. When we reached the top, Orlando stood for a moment, looking out over the small hedge maze that stretched below us; the branches along the path were brown and brittle. The wind rustled through the empty garden, but Orlando seemed immune to the cold.

"You didn't bring me out here to talk about the weather, did you?"

He shook his head, and his shoulders curved inward. He picked at the hem of his shirt with restless fingers. After a long moment, he asked, "How does my story end?"

"What?"

He turned around, his face bleak. "My story. The story of Orlando. What happens next?"

I bit my lip. "You shouldn't ask me that."

"But you know what happens. You've lived it."

Shaking my head, I felt my heart sink. "That's not how it works. The rules say you shouldn't know your own future."

"Why not?"

I knew the answer; Leo had told me the same truth in another time. "Knowing what the future holds for you could influence your decisions and your choices; it could change your life irrevocably."

"What if I *want* it to change?" he asked quietly.

"You can't change your past—"

"You are. That's why you're here, isn't it? To change the past?"

I pressed my lips together and exhaled through my nose in

twin plumes of cold air. "That's not exactly true. What I need to do here isn't changing the past so much as making sure time stays on the right course. If I fail, then, yes, things will change—but not in a good way."

"And my future? Can I change that?"

I opened my mouth with an automatic answer, but then paused. If I closed the loop as I was supposed to, then the future would unspool out as it had once before. And that meant Orlando would see more than five hundred years of the world pass by until he would be transformed into Leo and would open a place called the Dungeon where one equally cold January night the band Zero Hour would play a song that would change my life.

I knew that once the loop was closed, what had happened once would happen again—the good *and* the bad—all the way up to the point when I entered the time machine door. But once we returned home and the river was stable and whole, well . . . what happened after that was unknown. That was part of why I had come here: to protect the uncertainty of the future. To keep all our lives full of possibilities.

But Dante had already started to change things by finding his brother, by returning to his parents' home. Maybe events were already in motion that would result in an unimagined future. Maybe Orlando could be set free from his destiny as Leo.

In my heart, I knew the answer to Orlando's question, so I gave him the truth he deserved to hear, the truth I chose to believe. "Yes," I said. "You can always choose to change your future."

Orlando held my eyes with his for a long time. The wind ruffled his dark hair and bit at his cheeks until they turned red. A mournful howl followed in the wind's wake; I wondered if a storm was coming.

I pulled Alessandro's coat tighter around my throat, waiting, but for what, I didn't know.

Orlando remained as still as a statue. "I was positive I was going to die on the bank. I wasn't sure I even wanted to live if it meant I would have to face such desolation alone. And then I saw you come through the door, and you brought with you so much light and life." Orlando spoke haltingly, each word limping along after the next. "When I saw you, I thought . . ." He shook his head and looked down. The moonlight turned his blue eyes to gray. "I thought I might have a future after all. I thought I might find some happiness somehow—even after everything that had happened. But then I saw you with him— how you were with him at the shop, in the wagon, here at the house—and that's not how my story is going to end, is it? It will be you and Dante . . . not you and me."

Understanding cut through me and left me feeling breathless and bleeding. A memory surfaced: Leo sitting in my living room, explaining to me about the rules that would keep me safe. His voice rang in my mind through the long distance of years: *The story for you is more complicated. It begins the same way—young lovers taking a midnight trip to a park—but the ending is very different.*

Orlando and I weren't lovers—at least, not with each other—and the park was a simple, sculpted garden maze, but Leo had told me the truth then, as he always had. This was a complicated story. And the ending to the story of Abby and Orlando would be very different from the ending to the story of Abby and Dante. There was no way around it.

I wondered how I had missed seeing the truth of how Orlando felt. Perhaps I was as blind as Dante was, but in my own way.

"I'm sorry," I said, feeling my insides freeze solid until they felt colder than the wind blowing around me. "I didn't mean to hurt you. It's just—"

Orlando reached out to touch me, but at the last minute he let his hand drop. "I know. I don't think you could hurt anyone even if you wanted to. That's not who you are. I just needed to know the truth." He looked up at the star-speckled night sky and swallowed. "You love who you love. I understand that. And a powerful love can shape your whole life. What you share with Dante . . . it's powerful. It's worth protecting."

"Orlando—" I started forward, reaching for his elbow, but he pulled away before I could touch him.

"Dante told me about the locket. I don't pretend to under-stand everything he said, but I know that if he is going to sur-vive, he needs *you*. He is my brother, and I love him, so I will do whatever I can to help. Even if it means choosing a differ-ent future for myself than I might have wished."

I couldn't speak. All my words had vanished into the night.

"I'd rather he didn't know about . . ." He gestured elo-quently from himself to me, somehow managing to encompass the hill, the garden, the entire world around us. "Please. It would only hurt him."

Still reeling from his declaration, I tried to process what it all meant and what it might change, if anything. But whatever happened, I knew I would honor Orlando's wishes; I wouldn't tell Dante about our conversation. As Leo had once told me, it was not my place to tell another person's secrets.

"I don't want you to be hurt either," I said quietly. "Orlando, you are as much a part of my life as Dante is, but in a different way. And you will *always* have a place in my heart, I can promise you that."

"I thought I wasn't supposed to know what waited for me in my future," he said ruefully, "or how my story was going to end."

I shook my head. "Trust me when I say that your story is a long way from being over."

A sudden flood of light poured from the house as the door swung open.

"Abby!" Valerie ran toward us, waving her hands in the air. "Abby! Come quick! Something's happened to Dante!"

CHAPTER
20

Orlando beat me back to the house, but only by a step. He thundered into the main room and rushed straight to Dante's side.

Dante had collapsed, sprawled facedown on the floor. In his fist was the crumpled cloth of the bandage.

I grabbed Valerie by the arm. "What happened?"

She covered her mouth with her hands and shook her head.

"Valerie, talk to me. Tell me what happened!"

Orlando rolled Dante onto his back. His face was ashen, covered with the dried poultice his father had applied to his eyes. A dark red streak of blood dripped from Dante's nose.

"Dante!" he called. "Can you hear me? Wake up." Orlando listened to his chest, checking for any other wounds before wiping away the blood from his brother's face.

I let go of Valerie and fell to my knees on the floor next to Orlando. I grabbed Dante's hand, horrified to feel how limp it was in my own.

My heart pounded in my chest, echoing in my ears,

throbbing in my wrists. The edges of my vision turned fuzzy. I sucked down a deep breath, hoping it would help steady me.

"I don't know what happened," Valerie said in a rush. "We were talking about how pawns are really queens in disguise, and then he clutched his head like it hurt and then he ripped his bandage away and then he fell to the floor." She bounced on her toes with restless anxiety.

"Was it Zo?" I asked, pinning her in place with the intensity of my gaze. "Was Zo here?" This reminded me too much of when Zo had broken the locket the first time. I wondered in a rush if Zo had somehow managed to keep part of the locket and had attacked Dante from a distance. I pressed my hand tight to my chest, feeling the weight of the locket against my heart. No, I still had it. It was still safe.

But Dante was in danger.

"No." Valerie gnawed at her fingernails, her eyes blurry with tears. "There was no one here but us." She looked at Orlando. "He's going to be okay, right? He has to be okay. There are too many stories that need him."

"I don't know," Orlando said grimly, meeting my eyes over Dante's body.

I rubbed my thumb over the back of Dante's hand. I could feel his heartbeat through his wrist, faint and achingly slow. His breathing was shallow, the air raw and rattling in his throat. Sweat soaked through his clothes. I could see the knots in his muscles as his body tensed and twisted in pain.

"What can we do?" Orlando asked me in a low voice. "Whatever is happening—can we stop it?"

"I don't know, but we have to try," I said.

"Tell me what you want me to do." Orlando squared his shoulders, a soldier ready for battle orders.

But I didn't know what to say. What would help? What would hurt? Was there even anything I could do that would make a difference?

The wound in Dante's heart was bleeding out time.

But I knew a way to stop time. At least a small part of it. I had built a shell of time that had trapped Zo and stopped him in his tracks. Maybe I could build a smaller shell that could do the same for Dante by protecting his heart and stopping the unchecked flow of time.

I just hoped it wouldn't also stop his heart.

A spasm contorted Dante's body, pulling a guttural groan from his throat.

A hard resolve wrapped itself around my spine. My doubts didn't matter. The time for hesitation was over; it was time to act. I had to do something, or I knew I would lose Dante forever.

"Stay with him," I told Orlando, pushing myself to my feet.

"Where are you going?"

"To the bank."

"Wait—"

But I didn't.

In an instant the world disappeared around me, and I was standing in a barren wasteland. I caught my breath, feeling the familiar release of pressure in my body that signaled I had transitioned to the bank. My trips had never been that fast before, that automatic.

The bank was untouched: still flat, still empty from horizon to horizon.

But the river was boiling in turmoil.

The unspooling of the river Orlando and I had seen before was even worse. The thin streams of the broken river had grown into thicker branches, snaking out in all directions from the main flow. The once silver-white waves of the river had shadowed to gray, though a few were as sharp and black as shark fins.

I tried to block out the terrible sight and concentrated instead on listening for the music of time that I had heard before when I had summoned the shell of time that had trapped Zo.

There. The chimes were faint, muffled, and on the verge of dissonance, but they were there, and the language that lived in the echoes sounded clearer to me than ever before. If I focused, I could hear the shape of the words as they formed and reformed, flowing in a seamless stream of sound and meaning.

I remembered how Dante said he thought I had been given the gift of languages. I had thought he meant my ability to speak and understand Italian, but maybe it was more than that. Maybe I could also speak the language of the river. Of time itself.

The chimes shivered around me, and I recognized in their melody the unmistakable sound of truth.

I smiled, filled with a renewed confidence and strength. If this was my gift, my power, then I would choose to use it to help those I loved.

I remembered the strange half-word, half-chime sound I

had spoken to summon the shell for Zo. I needed something similar for Dante, but I didn't want something to trap or to hurt, but something to bind up and bandage.

Striving to find that balance of stillness inside of me, I listened to all the variations of the music as it flowed above the churning of the river, picking out exactly the tones I wanted in order to create the word I needed. *Protect. Save. Return. Heal.*

Exactly. I spoke the chord of meaning and felt a sudden rush of light flood through me. At the same time, a drop of light lifted from the river, hovering like a star above the silver-gray thread of time.

I reached out and touched the edge of the star. The light responded, echoing back to me the music I had used to create it.

I stepped forward into the river and directly back to Dante's side. The quick trip left me feeling unbalanced, my blood buzzing from the soles of my feet all the way to the top of my head. My ears still rang with the echoes of unspoken time.

But it had worked. I had returned with the drop of light in my hand. I could feel the power of it throbbing like a beating heart.

"It's beautiful," Valerie sighed in wonder.

Orlando looked up at me, his mouth opening in amazement. "It's impossible."

I knelt by Dante's side and placed my hand on his forehead. The light flowed from my hand directly into Dante. A glow seemed to flicker beneath his skin, burning with a bright light as it traveled down from his head, spreading across his chest, over his arms, and down his legs.

A ripple of pain shuddered through Dante's body, turning his muscles rigid. His breath caught, his chest lifting as his back arched off the floor. His face twisted, hard lines of pain etching grooves on either side of his mouth.

"What did you do?" Orlando demanded.

"Wait!" I ordered, my eyes still fixed on Dante. "Look."

The light seemed to burn the brightest across the scar that had blinded Dante. As we watched, the jagged edges of the wound smoothed out. The skin around his eyes faded from an angry blood-red hue to a softer pink. The length of the wound began to shrink, the thinnest ends knitting together tightly.

Within moments, the slash across his eyes had shrunk to half its original size, reduced to a sharp, thin line where it had once been a wide, ragged gash.

The light flared one more time. I winced at the brightness and looked away. When I looked back, the light was gone. But so was the scar. The last inch of the wound that had cut through Dante's skin had closed.

Dante's body relaxed in an instant, his muscles turning slack and his breath slipping out in one long, slow exhalation.

Orlando and I both instinctively moved back, giving him the space he needed. Valerie hovered around us, a nervous bird too unsettled to land.

In the silence that followed, Dante's eyes opened.

The gray film that had clouded over his vision had vanished. His eyes were clear and bright.

I saw him see me—really see me—and my heart threatened to stop.

He blinked slowly, as though waking up from a hard sleep. "Abby?" My name sounded dusty in his mouth. "Is that you?"

I leaned over him, cupping his face, touching his forehead, his cheeks, his nose, his lips. "I'm here. Are you all right? Can you see?"

He pushed himself up into a sitting position, his arms shaking with weakness.

"What about your heart?" I started. "How does it feel? Is it healed too?"

"Dante?" Orlando said quietly, moving into his brother's field of vision.

Dante's eyes opened even wider and his face turned winter white. Without a word, he reached for his brother and locked his arms around him.

I leaned back on my heels, tears spilling down my face. I didn't brush them away, though. I wanted to remember everything about this moment: the feel of my tears, the sound of Dante's voice as he said his brother's name, as together they called out for their parents, and the deep, overwhelming joy that filled my entire being.

❋

We stayed up the rest of the night talking, each of us amazed and awed by the miracle that we had witnessed. I knew Dante and Orlando had a lot of questions for me about what I had done and how, but with their parents in the room, such questions would have to wait. I didn't mind, as I wasn't sure I fully understood myself what had happened. All I knew was that Dante could see again.

I wanted to ask him about his heart, but with his parents' unending attention focused on him, I didn't have a chance. Dante knew I was worried, though, because at one point, when he had been released from yet another hug by his mother, he quickly touched his chest, then his lips, and blew me a kiss.

We told Alessandro and Caterina that it must have been Alessandro's poultice that had healed Dante so completely. It was easier than trying to explain what had really restored Dante's sight.

Dante, for his part, couldn't stop looking at his family. I could see the gratitude in his face, the recognition that against all odds he had been given an unexpected gift, and the resolve that he was not going to waste even a moment of it.

As the sun rose, I felt exhaustion begin to steal over me. I closed my eyes, capturing one last image of Dante's face close to my own, smiling. The sound of his voice whispering my name followed me into the darkness of sleep.

I felt a gentle touch tilting my face up, and a soft and slow kiss on my lips welcomed me back to the world.

"Good morning," Dante said.

I blinked as he moved away and a beam of sunlight fell across my face.

"Or should I say, good afternoon?"

"What time is it?" I rubbed at my eyes.

"Time to wake up," he teased. "Father, Orlando, and Valerie have already left for the shop, and Mother has been up for hours."

I vaguely remembered falling asleep in the main room and Dante picking me up and carrying me to a soft bed, covering me with a warm quilt, and closing the door behind him. I still wore Caterina's gold-brown dress, but my sneakers were lined up neatly by the open door.

Dante sat down in a chair next to the bed and picked up a pen and paper.

I stretched and wiggled my toes underneath the quilt. I wasn't quite ready to leave the warmth of sleep. I rolled onto my side and watched Dante work. I loved seeing his skin unmarked by scars and his bright eyes healed.

"Will you tell me something?" Dante said as he continued to write on the paper in his hand.

"Anything."

"How did you restore my sight?"

It was a complicated answer, and it took quite a while to explain how I had healed Dante with a touch of light, as well as what I had learned about the language of the river.

Dante listened intently and asked a few specific questions at key points.

When I finished, I closed my eyes, remembering how it had felt to hold a healing piece of the river in my hand. The scratch of Dante's pen on paper sounded like music, a lullaby that threatened to pull me back asleep.

"Dante?" I asked dreamily.

"Hmm?"

"So, did it work?"

"Did what work?" He continued writing, but I saw a smile play around his mouth.

I propped my head up on my elbow. "Your eyes are healed. Is your heart healed too?"

Dante paused in his work, then forged ahead. "For now."

I sat up in alarm. "So it *didn't* work?"

"I didn't say that." Dante set down his pen. "So much of what has happened to me—to us—has never been done before. I don't fully understand what you did, so I don't know how long the effects will last. So I'm focusing on what I know to be true: I know that, for now, I can see. I know that, for now, it feels like the hole in my heart has been bandaged up. I feel like I'm still losing time, but it's more like a slow leak instead of a flood." He looked at me with his clear gray eyes. "You have done an amazing thing for me, Abby. Thank you."

I relaxed, leaning back against the pillows again. I had hoped that Dante's heart would have been completely healed, but I knew he was right. We were in uncharted territory and there was no telling what the long-term effects might be. I would follow his lead and be grateful for what I had now and keep working toward what I wanted to happen in the future.

I listened to the sound of Dante's pen. "What are you writing? Are you keeping a journal?"

"Sort of."

"I'm sorry," I said in a hurry. "Journals are private; I understand. We don't have to talk about it."

"No, it's not that." He hesitated a moment. "I'd planned to show them to you when I was done, but I wasn't sure how you would react or what you would think of them."

"Them?" I repeated. "So it's *not* a journal?"

"They're letters," he said, looking at me a little shyly. "I'm writing letters."

"*Love* letters?" I grinned. "Dante di Alessandro Casella, are you writing me love letters?"

His shy smile teetered close to a tease. "They are letters of love, yes. But they are not addressed to you."

My eyes widened.

"They are *about* you," he hurried to finish.

"Go on," I said warily.

"I told you we were close to the time when you need to stand at the dungeon door and close the loop. But after that happens and we leave this time, I'm never coming back. Not for holidays or birthdays, not for weddings or funerals. I'll never walk these hills again. I'll never pass by the window and see my mother in her chair, sewing by the fire. I'll never ride with my father through town, or work alongside him at his shop."

"You don't know that," I said. "Once the river is stable again, you could come and go as you please, if you wanted to."

"That's just it." He leaned closer to me. "I won't want to. Coming back here—even to visit—will mean leaving you behind, and I swore I would never do that again." He picked up my hand and laced his fingers through mine. "When I say good-bye to my parents for the last time, I know it will be *for the last time*. But they won't know that."

"The letters are to your family," I said in quiet realization.

He nodded, his eyes holding mine. "I don't want them to worry about me. I want them to know that I'm healthy and happy and whole, even if I'm . . ." He cleared his throat. I saw his hand move as though he might touch his chest, but in the end, he didn't. He didn't have to; I knew what he was thinking.

"Whatever happens to me," he continued, his voice steady, "I want my parents to know the good parts of my story. But I won't be here to tell them, so the letters will have to do it for me. I've written enough to have one delivered every year for the next five years."

"Why only five years? Won't your parents be worried when the letters just . . . stop?"

Dante was silent for a long time. "My parents won't be around to expect a sixth letter."

"Oh." My heart ached at the thought of Dante's loss that was already so close and drawing closer.

He drew in a deep breath and held it. "Knowing the future is sometimes a burden I'd rather not bear."

I traced the back of Dante's hand with my fingers. "So, what did you write in these letters? You said they were about me."

Dante made a sound halfway between a laugh and a cough. "This is the part I wasn't sure you would like."

"Uh-oh, should I be worried?" I asked with a smile in my voice.

"Well, first I wrote about after I returned to da Vinci's

studio, how you and I began courting," Dante began slowly, his palm pressed against mine.

"And?"

"And then, in a letter that will arrive in a few years, I wrote about how you had accepted my proposal and that we are to be wed the following spring."

"And?" My voice squeaked in a high note of surprise and disbelief.

"And then, in the last letter, I wrote about how we are expecting a child. You think it will be a boy and want me to ask permission to name him Alessandro, in honor of my father. But I am sure it will be a girl, and that we will name her Sofia."

I gulped down my words, speechless with emotion. "Married?" I managed. "And a child? In five years? But I'll only be—what?—twenty-three?"

Dante's blush turned to dark red. "Well, I may have . . . accelerated the timeline a little. There's no rush, of course. I know you want to go to college and . . ." His words tripped over themselves in his hurry to explain. He was usually so calm, it was strange to see him so flustered. "Anyway, I know my mother would be pleased at the thought of a grandchild. Even one that is only a wish of pen and paper." He looked down at the letter in his hand and then back up at me. "Don't worry, Abby. I didn't write what was *going* to happen. Just what I thought *might* happen." Then he added in a low voice, "What I *hope* might happen."

I blinked, still reeling from the idea of my life unfolding in a series of letters. "But Sofia?" I echoed, my tumbling thoughts catching on something familiar. "I know that name. I heard you talking about her to Zo once on the bank, a long time ago. Did you see her in the river? Is she—" I could barely get the words out. "Is she going to be our child?"

"She could be," Dante said quietly.

"But you don't know," I stated.

He shook his head.

"Didn't you see my future in the river?"

He shook his head again. "I haven't looked. And I'm not going to."

"Why not?"

"I'm tired of knowing things I shouldn't. I'm tired of wondering which possibility will prevail. But most of all, I don't want to second-guess your decisions. I want you to be able to choose your own future by yourself."

I thought about everything Dante had told me: how his wounded heart was better but not yet whole, about the letters that sketched out his hopes and dreams, about the shape of our future together. I thought about the possibilities and the potential that waited for us. "But I'm *not* by myself," I said. "Not anymore. And the future I choose will be the one that has you in it."

A small smile curved Dante's lips. "So, does that mean you'll say yes when I *do* ask you to marry me?"

"When the time is right," I replied with a grin, "ask me and find out."

CHAPTER
21

Dante and I were outside in the garden, enjoying the sunshine and sharing stories, when a small carriage rumbled up the front walk. When Dante looked up and saw the pattern of stars on the side of the door, he stopped in his tracks.

"What?" I asked. "Who is it?"

"The court's men," he murmured. He took my hand and quickly led me back toward the house.

I kept my face down as well. We both had good reasons for wanting to avoid contact with anyone from the courthouse. Me because I had escaped from there not too long ago, and Dante because, according to their records, he was already locked up in the dungeon awaiting trial. How could he explain away the fact that he was in two different places at the same time?

We had just reached the door—Dante even had his hand on the latch—when a voice called out.

"Excuse me, miss? May I speak with you?"

I stopped short. I knew that voice. Glancing up, I saw a short man standing in the center of the pathway. He wore a heavy winter coat, and the stars on his collar matched those on the carriage. His boots were polished to a high shine, and over his shoulder he had a familiar-looking satchel.

"Miss?" he asked again, a little louder.

Dante whispered low in my ear. "He's seen you. If you don't answer, he'll be suspicious."

My heart skipped a beat. "But it's Angelo's assistant —Domenico."

Domenico took a few steps closer toward us. Dante shifted toward the shadow of the house, but his movement must have drawn Domenico's attention because he called out, "Sir? Yes, hello. I'm looking for someone. I was wondering if perhaps you could help me."

I exchanged a glance with Dante and shook my head. Now that Domenico had seen us both, there was nothing we could do but play along and hope for the best.

I turned around and gave Domenico a bright smile. I hoped that since my hair was down and I was wearing a dress instead of a T-shirt and jeans, Domenico might not recognize me.

No such luck.

He took a step back, tilting his head like a bird and peering at me with muddy brown eyes. "I know you," he said in astonishment, blinking in surprise. "You were at the courthouse. With Orlando di Alessandro Casella."

Before I could reply, Domenico clutched his satchel to his chest and began rummaging through the contents. "But he is the man I'm looking for. Is he here? It's important that I speak with him."

"I'm sorry; I can't help you," I said, grateful that Orlando was legitimately out of the house and out of harm's way. It was bad enough that Domenico had found me and Dante; I didn't want to jeopardize Orlando's safety too.

Domenico looked up from his search, glancing between me and Dante. "But isn't this the Casella home?" His face turned an embarrassed shade of pink. "I'm sorry. It's just that you look so much like him"—he gestured to Dante—"I just assumed . . ." He trailed off and studied Dante more closely. His forehead creased in confusion.

"Why are you looking for Orlando?" I asked, hoping to distract Domenico's attention away from Dante. "Has he done something wrong?"

"That's just it. He's done nothing wrong. I simply wanted to give him a message." He cleared his throat. "Are you sure you don't know where he is?"

He looked up at me with such hope in his eyes that I felt my resolve crumbling.

"I'm his brother," Dante said carefully. "You can give me the message."

Domenico hesitated, as though wary of trusting us too much.

"There are no secrets between my brother and me." Dante's voice was low but strong. "I know the truth of his past."

The wariness in Domenico's eyes retreated. "In that case, when you see Orlando, would you please tell him how sorry I am?"

Now I was the one to blink in surprise.

"Tell him that what was done to him . . . it was wrong. No

258

one should be made to suffer as he did." He dove back into his bag and rustled through a few more papers. "I have been looking for him everywhere in order to give him this." He held up a large envelope in both hands.

"What is it?" Dante asked.

"He was promised a new identity—among other things—in exchange for his . . . assistance." The pink blush of embarrassment deepened to the red of shame. "Angelo has refused to fulfill his promise, but I am a man of honor, and if this, in some way, can help Orlando, then it is my duty to help him however I can." He cleared his throat again and straightened to his full height, even though it meant he only reached my shoulder. "A promise is a promise, and I would like to make amends, though I know it will never be enough."

"You are a good man," I said. Tears filled my eyes and I reached for Dante's hand. "We would be honored to give him that message."

Domenico puffed his chest out with the praise and bowed low. "Thank you, my lady."

He handed the envelope to Dante and then turned to leave.

"Wait," I called out. "You won't . . . I mean, I'd appreciate it if you didn't tell anyone you saw me here."

Domenico smiled knowingly. "Angelo put me in charge of finding Orlando and the girl who had escaped with him from the courthouse. Now that I have found you"—he bowed once more—"I believe I can safely say that no one else will come looking for you." He nodded to Dante, then climbed into his carriage and drove away.

We both looked down in silence at the envelope in Dante's hands.

I touched the corner edge. "This is what will save Orlando, isn't it? This will allow him to go somewhere new, become someone new. Until he ultimately becomes Leo in all those years to come."

He nodded. "It's strange to think that the papers in this envelope will change his life yet again. Part of me wants to keep them a secret—as if, by pretending nothing has happened, we can all stay here, together as a family, instead of being swept apart by the river." He sighed. "But the other part of me knows that by receiving these papers, Orlando will have the choice of what—and who—he will become. I can't deny him that choice."

"But you know he'll be okay," I said, giving his arm a reassuring squeeze. "Eventually."

After a time, Dante drew me close and pressed a kiss to the top of my head. "I'm so sorry, Abby."

"What for?"

"For not fully understanding what you are going through. I might be afraid of losing my brother—my family—but it's already happened to yours. I should be doing more to help you bring them home."

"You don't have to apologize, Dante. It's strange to say it, but we haven't exactly had time to focus on the problem."

"I should have made time."

I bit my lip, thinking back to the ghostly images I had seen of my family back on the bank. I felt the hard pull of longing. "Could we try now?" I asked.

Dante didn't say anything; he simply folded the envelope into his pocket and, with a grin, flickered me to the bank.

I knew the river had been struggling and unstable, but I was surprised to see how much worse it had gotten even during the short time since I'd last been to the bank.

"Oh, no," I gasped. "This is terrible."

It was actually worse than that. The river had continued to unspool, fraying and thinning until it looked less like the winding Mississippi and more like the flooded Nile delta. It had been transformed into a swamp, complete with pockets of flickering lights and tide pools filled with sluggish images.

Dante surveyed the river in both directions, his mouth a grim line. "I'm sorry, Abby. Trying to save your family now might be the worst thing we could do."

My heart sank, but I knew he was right. As much as I wanted my family back, I didn't want to do the wrong thing at the wrong time and have them suffer even more for my mistake.

"Is there *anything* we can do?" I asked.

He was silent for a moment, pacing along the edge of the bank. "It seems to be weakest here and here," he said, pointing out two of the very thinnest spots where patches of silver threads lumped together in a sluggish knot. "But the river seems to be cleaner upstream, which is odd."

I walked along next to Dante for a measureless moment of time until we came to the point where the river slowed to a trickle, as though the flow had been blocked by a boulder midstream. "So what happened here?" I asked.

"The door happened." Dante crouched down to get a

closer look at the river. "Before here, the river is fine—see, it's clean and protected all the way back—but after here, the river has suffered from our interference."

I knelt next to Dante. "So when I go to see you in the dungeon, this is the point in the timeline that I'll be saving." It felt a little strange to be so close to such an important moment and yet still so far away. "And once I do, do you think the river will be stable enough that we can save my family?"

Dante nodded. "This is the hinge. The point where everything changes."

We watched the ebb and flow of the river for a moment. "What happens if you don't go through the door?" I asked curiously. "I know that you seeing me at the door is important and is what will close the loop and protect the river, but after that happens, will you still have to go through the door?"

"Yes, I will."

"Why?"

"Think of it as a lock and a key. Seeing you at the door is the key to saving me. My going through the door is what will lock the river into place. Together, we will be able to finally restore the river to its full strength and protect it from any further interference. It will take both of us." Dante shrugged. "If you don't go to the dungeon, or if I don't go through the door, then none of this will matter. The river will be destroyed beyond anything Zo could hope to do to it."

The thought sent a chill through me. As much as I didn't want Dante to have to suffer the pain of going through the time machine, I knew he was willing to do it if it meant that, in the end, the river could be saved. I had made the same choice when I had decided to come through a time machine of my own. I had chosen to accept the good and the bad. I just hoped the good would be so much better that it could outweigh the bad.

"So, here, on the other side of the river, there is a version of you, already in prison, already waiting for me—you just don't know it yet."

He nodded again, but slower, sadder.

I took his hand. "I wish there were something I could do to help. A way to tell the other you that you'll be okay, to give you some hope."

"*You* are my hope," he said. "You always have been; you always will be."

A flash of light appeared a little ways down along the bank. I looked up, wondering if it was the ghost of my family again, but the horizon line was empty. Instead, I saw a thread of the river peel off from the main flow. A quiet rumble rocked through the bank. The flat sky turned gray overhead.

Dante frowned and rose to his feet in one smooth movement. "Stay here."

I folded my legs beneath me, propping myself up with one arm. I watched as Dante walked away, his long stride purposeful and powerful.

A flicker in the river caught my eye and I glanced down. I wasn't expecting to see anything—the river was so muddled here where the boulder of the door blocked the flow of time—but, to my surprise, the image of a face surfaced, clear and sharp.

Dante's face.

I bit down on my lip, swiveling back to my knees so I could lean closer to the river.

The river offered up more of the image—just flashes, glimpses—but it was enough. I saw close quarters, black bricks, and thick bars blocking any escape. I didn't know if my thinking of him had summoned him, but I knew I was seeing the Dante who was in prison. The one I was destined to save.

Physically, he looked almost exactly like the Dante I knew. But the fear in his eyes made him seem younger and more vulnerable. He wore a dirty shirt, ragged at the cuffs and hem. He pressed his back up against the wall, tucking his bare feet as close to his body as he could. A steady drip of water leaked from the ceiling, the puddle next to him glistening like oil in the dim light. It looked like he was in the third cell from the end of the hall.

I could see him shivering from the cold.

I knew he had strength, but it was still raw and unformed. He hadn't been tried or tested yet, but I knew that it was coming. And that it would be harder than he'd ever imagined.

I glanced down the bank, but the other Dante was on his knees, studying a different section of the river.

Returning my gaze to the Dante in prison, I thought about how we were a team, the key to each other's survival. I knew I had to do something to help him. How could I not?

But the bigger question was, *could* I help at all? He was in the river; I was on the bank. I tapped my lips with my finger, thinking.

I remembered how I had once sent a message ringing through the void of the bank, challenging Zo after he had left my doll's head in a gold box for me—his sick idea of a gift. Surely, if I could send a message into the bank from the river, I could send a message into the river from the bank.

But what could I say? What message of hope could help strengthen Dante? What would give him the courage he needed to face the unknown? What would save him?

And then I knew.

I slowed my breathing, naturally falling into that meditative state where my thoughts sharpened and the counting came easy. The ever-present chimes of time warbled in my ears, whispering encouragement and direction. I fixed the image of Dante in my mind, concentrating on the exact moment I wanted to reach. I felt the familiar pressure of the bank building, heard the river chuffing like a lion's roar, but I continued to breathe, to count, to focus.

And when I felt the edges thin to the point of invisibility, I sent my message into the river with as much force as I could manage.

Feel the fear till the count of ten, then count once more to be brave again. I took a deep breath. *The counting will save you, Dante. Remember to count.*

The image of Dante swirled away into the river, and maybe it was my imagination, but I thought that the spot where he had been seemed a little clearer, a little smoother, than before. It was the best I could hope for.

CHAPTER
22

W hat are you doing?" Zo said.

My thoughts broke like glass and I whipped around, startled. I scrambled back, struggling to find my feet, but Zo's hand flashed out and gripped my wrist, holding me in place.

The drop of darkness in my mind quivered at his touch and all my words vanished in my throat.

His hand twitched on my arm; his skin was burning hot with the heat of fever, of sickness.

"Are you trying to change things?" he continued conversationally as he crouched next to me on his haunches. "All by yourself?" He looked down at the river where Dante's face had been a moment ago, but his eyes were slightly unfocused. "I was in the cell next to Dante, did you know that? All that muttering and counting and pacing. It about drove me crazy."

I looked over my shoulder, searching for Dante. Where was he?

Dante was following the broken thread of the river as it

wove its way downstream. He was too far away to hear us, too far away to see what was happening.

"Or were you trying to help *him?*" Zo nodded downriver at Dante's retreating form. "Because I don't think that's very fair."

My voice returned, rusty and hoarse. "Since when have you ever played fair?"

"Now, Abby, that hurts. Dante broke my guitar; I broke his locket. That is the definition of fair." He opened his mouth to laugh, but all that emerged was a dry gasp that ended in a cough. "And even though we are both wounded—both dying—you have helped only *him.* So now who is playing favorites?" Zo leaned in as though we were sharing a secret, a smile on his dry and cracked lips. "Is it because he's a better kisser?"

Growling, I yanked my wrist out of Zo's grasp and pushed myself to my feet, glaring down at him. "I helped Dante because I love him. But I don't expect you to understand that." I turned my back on him and took a step downstream toward Dante.

Zo's voice called out from behind me. "It doesn't have to be like this."

"Like what?" I tossed over my shoulder without looking back.

I realized later that was my first mistake. Had I turned around, I would have seen Zo coming for me and I might have been able to avoid him.

My second mistake was in not calling out for Dante as soon as I had found my voice again. If I had, he might have heard me. And then he might have saved me before it was too late—before Zo's body hit mine, before he wrapped his arms tight around me and flickered me into the unknown.

❋

The spires of the Cathedral of the Angels pierced the sky above me. I landed on my back, my head aching and my vision off-kilter as I struggled to catch my breath after such an abrupt transition. I hated traveling with Zo; he lacked Dante's grace and finesse.

Zo's face hovered over me, his body pinning me down. He grinned and ran his hand down my cheek and along the curve of my neck. "Well, now, isn't this interesting?"

I didn't want to be here, and I wasn't going to stay. I steeled myself to jump to the bank, but nothing happened.

Zo slid his hand down my side and locked my wrist in his fist. "You're not going anywhere, my sweet. Not yet. Not until I say so."

At the sound of his endearment for me, the black spot in my mind woke and acquiesced to his command. I had hoped the dark block was gone for good, but now I felt it return, cutting me off from the bank as easily as closing a door. I gritted my teeth at the pain that accompanied Zo's touch in my mind. A trickle of sweat traveled down the back of my neck.

"Get off me," I snapped, shoving hard at his chest with my free hand.

He rolled to his feet with a dark chuckle and yanked me up by my wrist, still holding me tight against his body.

But being that close to him, I could tell how sick he really was. I could hear his breath rattling in his throat. Sweat coated his skin. He kept bending and flexing the fingers of his left hand as though wanting to make sure he could still feel them. I suspected that holding me here was taking all of his remaining strength.

I looked around at my new surroundings, hoping to see something that would help me escape, but we were alone. I couldn't see anyone else close by. Zo had brought me to an empty plot of land outside the cathedral walls. A bitter wind blew through the wrought-iron fence that encircled the small area. A few statues had been scattered over the uneven ground: a pretty girl, a man kneeling in prayer, a hooded figure, a crying angel. The shiver that ran through me had nothing to do with the cold. We were in a cemetery. Why had Zo brought me to a cemetery?

"Let me go," I demanded. I tried to concentrate, to send a message to Dante on the bank, but Zo's block made it hard for me to focus or find my balance. My thoughts kept scattering like leaves on the wind.

Zo shrugged one shoulder. He didn't seem bothered by the cold. Or my demands. "I might. After you have helped me."

"I won't help you," I snarled. "Ever."

"You don't even know what I want," Zo said casually.

"I can guess."

Zo arched an eyebrow in invitation.

"You're sick. Dying. Just like Dante was." I swallowed at the memory of Dante collapsing to the ground, of him lying so still and cold in my lap. "But he's better now. And you want me to do the same for you."

Zo grinned, his teeth dull against his grayish lips. "Very good. I must say, I was surprised when I saw what you had done. I'd been watching you for some time, and when the ripples in the river showed that you had not only healed Dante's vision but patched the hole in his heart, well, I knew then that if it was good enough for Dante, it was certainly good enough for me."

"If you think I'm going to help you like I helped Dante, you're a fool."

Zo's face darkened in anger.

I watched warily as he took a breath and slowly regained his control.

"You said you would do anything for me." His voice took on the same silky tones he had used in the cathedral to convince me I loved him, his words underscored with the same song I had heard before. Even though the song wasn't as strong or as seamless as it had been before, the darkness in my mind responded, urging me to surrender, to obey.

I shook my head, dislodging the compulsion that was building. Zo might be strong enough to keep me from escaping, but he wasn't strong enough to make me do anything else he wanted. Not anymore.

"You *made* me say that, so it doesn't count." I tried to yank my arm away, but Zo simply held on tighter. I could feel the bones in my wrist grinding against each other.

A muscle jumped near his eye. He thinned his lips in

displeasure. The darkness in my mind faded to gray as he abandoned his attempt at forced obedience.

"A promise is a promise, no matter who makes it." Zo looked down at the headstone closest to him. A small angel statue stood behind it, her wings extended to offer shelter to the name carved into stone: *Angelica Giardini*. He shoved me forward, closer to the grave. "*She* made me a promise too. Then she broke her word. And now she is here." He hauled me back around to face him. His black eyes burned. "Do you want that to be your story?"

I swallowed. I had seen Zo in many different situations and with many different emotions. I had been threatened by him more than once. But I had never seen such raw violence in his eyes. I saw it in his face: not only the promise of pain, but an eagerness to inflict it.

He was clearly a man on the edge, desperate, and that made him even more dangerous than usual. I stopped struggling. Fighting with him would only make things worse. Maybe if I remained calm and at least a little cooperative, he would relax his guard and I could get away.

Or at least survive until Dante arrived.

"Who was she?" I asked, my voice cracking on the last word. I wrapped my arm around my chest, trying to hold on to whatever warmth I could. I could feel the tops of my ears and the tip of my nose tingling with the cold.

Zo touched the curve of the angel's wing. "She was mine, once. She promised she would make me happy and give me sons and do whatever I asked." He tightened his grip on me again, and I hissed in suppressed pain. "When she refused to marry me, I knew that all her promises were lies. She pretended to be an innocent flower, but she was poison."

"Is that why you killed her? Valerie told us the story of how the Flower Girl refused the Pirate King and how she was broken, body and soul," I blurted out before I could stop myself. I winced. What had happened to trying to be cooperative? I braced myself for his reaction.

But Zo didn't lash out at me. Instead his face tightened. The rattle in his chest grew deeper until it sounded like a growl. "She betrayed my trust. She humiliated me. She made me look like a fool."

"And that was the worst part, wasn't it?" I said, with dawning realization. "It wasn't that she broke your heart. You probably didn't even love her—not really. It's that she refused you. She was no longer something you could own. It's never about love with you, is it, Zo? It's about possession. That's why you want me to help you. Why you want *me* at all. Because you know you can't have me."

Zo clenched his jaw, anger flashing in his eyes. "Let's make this simple, shall we? I blinded Dante, and he should have stayed blind. I broke his locket, and he should have stayed broken. But instead, you healed him. You defied the wishes of a Master of Time. It's only fair that you even the scales by restoring to me what belongs to me." He grabbed me by the shoulders and pulled me close to him again. "You owe me. After everything we've been through. Everything you've done. You owe me this."

"I don't owe you anything," I said. "And you won't get what you want. Not from me."

Zo shook his head and smiled, the predator back on the prowl. "Oh, but sweet Abby, you should know by now that I always get what I want."

Before I could react, Zo's mouth came down hard on mine.

I tried to recoil, shoving hard against his chest with both hands, my fingers automatically turning into claws. He may have been bleeding out time from an unseen wound, but he was still physically stronger than I was. I aimed a kick at his leg, hoping to connect with a knee or an ankle, but with my brain screaming and my body struggling, I missed. I would have fallen if he hadn't been holding me so tightly.

His mouth moved on mine in a smile. I could almost taste his amusement. It made me want to throw up.

He advanced, keeping me off balance and forcing me to take a step back. I felt the rough stone of the cathedral wall behind me. A small part of me was grateful for the support, but the rest of me hated the feeling of pressure all around me, of being trapped without being able to move, without a way out. His body was so close to mine.

Panic rose up in my throat. I didn't dare close my eyes. I didn't dare breathe. My vision started to turn black around the edges. I tried to twist out of his grip, but he seemed to anticipate my every move, countering me and keeping me pinned.

Was this how it was going to end, then?

Or was this just the beginning of something worse?

And then he was gone, his body ripped away from mine in one violent movement. I caught a glimpse of his eyes, a lightning flash of surprise in their dark depths, before he crashed to the ground a few feet away from me. I gasped out loud with sudden freedom, gulping down the cold air until the inside of my throat felt coated with ice. I scrubbed at my mouth with both hands, frantic to erase Zo's touch.

A dark shadow rose up in front of me, and I shied away in instinctive fear, my heart beating hard and fast in my chest.

As the light cut through the clouds, I saw who had saved me from Zo's attack.

Dante stood over Zo, his back to me and his feet spread wide to help him keep his balance. His hands clenched into fists. A halo of stillness settled over him, tightening his muscles. His body hummed with tension, focused and sharp. This wasn't the stillness he summoned when he was thinking or planning; this was a profound absence of thought. And, in the void, there was only action.

Zo scrambled back, attempting to leverage himself up to his feet, but Dante was quicker. He moved forward, bringing his boot down hard on Zo's hand.

I heard the sickening snap of bone, but Zo didn't scream in pain. Instead, he smiled up at Dante as though he had run into an old friend on the street.

"It's good to see you again, Dante. Frankly, I was beginning to wonder when you were going to show up. I was starting to think you didn't care—"

Dante leaned his weight forward, and another snap cracked through Zo's words.

His grin faltered for a moment, but then he drew in a shuddering breath and fixed it back in place. "I see you've decided not to play nice anymore."

"Shut up," Dante said, his voice the cold rumble of an avalanche. "Are you safe, Abby?" He threw the words over his shoulder without moving.

I nodded. Then, realizing he couldn't see me standing behind him, I said, "Yes." Then again, louder, "Yes, I'm fine. He didn't hurt me."

I felt more than saw a little of the tension leave his body. "Good," he said in a tone that was reassuring to me but that made Zo's eyes flick to Dante's face. He must not have liked what he saw because a few drops of sweat appeared on his forehead.

"Abby did a nice job healing your eyes," Zo said. "Impressive work. Just so you know, Abby," he called to me over Dante's shoulder, "I'm expecting the same level of quality when it's my turn."

"I doubt that will be happening anytime soon," Dante said.

"Oh, I don't know about that," Zo said with a grin. "Stranger things have happened."

"There's a lot you don't know," Dante said.

"I know you can't keep me here," Zo said, but his bravado sounded strangely flat.

"Watch me."

He shifted his weight, but instead of breaking another of Zo's fingers, he simply applied direct pressure on the two that had already been wounded.

"Hard to travel when you're in pain, isn't it?" Dante commented.

Zo dug his heels into the ground as he attempted to extract himself from under Dante's foot.

But Dante simply pointed at Zo's chest. "Stop," he said, "or I swear I'll make you wish you had."

Zo stopped moving, though his breathing quickened. Sweat dribbled down the side of his face. "So this is your big plan, Dante? You're just going to stand on me?"

"No," Dante said. "My plan is to do this."

And he reached down, grabbed Zo by the throat, and swung his fist hard across Zo's face.

CHAPTER
23

I wanted to step back from the sudden violence, but my back was already pressed flat against the cathedral wall.

Blood streamed from Zo's mouth and nose. Even unconscious, his hand curled protectively around his broken fingers. Since Dante had inflicted those wounds, I knew they would be permanent. Still, I had a hard time finding any sympathy for Zo's pain.

Dante straightened to his full height, shaking out his hand. He stepped over Zo's body and reached my side in a moment.

"Abby," he said, touching my arm. "It's time."

I blinked. Things had happened so fast, I felt caught in a whirlwind, my mind still reeling from Zo's attack and Dante's rescue.

The pressure of his fingers increased, adding to the urgency of his voice. "You have to get the door—now—before it's too late."

"It's time?" I repeated. Dante had warned me that it would be time for me to go to the dungeon soon. But now?

"When we were on the bank, I saw events start shifting, moving into place. I knew it was time, but when I turned around to tell you, you were gone." He glared at Zo's body on the ground. "I came as fast as I could. I'm sorry—"

Suddenly, Dante caught his breath and a grimace twisted his features. He clenched down on his jaw so tightly the skin turned pale.

"Dante?" I reached for his arm, feeling the pull of his muscles as a concentration of pain passed through him. "Is it your eyes, your heart?" We had worried that my healing effects might be only temporary, but I hadn't imagined they would wear off so soon.

He shook his head and exhaled slowly; I could see the effort it took him to maintain his control. "No. I can feel the river moving into place. Our window of opportunity is closing. The pressure is building. It's time," he said again. "*I* need help too, Abby, and you are the only one who can do it."

I knew I would have only one chance to save Dante and thereby save the river as well. It was why we had come all this way, endured so much. If I didn't go, all our sacrifices would be in vain.

I buried my face in Dante's neck. "I wish you could come with me," I said.

"So do I," Dante agreed, gathering me into his arms, his hands locking tight against the small of my back. "But it's not possible. I can't risk seeing my other self. And I can't risk leaving Zo alone—even unconscious. You'll have to go alone." He leaned back to look me in the eyes. "It's like you said: The me inside the dungeon can't wait to see you for the first time—he just doesn't know it yet. Go. I'll be here when you get back."

I kissed him hard and fast. "I'll see you soon," I said with a fierce smile.

I hurried out of the cemetery to the edge of the courtyard outside the cathedral. I looked in the direction of the court-house as though I could see through the buildings that sepa-rated us. A few people milled through the streets. A nearby vendor called out to passing customers, offering to show them his wares. Two children ran in circles, laughing and shrieking in a game of tag. The whole town was filled with people, and not a single one of them understood what was going on, the danger they were in. Their lives were in my hands too.

I took a deep breath and squared my shoulders. After all we had been through, all we had seen and done, I knew this was the moment that mattered. The fulcrum on which the fu-ture balanced. Stay or go, it was time. And time wouldn't wait for me anymore.

I turned my face toward the courthouse.

And I ran.

❖

I ran across the plaza without a passing thought as to who was around me or what they might think. The important thing was to get to the dungeon before it was too late. I kept my focus fixed on the courthouse. The sooner I got there, the bet-ter. I could feel time slipping away with every breath.

My heart threatened to beat out of my chest, so I counted my steps, pacing myself, forcing myself to find that still space of calm in the heart of the adrenaline storm raging inside me.

I remembered my midnight escape from this very same courthouse with Orlando, though it felt like it had happened to another person. Maybe it had. My trip through time had certainly changed me.

Thinking of that escape, though, made me slow my steps from a run to a dash to a walk. Domenico had said that the guards were not looking for me anymore, but still, I didn't want to draw too much unnecessary attention to myself. I still had a long way to go to reach the lowest basement of the courthouse, and although part of me wanted to run all the way to the door, through the hallways, and down the stairs to the dungeon, I couldn't afford to be stopped or caught or delayed by anyone.

Still, when I reached the front door of the courthouse, I walked through without hesitation.

A handful of people were in the hallway, but no one gave me a second glance.

Keeping myself close to the wall, willing myself to be invisible, I counted off more steps, keeping time with my measured breathing.

I turned a corner and was heading toward a staircase that would lead me down when I saw Domenico exit a room a little farther down the hallway.

He looked up and saw me, a smile appearing on his round face. "My lady, I had not expected to see you here today."

"I had not expected to be here today," I replied, trying to catch my breath. I brushed my hair out of my eyes, scrubbing off a line of sweat in the process.

His smile faded into concern as he took in my disheveled appearance. "Is everything all right? What's wrong?"

I didn't even know how to begin to answer him. "Would you be able to do a favor for me?" I asked instead.

He bowed. "I am at your service."

I hesitated, then said, "I need to go to the dungeon."

"The dungeon?" he exclaimed. "Why are you going there?"

"It's a long story," I said with a sigh. "But I need to see someone there and I can't afford to be late." A pair of guards walked past, their swords gleaming at their sides. "Though I'd rather not be seen along the way if I can help it," I muttered.

Domenico followed my gaze, his face drawn in thought. "This thing you need to do, it won't hurt anyone, will it?"

I shook my head.

"It will break no laws?"

I shook my head again. I was tired of things breaking. It was time to start fixing a few things instead.

"Follow me." He led me back into the main hallway and toward the last door in the row.

"Where—" I started, looking back in the direction of the staircase.

"This is faster." Domenico opened the door. "You did say it was urgent, didn't you?"

✖

"Are you sure about this, my lady?" Domenico asked. "Certainly I could help you with this task so that you wouldn't need to enter this place."

"No, it has to be me," I said. "But thank you for your help." Domenico's shortcut had been a single staircase that led from the main floor of the courthouse directly to the back door of the dungeon. It had saved me valuable time, and now I was where I was supposed to be *when* I supposed to be.

"The guards will not be pleased to see you," Domenico warned.

"This will only take a moment," I said. "I promise."

My heart quickened. Dante was so close. He was right there, on the other side of the door. I felt like if I closed my eyes, I could point directly at him even through all the layers of wood and stone and darkness that separated us. I pressed my hand to my chest, feeling the cloth packet that contained the broken locket. It was time.

I opened the door carefully; I didn't want to alert the guards by accident.

As my eyes adjusted to the dim light, I studied the layout of the dungeon. Not that there was much to see. So far beneath the surface, the only available light came from a row of torches on the wall and a few fat candles that did little to mask the scent of old food, dirt, and rot that hung in the air like an invisible cloud. I could hear the sound of dripping water from somewhere in the shadows.

The dungeon was one large room lined on either side by cramped cells, each one blocked with bars across the front. There were two guards standing at the far end of the room where there was another staircase leading up.

I stepped through the door, hesitant to touch the walls. I prayed I wouldn't slip in something unspeakable.

I shook out my hands, trying to still the trembling in my fingers. I wanted to take a deep breath, but I knew I didn't want that foul air inside my lungs. I wanted to be as clean—inside and out—for Dante's first look as I could be.

Everything hinged on this moment.

I took a step forward.

"Look here!" a guard shouted at me from down the row of cells. "What do you think you're doing?"

I could feel the river flexing around me as the broken spiral slowly began twisting into a healing circle.

The moment was here. The moment was now.

There was no going back.

And then everything happened at once.

I saw the guard heading straight for me, his partner rushing behind him.

The prisoners closest to the door noticed the activity and a wave of noise rose up and crashed over me. Voices yelling, whistling, begging. To me it sounded like the roar of the river falling over rocks.

A third guard trailed after the other two. I saw a blanket clutched in his fist.

The river shivered and shook as it bent back into place.

There wasn't much time left.

I scanned the cells along the wall, looking for the one that was the third from the end. Dante's cell.

One.

The light from the torches danced on the walls, casting long shadows of bars on the floor. Goose bumps lifted on my arms. I could see my breath in the cold air that was trapped in the dungeon along with the prisoners.

Two.

The wild cacophony of voices ebbed and flowed in the dungeon. Demands for freedom. Declarations of innocence. Sobs from broken hearts; screams from broken spirits.

Three.

My heart hurt from the relentless pressure of time closing in on me. My throat clogged with anticipation. My bones creaked with the strain of holding my body upright.

I rose up on my toes, holding onto the door frame for balance, and scanned the faces of the prisoners that I could see. They all looked so much alike. Dirty, ragged, worn out and worn down. They all sounded alike.

Wait—

Through the din, I could hear one voice offering up a litany of numbers.

Dante's voice. I would know it anywhere.

My eyes swung back.

There. That one was Dante's cell. He was there. *Right there*.

The sound of his counting cut off suddenly, and I could imagine him standing by the bars, his long fingers wrapped around the dull metal, his eyes ready to meet mine for the first time, for always.

I looked for a pair of gray eyes the color of stars at dawn, a face that I knew as well as my own, a mouth that I ached to see smiling at me.

What I saw instead, though, was Dante sprawled on the

floor of his cell, his arms flung wide, his wrists bare and unmarked by chains.

My rising euphoria collapsed into a broken cry of horror.

Standing over Dante's unconscious body was Zo, his golden chains cuffing his wrists, his wild, black eyes burning with pain and anger and hate. Blood streaked down his nose, over his mouth.

He looked at me for a split second before lifting a swollen and bruised hand in greeting. His two broken fingers were bent at odd angles; they looked like talons beckoning me to come closer.

In his other hand, he held a knife.

And in his grin, I saw a declaration of war.

I watched, frozen in terror, as Zo thrust down and plunged the needle-thin blade directly into Dante's heart.

And then he vanished.

CHAPTER
24

I was vaguely aware of the guards rushing toward me. One of them wrapped me in a blanket and bustled me out the door.

All I could see frozen in my mind was that moment when Zo's blade pierced Dante's heart. Every detail felt like it had been etched into my soul with acid. This was worse than when Zo had cut Dante's eyes and blinded him. Worse than when Zo had broken the locket and punched a hole in Dante's life. This was worse than anything I could imagine.

If Dante died, he would never go through the door, and it wouldn't matter if he had seen me or not. If Dante died, the circle we had sacrificed so much to close would break beyond repair, pulling the river—and everyone in it—into darkness.

I closed my eyes, but I could still see the way the torchlight lined the blade like fire on its journey downward. I could still see Zo's black eyes staring at me and the blood on his skin. I could still see Dante's unconscious body lying limp and still, the hilt of the knife standing upright in his chest.

The river shuddered and groaned with a sound like cracking rocks. I had been so close, but not close enough. One more moment, one more breath. One look. That was all it would have taken. Just one.

But Zo had timed his attack perfectly.

Dante hadn't seen me. The loop hadn't been closed.

And now Dante was dying and the river was spiraling into chaos.

✣

It wasn't until I felt Domenico's hand on my arm that I found my voice and my strength. Adrenaline shot through me like lightning, waking me up from my numbness.

"Let me go!" I shouted, struggling to break free from the blanket wrapped around me. "You don't understand. I have to go."

Domenico hovered nearby. "Be calm, my lady. You will be all right."

"No!" I managed to free my hand and I shoved hard at the guard holding me. "Let me go! He needs my help!"

The guard grunted but didn't budge.

"Who?" Domenico asked. "Who needs your help?"

I reached for the door, my fingers brushing the wood. "Dante," I cried. "He's been hurt. We have to help him. Please! Promise me you'll help him."

Domenico made a sharp gesture to the guard, who set me down and loosened his hold on me. "Tell me what happened."

I didn't answer him. As soon as my feet hit the ground, I bolted toward the door.

Crashing through, I headed straight for the third cell on the end. Dante's cell.

The guards followed behind me; I could hear them shouting at me to stop, but I didn't. I couldn't.

The prisoners in the other cells paced like wild animals, shouting and calling out. Hands reached out through the bars toward me, grasping, clutching.

I hit the bars of his cell hard. I wrapped my fists around the steel and shook, even though I knew they wouldn't bend or break. Dante's body lay in a lump on the cold floor. The silver hilt of the knife gleamed dully in the flickering torchlight. I tried not to look at where metal met flesh.

Looking over my shoulder, I saw Domenico trotting along behind the guards. "Open this!" I shouted. "Please!"

"Do as she says," Domenico ordered, motioning for the guards to step aside.

The head guard hesitated, his hand hovering by the ring of keys at his waist.

"Or will I need to report your disobedience to Angelo?" Domenico demanded, standing tall despite his small stature.

At the sound of Angelo's name, the guard jumped to action, shuffling through the keys until he found the one that opened Dante's cell.

The hinges squealed in protest as I yanked the door open almost before the guard had withdrawn the key.

The smell of blood had been masked by the other odors filling the dungeon, but now, so close to Dante's body, the coppery tang made my nose itch. A bright red stain spread over his chest; fat drops of blood made a puddle on the floor.

I knelt by Dante's head, trying not to think about another night when another Dante lay dying in my lap. My tears splashed on his closed eyes and trickled down his pale cheek.

I couldn't lose him. Not now. Not like this.

Domenico stopped short just inside the cell, surprise and horror mixing on his face at the sight of the knife and the blood. He turned back to the guard. "Fetch the physician. Now."

The head guard darted away. The other guards worked to quiet the other prisoners, checking the locks on the other cells, asking questions about who might have done this, and how.

"My lady?" Domenico took a half step forward. "Take heart, my lady. The physician is on the way."

"There's no time," I murmured. "It's too late. I was too late. Everlastingly too late."

The river creaked, bending around this unexpected rock that Zo had dropped in the flow. The pressure on me increased, a slow compression of my lungs, my bones, my heart. I grimaced and pushed the pressure back. I couldn't let it overwhelm me. I had work I needed to do.

Domenico knelt on the floor next to me. He peered closely at Dante's face, then up at me. "I met this man this morning," he said, astonished. "How is it possible that he is here, now?"

"It's not the same man," I said truthfully. This Dante hadn't had the experiences yet that would shape him into the man he would become—the man with whom I had walked in the Casellas' garden just this morning. In time, they would become one and the same, but for right now, they were two different people. And right now, I knew they both needed my help.

Dante had said that he could sense his other self, a distant echo that he couldn't ignore. I wondered if he had heard—or felt—the impact of Zo's blade. I wondered if, for a moment, that echo had sounded like a shout. Or a scream. I wondered if he was worried about the silence.

I made myself look at the knife and the blood that dripped from the wound. I had patched a hole in Dante's heart once already. I could do it again. I would. I had to.

"I don't understand—" Domenico started.

"I don't expect you to," I interrupted. I caught his gaze with mine and held it tight. "The world is full of impossibilities—some beautiful, some terrible—but sometimes, when you least expect it, they can become possible. Please, trust me, and don't interfere."

I couldn't go to the bank, not with Domenico watching my every move. I wasn't sure I even dared go halfway there as I had when I'd summoned the shell of time to trap Zo.

Maybe I didn't need to. Maybe, this time, the music could come to me.

I closed my eyes, striving to find my balance despite feeling like the world was unraveling around me. I breathed. I counted.

Blocking out the noise of the dungeon—the cries and moans—blocking out the smell—sweat, fear, blood—I focused on filling the emptiness inside me with stillness, with music.

I thought about the river, how it looked and how it felt

to stand beside it, but most of all, I thought about how it sounded. The rushing of the past to the future, the music of possibility, the language of time.

Faint chimes rang deep in my inner ear. My heart sped up in anticipation. I coaxed the music closer, listening for the melody I needed that could heal Dante. I heard the chord that would connect me to Dante, that would channel the healing power of the river to his heart.

Protect. Save. Heal.

I could almost see the words taking shape: the tall, straight lines, the bent and curved lines, the links that connected letter to letter and word to word, but unlike last time, when a bright star of healing had answered my call, this time there was only a glimmer, a spark. A deep shadow flowed behind the music, turning the words to darkness.

The river was sick as well, wounded and wavering. The music trembled, the notes struggling to stay together.

The spark wouldn't be enough. Not for a wound like this. But I didn't have the strength to demand what I wanted right now. I would take what I could get. I would do the best I could with what I had. I let go of the chord I wanted and focused instead on a single note, a single word.

Hold.

The note slipped free like a sigh. I opened my eyes a slit, squinting as the light I had summoned wreathed my hand. I had wanted a fierce golden blaze, a fire that could cauterize Dante's wound from the inside out, but all I held was a pale white flicker, no brighter than a wish.

Fear touched Domenico's eyes as he looked from me to my hand to Dante's chest.

I touched the cross-shaped hilt with my outstretched finger, and the light moved from me to the knife, making the blade glow an even brighter silver. The light pooled at the point of contact, capping the wound and holding it in place.

The flow of blood slowed to a stream, a trickle, a drip—a stop.

It wasn't perfect, but it would do. It would hold.

Dante was still unconscious, his eyes closed, his face pale. I was glad he hadn't woken up while I was in his cell. Yes, he needed to see me, but I didn't want it to be like this. Not under these circumstances.

I stood up, brushing away the dark smudges from my skirt. A coldness settled into the pit of my stomach, spreading out to encase me in a hard shell, like armor. "Don't move him," I ordered Domenico. "Don't touch him. Don't let *anyone* touch him but me."

"Where are you going?" Domenico asked, looking at me like I was part angel of mercy and part demon of destruction.

"Hunting."

As I ran across the plaza back toward the cemetery, I heard the echo of Dante's last words to me: *I'll be here when you get back.*

I hoped that was still true. I wanted to see him standing

at the edge of the cemetery, waiting and watching for me to return.

But Zo had somehow made it to the dungeon, and I feared he had only been able to do that because something bad had happened to Dante.

I bit back a bitter laugh. Something bad *had* happened to Dante—to both of them.

The world stuttered and jumped as the colors began bleeding into each other. The gray walls of the buildings around me brightened to a silvery sheen; the brown cobblestones under my feet darkened to a burnt orange. The blue sky overhead slid into a light shade of lavender.

The river twisted with a grinding sound like falling rocks.

The Cathedral of the Angels rose up before me. I dashed through the crowds of people in the plaza, none of whom seemed to notice that the world was falling apart. I knew they wouldn't, not unless the river fragmented beyond all hope of healing. If that happened, then for those people, it would be as if the world suddenly stopped. Cut off into nothing. It would be as though all of reality suddenly fell off a cliff into everlasting darkness.

I heard someone call my name and I looked around in confusion, shading my eyes from the light that suddenly felt as sharp as a blade.

Valerie ran toward me with Orlando close behind her.

Even at a distance, I could see the black smudges around her eyes, the pallor of her cheeks.

I stumbled to a stop.

"What are you doing here?" I asked as Valerie crashed into my arms.

"What are *you* doing here?" she replied, her voice frantic and shrill. "You're supposed to be with him. Who is with him if you're with us?"

I looked over Valerie's head at Orlando, who shook his head, struggling to catch his breath. "We were at Father's shop. Then she just turned and ran out the door." He frowned. "What *are* you doing here? Did something happen at home? Where's Dante?"

"Waiting for me by the cathedral—I hope." I kept walking toward the cemetery. There was no time to waste. Valerie clung to my arm; Orlando matched my stride. I quickly told them about my unexpected trip to the cemetery followed by my sudden trip to the dungeon and the violent appearance of Zo. When I explained how I had healed Dante in his cell—or at least held off his death—Orlando's face tightened and the lines around his mouth deepened.

"He'll be okay," I said, praying that I was telling the truth.

I rounded the corner of the cathedral and saw the iron gates of the cemetery rising up, black and tall. Orlando rushed through first, looking around quickly, but I slowed my steps, dragging my feet. I knew the truth. I had seen it the moment I looked through the gate.

The high clouds had vanished as though a strong breeze had blown them away. The air was still and heavy around us.

There was no sign of Zo.

There was no sign of Dante.

The cemetery was empty except for us—and the dead.

CHAPTER
25

"No, no, no! The story isn't supposed to go this way."
Valerie grabbed my arm. "The story is too dark. And the
darkness is hungry."

"Abby?" Orlando asked, returning to where I stood in
shock.

I couldn't speak. My whole being was consumed with a
single thought: He wasn't here. Dante wasn't here.

Our surroundings continued to dissolve into smears of colors. The buildings lost their outlines, and the ground, which
looked level, suddenly felt slanted.

Valerie whimpered. "The Pirate King was here. He stole
the River Policeman and now they are gone." She pointed to
the bone-white statues. "These are his people—his crew—but
they won't tell us anything. The darkness has taken all their
stories."

A low rumble ran through the ground beneath my feet.
The world blurred, rocking on its axis before settling back
onto its foundation. But when it did, everything looked a
little flatter, the edges more sharply defined. My head hurt
trying to assimilate this new two-dimensional reality into my

three-dimensional expectations. My heart hurt trying to assimilate the fact that one version of Dante was dying in prison and the other Dante had vanished.

Cracks appeared in the foundation of the cathedral, spreading upward like the thin veins in a feather or a leaf. Another shock wave rumbled deep underground, the stones groaning as they rubbed against each other.

"It's not safe here," Valerie said, tugging on my arm. "We should go."

"Go where?" Orlando asked.

They both looked at me for an answer, a decision. But I didn't know what to say. Zo and Dante could have gone anywhere. But where? When? The river had been rocked to its foundation. Where would Zo have dared to go with the river already so dangerously unstable?

I looked up in sudden certainty. "The only place we can." I grabbed Orlando's hand with mine, linking the three of us together, and then I traveled to the bank.

Where I saw Zo waiting for me.

❖

"So good to see you again, Abby," Zo said, a twitch pulling at the corner of his eye. A dark shape lay beneath his feet. Dante was sprawled on his back on the bank, his eyes closed and his breathing shallow.

I felt my breath freeze in my lungs. He was the mirror reflection of the Dante I had left behind in the dungeon. Both wounded. Both bleeding. But both still holding on to a thread of life.

"You'll have to excuse Dante's poor manners. He's not feeling like himself at the moment." Zo stepped over Dante's body and sauntered toward me.

I tensed. I wanted nothing more than to bolt past Zo and head directly for Dante's side, but Valerie tightened her grip on my arm and held me in place.

"Don't go near him," she growled. "He'll hurt you." She bared her teeth at Zo, glaring.

Being this close to Zo made the stubborn black spot in my mind flicker to life again. The link wasn't as strong as before, but I could still feel the dark buzz of it echoing through me. I pointedly ignored it.

Orlando stepped forward to block Zo's approach, his chin raised, his mouth a flat line.

Zo stopped, a grin blazing across his face like a scorch mark. He looked at the three of us, one after the other, before his gaze came to rest on me. "I know what you're thinking, Abby. You've always been so blessedly transparent. And the answer is yes, I know exactly what I've done—what I'm *doing*."

Now that he was closer, I could see that he had cleaned off most of the blood from his face, but dark smears lingered around his mouth and nose. He held his right hand carefully, his two broken fingers still bent at awkward angles. His dark hair hung in sweat-dried clumps, the white fringe making him look like an old man.

"How did you get away?" I asked. "Dante knocked you out at the cemetery."

"*Down*. Dante knocked me down, not out. And while he was right about how much it hurts to travel when you're in-jured, he was wrong about it being impossible." Zo shrugged, scratching at his arm. Bits of his skin flaked off under his nails. "I heard him tell you to go to the dungeon. It was a simple trick to be where I needed to be and do what I needed to do." His grin burned. "I didn't even have to do anything to Dante. I simply left. I knew he wouldn't follow me and risk seeing his other self in the dungeon." He tossed a sneer over his shoulder at Dante's prone body. "Coward."

"What about you?" Orlando asked. "Weren't you afraid to see your other self?"

Zo's grin grew even wider. "I wasn't in any danger. My other self was already in the machine. For once, the timing worked to my advantage."

Valerie shook her head, muttering, "You shouldn't have done it. You shouldn't have hurt the River Policeman."

Zo ignored her. "When I went back to the cemetery, I expected some kind of retaliation, but Dante was as you see him. Useless." Zo spat the word at Orlando, who bristled, nostrils flaring. "I didn't much care. It made it easier to bring him here. And, I'll be honest, it was kind of nice knowing I'd killed two birds with one stone," he said. "Or, in this case, two Dantes with one knife."

"He's not dead," I shouted. "Either one of them."

Zo shrugged as if that were a minor point.

"But why bring him to the bank?" Orlando asked.

"Why?" Zo repeated, astonished. "I knew if I brought Dante here, the rest of you would follow like obedient little sheep." He waved his left hand to include Orlando and Valerie. "And that's what I wanted. I wanted all of you to see this." He gestured toward the river and laughed, the noise falling somewhere between a sharp cough and a chittering giggle.

My stomach turned, both at the sound of his sickness and at the sight of the river.

The river was a disaster. The once-powerful flow of time now gurgled and spat, a foamy film popping on the surface like bubbles of tar. Streams and spiral eddies branched out in all directions, creating a swamp of gray and white, of past and present. The bank felt soft underfoot, almost like quicksand. A flat light hung low over the bank and flickered madly in random patterns that made my eyes hurt.

"Beautiful, isn't it? Take a good look, as I doubt there will be a repeat performance tomorrow." He laughed again. "I doubt there will *be* a tomorrow."

A stench rose up from the sluggish river, and sulfur coated my nose and throat with the taste of rotten eggs, making me gag.

Valerie covered her mouth, her skin turning a sickly shade of green.

"We have to stop this," Orlando said to me in a low voice.

"I'd like to see you try," Zo challenged with a hard glint in his eye. "The river—like so many of us—is dying." He turned on his heel and walked back to the edge of the river. "And if the river is going to die, then I want to watch every last moment of it, up close and in person with my good friends by my side." He nudged Dante with the toe of his boot; Dante's arm rolled off his chest, his hand landing next to the river.

I bit my lip. Dante's body was dangerously close to the border where bank met river. I knew that if he fell in, or if any one of the many silvery-gray threads of time touched him, he would be pulled back into the river. And if he was in the river when it stopped flowing . . .

I turned to Orlando, pitching my voice low so Zo wouldn't hear it. "You get Dante," I said. "I'll take care of the river."

Orlando had already taken two steps before I finished speaking.

I reached out for the music that I knew lived in the ebb and flow of the river. Even though it was slow and soft, I knew there was still power there.

"And, Abby?" Zo said without turning around. "If I hear one word—one note, one sound—from you, I swear I'll push him in." He wedged his foot beneath Dante's shoulder and lifted. Dante rolled even closer to the edge. A thread broke away from the main river with a snap, the grayish trickle heading for Dante's hand.

The words died on my tongue.

Dante suddenly moved, twisting back around to clamp his hand around Zo's ankle. "You do," Dante rasped, "and I'll take you with me."

Zo stepped back in surprise. Dante let go and rolled to his feet in a single fluid motion. He stayed hunched over, ready to move whichever direction Zo did.

Orlando skidded to a stop and attempted to grab Zo by the shoulders, but Zo ducked and backed away, out of reach of both brothers.

Orlando lunged forward and Zo danced away, preserving the distance between them.

Zo winced in sudden pain, pressing his hand to his head. A grimace pulled his mouth tight.

Dante touched his chest, rubbing a small circle over his heart. He tried to mask the ragged pattern of his breathing, but I could tell he was in pain. He and Zo glared at each other for another moment. Then, still wary and on edge, Dante and Orlando stepped back, their aggressive stance softening slightly.

It was as if an invisible barrier had sprung up between them, a line neither side was willing to cross just yet.

The river wheezed in the background, the last gasp of a dying man.

"Welcome back to the land of the living, Dante." Zo's laugh rasped in his throat. "But I'm afraid it's too little, too late. The meeting at the dungeon didn't happen. So even if you and your little friends think that you can somehow manage to heal the river, you've still missed your chance. You'll die in prison, or you'll be sent through the time machine with your sanity already broken. Either way, the river dies, and I win."

I took another look at the sluggish stream. The images that once had flowed past faster than the eye could follow now drifted in slow eddies, random moments out of focus and smeared with color. Even the music that I could hear in my inner ear sounded softer, slower. The words had lost their meaning, the sounds communicating only pain.

"But if the river dies, then so will all of us—including you," I said to Zo.

"Ah, that's where you're wrong. You are not part of the

river anymore, Abby. You and Valerie and Orlando are tied to the bank. Dante and I—well, we have gone *beyond* the river. As long as we are on the bank when time dies, we'll be just fine. We'll survive."

"But then we'll all be stuck on the bank—forever," I said. I swallowed hard and forced myself not to look at Valerie. I knew what happened to people who stayed on the bank too long. Zo and Dante didn't have that threat hanging over them anymore, but the rest of us did. I felt a little like we had just walked into a trap.

Zo shrugged. "It may not be the life I would have chosen, but it will still be a life. And it will still be *my* life." He rubbed the sweat off his forehead with the back of his hand.

"The Pirate King never forgets, and the Pirate King never regrets, yet we all will pay for the Pirate King's debts," Valerie sang in a small voice.

"Why?" Orlando asked. "Why do this, Zo? Killing the river . . ." He shook his head in confusion and horror.

"He tried to control the river and failed," Dante answered bitterly before Zo could speak. "He even tried to redirect it to be something else and failed. There was nothing left he could do but this."

Zo's face darkened, a snarl hovering at the corner of his mouth. "If I can't have it, no one can."

Valerie shook her head. "But it doesn't belong to you. It doesn't belong to anyone."

"I am a Master of Time," he shouted. "It *all* belongs to me!"

"No," Valerie said. "Not everything."

I caught her eyes and saw a bright light rising up in their

depths. I recognized that light. I'd seen it on occasion before when the old Valerie—the Valerie before the bank—had been able to peek through the cracks in her mind. For the moment, she was as sane as she had ever been.

Valerie started giggling, a slow hint of amusement that built into a loud laugh, shaking her shoulders and bringing tears to her eyes.

"Stop laughing," Zo snapped, his eyes flat with rage.

"I don't have to do what you say." Valerie wiped at her eyes and sauntered toward Zo, daring to breach the no-man's-land separating us. "The River Policeman said that the chains between us are broken. So, you see, you're wrong. Not every-thing belongs to you." She stood in front of Zo and spread her arms wide like wings. "I don't. And being free of you feels wonderful. In fact," she purred as she walked all ten of her fingers up the front of his shirt, "I think the only thing that can make me feel any better is this."

She pulled her hand back and slashed her nails across his cheek. Four red welts rose up in parallel rows. A hard mask descended over her face. "You hurt me." She cut him again, this time across his other cheek. "You hurt my friends," she said, all laughter gone from her voice. She grabbed his chin and forced him to look at her. "Never again."

Zo gaped at her, blood trickling down his face.

As Valerie turned and began walking away, she smiled at me in victory.

With her back to Zo, she didn't see him straighten to his full height. She didn't see him curl his one good hand into a fist. She didn't see him spring forward with murder in his eyes.

CHAPTER
26

I didn't stop to think. I shouted "No!" at the same time that Dante sprang forward, attempting to block Zo's attack. "Stop!" But this time, the word that came out of my mouth carried with it the shimmering chimes of the language of time, and the music that had been mumbling in the background came to life at my call.

Valerie had a moment to look at me in startled surprise before Orlando wrapped his hand around her arm and yanked her forward into his arms. He immediately pivoted on his heel, using his body and his back as a shield.

Dante swung at Zo, but instead of hitting muscle or bone, his fist hit the leading edge of a fast-moving, shimmering wall of light that rose up in front of Zo and wrapped around him, trapping him in a column of music and light.

Zo skidded to a stop, cautious and wary. He looked up at the open top of his prison where the ends of the strands of light wavered and rippled like a curtain.

Dante stepped back. He looked at me in surprise. "Abby?"

I shook my head. I hadn't intended for that to happen.

The column didn't seem as strong as the shell of time I had summoned back at the apothecary shop.

Zo kept his eyes on me as he touched the flowing light with a tentative finger. When I didn't react, he pushed his whole hand into the light. I could see the curtain bending around the pressure, and I knew it would break at any moment.

I may have stopped Zo, but I hadn't *contained* him.

"No!" I yelled. I couldn't let him break free. I reached for the music, for the stillness of time that had answered my call in the past. But the river was weak—fragile and spent. I knew I couldn't do it alone. "Dante, I need your help."

Dante was at my side in an instant. He took my hand. Our fingers touched, gripped, held.

Still, I hesitated. Dante was wounded; more, he was linked to his other self, who was also wounded. If I lost either one of them, I would lose both. Could I honestly ask him to risk his past and his future to help me?

Dante met my eyes, and I didn't have to say a word. "Tell me what you need," he said quietly, "and it's yours."

Power thrummed through him, and I felt more than saw a shimmering arc of light flare into life around the two of us, linked by our joined hands, from head to foot. It seemed to burn the brightest over his heart.

"*I* am yours," he said. "Always."

I nodded, grateful for Dante's strength and his unwavering belief in me. I concentrated, listening for the secret language of the music of time, drawing the notes I needed to me like filings to a magnet.

Contain. Imprison. Block.

As each word blended into the next, creating one unbroken sound, I could feel the music grow stronger around me. The roar in my ears sounded like a scream. I hoped it wasn't mine.

The curtain surrounding Zo flickered. He was almost through.

It wasn't enough. I needed more. We would need more in order to build a strong enough shell to stop Zo.

Remove. Erase. Eliminate.

I felt Dante gripping my hand tighter and tighter, but the feeling was a distant pressure buried beneath the endless stream of the river of time that flowed into him, through him, and onward into me.

Though I felt weak, I knew that Dante, as a Master of Time, could handle the raging influx of power I was channeling through him. The balance was perfect. Each of us relying on the other to provide support and strength. Each of us drawing power from the other, and both of us offering up the best of what we had.

I closed my eyes, focusing on finding the precise moment, the word that would resonate with enough power to stop Zo once and for all.

Finish.

The music responded with a sound like a lock clicking into place. I felt Dante spring the trap and heard the crash of the newly formed shell as it hit the ground.

The sound of Zo's rage roared past me like a train.

I opened my eyes to see that the curtain of light was gone,

replaced by a clear but solid wall that had arced up and over
Zo, trapping him in a thick shell.

Zo glared at us, pacing the small footprint of his domed
prison. His body shook with barely contained rage. He pressed
his hands flat against the curved wall. Without breaking eye
contact with us, he smashed his fist against the shimmering
wall that separated us.

Dante and I both winced, but nothing happened.

I think Zo was as surprised as I was. He shook out his
hand, looking from Dante to me with suspicion.

"What happened?" I asked. "Usually it hurts when he does
that."

Dante arched an eyebrow toward me. "Did you want to
feel the pain?"

"No," I said. "Of course not. Tell me what you did."

"Nothing," Dante said. "I was simply the catalyst for you.
What did you do?"

"Nothing," I echoed. "I just wanted to build another shell
to stop Zo. Maybe . . ." I frowned in thought, feeling my way
through a new idea. "When I created the shell at the apothecary shop, I did it by pulling some of the timelessness from
the bank. That's probably why Zo could hurt me. I was linked
to the shell because I'm connected to the bank. But this time,
we're on the bank, so maybe this shell was built by using some
of the time from the river."

"And so it's linked to the river, not to either one of us,"
Dante finished.

"Are you all right?" Orlando asked, coming up next to us.
Valerie clung to his arm and refused to let go.

I nodded. Exhaustion weighed me down. I leaned against Dante's body for support. He wrapped his arms around me, holding me up. I could feel his muscles trembling with the strain, and I hoped what we had just done hadn't aggravated his injury. Pressing my hand to his chest, I could feel his heart beat. Slow and steady, but, I feared, not as strong as before.

Zo tapped on the glass wall. "Abby? Dante? I just wanted to say thank you," he called out. "By linking this to the river, you've given me the key to escape. After all, I also know how to make the river do what I want."

And he opened his mouth, but not in laughter this time. In song.

Even though Zo didn't have his freedom or his guitar, even though he was sick and dying, he still had his music. And he still knew how to use it.

The song rose in volume, a strong melody, but there was something off about it. A sharpness to the notes that rendered it just this side of discordant.

As Zo's voice picked up the tempo of his song, he touched the interior wall and the shell bulged and flexed. He closed his eyes, clearly struggling to summon the power he had wielded so effortlessly in the past.

The music rumbled from deep inside his chest, rising in a tide of notes that spiraled up higher and higher, pushing against the inside of his prison. In some ways it was similar to the music I could hear running under the roar of the river, but in other ways, it was different. I had listened to the river's music and asked for help; Zo demanded.

I saw a hairline crack appear along the surface of Zo's shell, and I took a step back.

"Dante," I warned quietly, pointing out the black thread against the silver.

"I see it," he said.

"We can't let him escape," I said. The music pressed on me, a suffocating weight.

"I know."

"What can we do? I don't think I'm strong enough to build another shell."

Dante took a deep breath, looking at the three of us standing before him, then he glanced at the river. The silver had turned to the gray of a corpse. A few of the threads that had peeled away were going dark, the blackness slowly eating away at what little light remained.

Dante touched his chest just once. I mimicked the motion and touched the locket next to my heart. "Dante—" I started, but he held up his hand.

Stepping toward the crack in the shell, he simply said, "Count for me."

I felt tears well up in my eyes.

The poem he spoke was gentle and rhythmic, a soothing balm that ran counterpoint to Zo's driving song.

Zo opened his eyes; when he saw Dante standing outside the shell, his song shifted in intensity.

I counted out loud, trying to match the numbers with my heartbeat, even though I could feel my body and my breath racing. Orlando and Valerie stood beside me, and their voices joined mine in a chorus of counting.

Dante's voice remained slow and steady, but it sounded deeper, resonating with power. The poem seemed to take on weight, a shape and substance.

The flat light of the bank flickered, the pressure around us turning thick. The air crackled with the power that had been unleashed, humming with the power still to come.

The hairs on my arms and the back of my neck lifted as though lightning was about to strike. Still, I counted. One number after the next. After the next. I held Valerie's hand, and she still held Orlando's. I felt stronger knowing my friends were with me.

I fixed my eyes on Dante, listening to his words, his voice, with everything I had inside me. My body thrummed with the power of his poetry.

Still, I counted.

Zo clenched his jaw, struggling with the effort of forcing his song to bend the world to his will. He ground out the notes between his teeth, spitting them at Dante. But it wasn't enough.

The crack in the shell slowly reversed direction, filling in and smoothing over. The bulging wall stopped breathing and grew strong and straight.

Dante's words continued in an unending flow. The rhythms and rhymes created images in my mind: the winding path of a labyrinth, a spiral shell, stars scattered in constellations across a night sky, a half-sun, half-moon circle, an hourglass spilling sand with a sound like crackling flames.

I frowned. Something was wrong. The shell around Zo seemed smaller than it had been before, as though the space inside had been compressed. Zo's eyes were closed; he hadn't noticed the change.

Zo continued to sing, his voice as sweet as an angel's hymn, though the words he offered up were dark and dangerous. Promises of pain. Threats to bind, to bend, to break.

The shell of time shuddered. As I watched, it grew even more compact, ratcheting tighter and tighter in response to Zo's music.

My numbers turned to ash in my mouth and blew away as I exhaled a low moan. The bubble around Zo was about to burst—not outward, to release, but inward, to crush.

"Dante!" I called out, and I ran forward, grabbing his arm and pulling him away just as a horrible tearing sound came from inside the shell.

The ground beneath Zo's prison cracked open between his feet. A shimmering black light flowed into the confined space like water in a glass.

I gasped. A section of the river had broken free of the main flow and was seeping up through the bank, surrounding Zo's feet in a corrupted and poisoned puddle of time.

Zo's music suddenly stopped and he opened his eyes, looking around wildly. "What have you done?" he shouted. The walls had collapsed in on him so much that he had to hunch over, his back pressed against the curved dome. "Let me out!"

"I'm sorry," Dante said, shaking his head. "It's too late."

The gurgling river sloshed over the tops of Zo's boots.

Dante and I watched in horror as the outline of his boots softened and melted in the rising river, disappearing into a blackened emptiness.

"You built this, Dante." Zo pounded on the wall but nothing happened. "You break it."

"I can't," Dante said.

He turned frantic eyes to me. "Abby. You have to help me. You owe me."

The lingering touch of Zo's mind inside mine urged me to obey. The compulsion was still there, but Zo wasn't strong enough anymore to enforce it. I remembered the words to Dante's poem, the one that had restored my memories, and as I filled my mind with his words and his voice, the final drop of Zo's darkness vanished. Zo's hold on me was gone. "The shell is part of the river," I said. "We can't break it without breaking the river. It'll destroy everything."

"It's destroying me!" Zo shouted. The water level had crept past his ankles, rising up his legs, threatening his knees. Everywhere the river touched, Zo was being washed away. Erased. Unraveled.

He looked to Valerie, but she merely looked back, her face expressionless.

"Orlando—" Zo choked. "We were friends, once. Brothers-in-arms. We were the Sons of Italy. We were going to change the world. Remember how you agreed to follow me? You swore you would obey me." He banged his fist against the shell. "I order you to help me. Get me out of here. I promise, I won't hurt you. Any of you."

Orlando began shaking his head before Zo had even finished. "I know what your promises are worth."

Zo backed up as far as he could inside the shell, but it had shrunk so much in size that there was nowhere for him to go. He braced his good hand against the curved wall next to his head and lifted his foot above the level of the sludge, but when he raised his knee, his leg ended abruptly midcalf. There was nothing there. No blood, no wound. Just an emptiness intent on slowly devouring him.

His prison would become his tomb. And we all knew it. Especially Zo.

The rising water came faster and faster, a black hole of nothingness.

Knees, thighs, hips. Half of Zo was gone, buried in the water that he couldn't avoid, couldn't touch, couldn't escape.

Zo howled, his eyes wild and raw. His hand slipped off the wall, splashing into the water and disappearing in an instant. He looked down in stunned disbelief. His two broken fingers were gone, along with the rest of his hand. His arm ended abruptly at the elbow.

Then the panic that had burned in his eyes turned to anger and loathing. His mouth twisted into a snarl, his lips pulling back over his teeth. His face darkened.

"Go to hell," he growled. "All of you."

And then, in one swift motion, he dunked the rest of his body into the water.

A wave of black corruption closed over his head, swallowing him completely.

When the trapped river had reached the top of the shell, the shell bulged under the pressure, bending but not breaking. Then, with a sound like a pulled plug, the river water drained away down through the bank until it had vanished.

A deep silence settled over the bank.

Dante cautiously approached the empty shell.

"Careful," I warned.

He nodded, reaching out his hand. I caught my breath. Before he could touch the shell, however, the clear wall shattered, falling to the ground like so many shards of glass. One of them flew past me, cutting my cheek with razor precision, leaving behind a trail of fire that burned.

A blue-white glow surrounded each piece of the broken shell of time, flaring hot and then dying away, leaving behind only a shine like an oil slick and the lingering sound of music.

CHAPTER
27

I couldn't tear my eyes away from the spot where Zo had disappeared. The shock of what had happened hit. Hard. My mouth felt dry; my stomach tightened. My whole body shook.

Dante gathered me into his arms, pressing his hand to the back of my head.

"Did it work?" Valerie asked in a raw voice. "Are we safe?"

"It's finished," Dante said. "Zo's gone. And he's not coming back."

Valerie sighed in relief.

"Are you all right?" Dante asked me, rubbing his hands in circles over my back.

I nodded, but I wondered how much of that was the truth and how much was a wish. I feared the image of seeing Zo unraveling from time would haunt my dreams forever.

"You might be all right," Orlando said, "but what about the river?" He pointed to the ground at our feet. The once wild rush of time was barely flowing anymore; the river that had once been as clear as glass had darkened to a clogged green and black and gray.

The stench had grown worse, the sulfur now layered with rotten meat and burned flesh.

"But Zo's dead," Valerie said. "Why didn't the river get better?"

"Because the loop still needs to be closed," Dante said, his face drawn and pale. "And if I die—either here or in the dungeon cell—the loop will never be closed."

I frowned. "I thought it was too late to go back to the dungeon. Do you think, if the other you sees me there, that will be enough to fix the river?"

Dante paused in thoughtful stillness. He studied the river as though he could see through the murky shadows all the way to his other self. "I don't think so," he said quietly. "A wound of this magnitude will require something of equal magnitude to heal it."

"Like what? It's the end of time, Dante. How can we fix it?" I coughed, feeling the thick air weighing down my lungs like lead.

"I know how," Orlando said softly.

I whirled on him, a sharp hope burning in my heart. "What? What can we do?"

"Not *we*," Orlando said. Then he pointed at my chest. "*You.*"

"Me?"

He nodded.

"You have a plan," I stated.

"I have an idea," he corrected. "It might not work."

"Whatever it is, I'll do it. I can't simply stand here and watch the river die."

"It means traveling to a place where no one has ever been before," Orlando warned.

"Where?"

Orlando pointed upstream. "There."

"What's up there?"

"The beginning of the river," Orlando answered, his voice calm and controlled.

Fear pulled into a tight knot in my stomach. "What?" I breathed.

"If you walk back along the bank far enough, you will find the point where the river begins. And when you do, you will be able to heal the river."

The idea staggered me. "Why would you think I could do something like that?"

"Because you can speak the language of time," Dante chimed in.

Orlando lifted one shoulder in a shrug. "I saw what you did to heal Dante. What you did to Zo. It has to be you, Abby. You're the only one of us who can." He looked back at the sludge that crawled past our feet. "And it has to be now."

I swallowed. "But, once I get there—assuming I even can—what am I supposed to do there? Heal the river? I wouldn't even know where to start."

"You'll know," Orlando said.

"How can you be so sure?"

"Dante said that we all have a gift here on the bank. Mine is that I can see the light of the river. I have seen that same light around you. The river wants your help, my lady. It needs it."

"You can do it, Abby," Valerie said.

I looked up at Dante's face. His clear gray eyes were steady and sure. That small smile that was mine alone curved his mouth.

I swallowed and held out my hand to Dante. "Will you come with me?"

"Yes." His answer was instant.

"Will you catch me if I fall?"

"No."

I pulled back, surprised. There was a finality in his voice I hadn't heard before. And then what he had said hit me, making me blink in confusion.

"What? Why—?"

Dante cupped my face with his hand and brushed his thumb across my lips, silencing my questions. "You will not fall. You will not fail." He brought his other hand up to frame my face and looked directly into my eyes. "I won't catch you, Abby, because I won't need to. You were always meant to fly."

I caught my breath, feeling a swell of emotion rising up inside me. I nodded, then turned to Orlando.

"I'll do it. I promise."

I hugged Valerie and Orlando in turn. Then I took Dante's hand in mine and together we walked along the edge of the river, heading upstream, heading into the darkness. Heading toward our future.

CHAPTER
28

The darkness is absolute.

She remembers how the sky above the bank had turned black once before, when the river had been redirected and washed away her family, her past, her life. But this is even darker than that. This blackness breathes. This darkness waits.

She is only a thought. She is a shape without form. She is drifting without moving. She is alone in a darkness that is as tight as a drum, taut as a string.

The tension hums, not quite a sound. Not quite a song.

There is only the waiting. Endless waiting.

She wonders if this is the end. Or the beginning.

After a timeless moment, she realizes this is the *before*.

The moment *before* the beginning. This is the anticipation.

This is what they came for. To find this moment, here at the beginning of forever.

And she knows *exactly* what to do.

Her mouth shapes his name, and her mind rings with re-membered echoes. His voice, dark, like chocolate, but also light, like citrus. There are no words yet, just sounds inside her mind, just feelings inside her heart: a laugh as bright as a wish, a sigh as soft as a secret. A kiss as solid as a promise.

She conjures him. Claims him. She speaks his name: "Dante."

The darkness shivers with the sound. A silver chime blooms like hot glass, turning the darkness from black to gray. Like smoke. Like stars.

The space next to her suddenly has depth and dimension.

And he is there. Present in a way he wasn't before.

She is holding tight to his hand, the only point of contact in this terrible void. He is close. She can feel the heat from his body. She inhales the scent of his hair, his skin. She listens to his body move, breathe.

The glassy chime ripples outward, resonating through the darkness, reaching . . . searching.

And then, his voice . . .

"Abby."

The two sounds meet, merge. They are one. They are whole.

And she feels herself take shape in the darkness, take on depth and dimension.

They are no longer lost in the darkness. They are united. They are together, one harmonious whole.

The sounds of their names spiral upward together, filling the blank spaces around them with light and life and music.

The gray lightens to gold, smoky and muted, but light nonetheless.

She can see more of him now. But only an outline.

He is darkness against the emerging light. His hair is the black of closed eyes at midnight. It is swept back from his face, curling against his neck. His skin is shadowed and smooth. His body is long and lean, the shape of strength, of contained confidence.

There is a power in him. She can feel it pulsing through their linked hands. She is surprised to realize that the power is in her too. It feels the same as his, but different. As though they have both taken a small part of themselves and, in sharing it with the other, have been rewarded with more than before.

She feels hollowed out, but not empty. She is filled with the echoes of her name from his lips. She is amplified.

The music grows, each note high and clear.

He takes her hands in his. His thumbs rest in the curve of her palms.

She looks into his eyes, and she can feel her heart beating in her chest, each thump as bright and sharp as a diamond. Her breath is like silk in her mouth. Her lips are dry, but her bones feel like water.

Anticipation burns.

He moves closer. She moves to meet him.

Hands and fingers intertwine. Her head rests on his shoulder—the perfect height. His hands support her back—the perfect balance.

They breathe together. Their hearts find the same rhythm. The music encircles them, envelops them, encases them. She feels like dancing.

She can feel the *rightness* of the moment.

It is time.

She steps back and withdraws, from next to her heart, a second heart. *His* heart. A silver shape that had been cracked open.

The heart is empty except for a small key, yet she still feels a heat spilling over her fingers like blood.

She listens to the music that has been born into the space around them. She can speak this language, this music, and so she listens and finds the words she wants to say.

Whole. Together. Renewed.

The note she speaks is all of these words, but mostly it is *love.*

When she looks down at the heart in her hand, the fractures have disappeared. The cracks are no more. The heart is whole again. Better—it is as though it had never been broken.

She smiles. She knows how important it is to be whole before you can be healed.

A light shines from inside the heart. A brightness that pushes back the darkness like the birth of a star—or a sun.

She holds the locket in her hands and then presses it against his chest. The light penetrates into his skin, casting a glow from the inside. It centers over his heart, rises up behind his eyes.

She speaks once more. The music of healing. The sound of permanence. The words of strength.

The light flares—inside and outside his skin—and she knows it is done. He is healed. He is strong. Better—it is as though he had never been broken.

And then, from out of the distant darkness, a wave of light.

As the light crashes down around them, sparking like fire,

flowing like liquid, the music spirals upward on a rising scale, each note glittering with promise and potential.

The light fills the void. There is a bright point on the ground next to where they stand. The point lengthens, elongating into a line that grows thicker and wider until it is a trickle, a stream, a river that flows away into the distance, burning away the darkness as it goes.

It is instantaneous, yet she can feel the exact moment when it happens. The moment when the river of time begins to cut through the bank on its way to the future and forever. When timelessness changes into time.

But before the first tick of time registers, before the river moves with the first ripple of life, in that moment when the light is the brightest, she sees him clearly—who he was, who he is, who he could be. She sees all of him, and he is beautiful. She knows in that moment that she holds his soul in her hands, in her heart, and she is honored by his trust.

She looks deep into his silver-gray eyes and willingly offers her own soul to him in exchange.

She places the newly mended, perfectly whole silver heart in his hand.

His eyes glisten like stars, like moonlight. He lowers the locket into the river. It slides into the light; he lets it go. As he withdraws his hand, a ripple extends outward from his touch. And another ripple extends beyond the first. And then a third follows the second. And on and on and on until the river of light is teeming with ripples, bubbling with life.

It has begun. And there is no calling it back, no stopping it.

The time that pours into the river is forever protected.

The music is everywhere. The music is everything.

The song the river sings is filled with the language of *life* and *love* and *light*.

He takes her into his arms.

Being held by him is as soothing as ice on a hot day. As comfortable as silence.

As intimate as a midnight kiss.

This is what they came here to do. To restore the balance. To cleanse and be cleansed. To be united and reunited, bound together by a power that will last beyond time.

He places his hands on either side of her face. His eyes are endless pools of light, shimmering with the glow of new-born stars. His mouth curves in a small, secret smile.

"Make a wish, Abby," he says.

She thinks about those words for a long time. Does she know what to wish for?

Yes. She does.

She holds it in her mind, looking at it from all angles. Past. Present. Future.

It is a good wish.

Her wish flies from her lips in a language both specific and sure. A chime of *release*. Oh, but there is so much more. She knows it will be years—centuries, even—before the last piece of the wish comes true, but she knows that it will. And she knows that it will be happiness when it does.

When he kisses her, it feels like the first sunrise, it feels like the beginning of her life, it feels like coming home.

CHAPTER
29

"Abby?" a voice summoned me up from the depths of a dream.

The dream was of light. A bright, white, energizing beam of light that seemed to shine straight up from the deepest part of the river and turned the whole world electric.

In the center of the light stood three people I immediately recognized: my mother, my father, and my sister.

They were whole; they were together. The light spilled down the river, washing over them, carrying them downstream. But I wasn't worried about them. I knew in that strange logic of dreams and wishes that my family was restored to me. They were returning home to their proper place and time.

I opened my eyes to find myself cradled in Dante's arms, my legs stretched out on the ground. My toes looked oddly far away. I wiggled them to make sure they were still attached. My whole body was filled with light, buzzing with a warmth that felt like white gold.

"The river?" I whispered through lips parched dry as bone. "Is it safe?"

Dante nodded. "Yes, Abby, it is."

"What about you? Are you safe?"

This time when Dante nodded, tears slid down from his eyes. "Yes, I am."

I touched one of his tears in amazement. In all the time I'd known him, I had never seen him cry before.

"Thank you," he said. "For healing my heart. For making me whole."

"And the you that Zo stabbed in the dungeon . . . ?"

"His heart is whole as well."

"So, is that it?" I asked as the first hint of exhaustion crept closer. "Are we done? Can we go home now?" Knowing that my family was back where it belonged and that Dante—all of him—was whole was a huge weight off my soul.

Dante smoothed a stray curl away from my eyes. "Almost."

I looked up into his face. "Let me guess. I still need to go to the dungeon, don't I?"

"If you wouldn't mind," Dante said with a small grin. "I know I would really appreciate it."

"Not at all," I answered, reaching up to wipe away his tears. "In fact, nothing would make me happier."

✤

I left the bank and returned to the dungeon. Part of the wish I had made at the beginning of time was to have a second chance to make this moment right.

In the third cell along the wall, right where he was supposed to be, was Dante. No wound on his chest, no scar to cover a broken heart. He was unmarked and untouched. And with the river cleansed and stable, he probably had no idea anything remarkable had even happened. For him, time had simply flowed as straight and steady as it always had.

As I stood in the doorway, my hand on the frame for balance, I thought that Dante looked exactly as he had when I had glimpsed him in the river and urged him to survive by counting. Still young, still innocent—but with an inner core of strength that would shape him into the man he would become past the door, past the bank.

He was still my Dante, forever and always.

My eyes met his, and I felt like the summer sun had crashed into the dungeon, bringing with it light and life and warmth. I was filled with the promise of a future flowing straight and clean.

I held his eyes with mine for one more moment, and then I smiled.

I saw Dante's knees buckle a little. He clung to the bars, using them to hold himself up. The torn cuffs of his sleeves slipped down his arms and I saw that his wrists were still bare of any chains.

The river clicked into place with a sound like a door closing.

I wanted to laugh and cry and dance all at the same time. It was done. I had seen and been seen.

The river was whole. Dante was saved. And the circle was finally closed.

"Is it my turn?" Valerie asked Dante as Orlando and I joined them by the fireplace hearth later that night after Alessandro and Caterina had said good night.

Orlando leaned against the wall, his arms folded across his chest, watching intently.

"Yes, it is your turn," Dante said gently as he helped her sit in a chair. He knelt in front of her and took both of her hands in his.

I sat next to Valerie, so close that our knees touched. My palms felt cold and sweaty, and no matter how many times I swallowed, I couldn't quite clear away the cotton in my mouth. Dante said that now that Zo was gone and the river was back to normal, healing Valerie would be easy. I hoped he was right; I hoped she would let him.

"Are you going to sing to me?" she asked, a worried line creasing her forehead.

"No, it's not a song," Dante said.

The line deepened. "Is it a story?"

Dante shook his head.

Valerie relaxed. "Oh, good. I have all these songs and stories in my head and I'm tired of listening to them all."

"I'm sure you are."

"At least the stories have happy endings again. For a while there, I was afraid they would all end in darkness." She turned to look at me briefly. "I'm glad the darkness didn't get you."

"Me too," I said.

Dante glanced at me, and I nodded. He took a deep breath

and squeezed Valerie's hands. "I have a poem for you, Valerie. It's a very special poem. Are you ready?"

Valerie shifted in the chair, straightening her spine and settling her shoulders. Then she tilted her head to the side, first right, then left, like a bird. "Something's missing." She frowned. "I'm missing something that belongs to me."

"What, Valerie?" I asked. "What are you missing?"

"My key." She twisted around to pin Orlando with a narrow gaze. "I gave it to him." Untangling her hand from Dante, she held it out toward Orlando. "I need it back now, please. I need to be whole before I can be healed. You do still have it, don't you? You promised to keep it safe."

"If I promised, then yes, I still have it." Orlando reached behind his back and then held his closed fist over her open palm. He spread his fingers. Nothing fell out of his hand, yet Valerie made a scooping motion, bringing her palm directly to her chest and pressing the invisible key to her heart. "Thank you. I feel better already." She smiled at Dante. "Okay. *Now* I'm ready."

Orlando leaned forward, his eyes bright with curiosity.

Dante's voice started out small and soft.

> *Your heart beats,*
> *The heat now departs.*
> *The light remains to fill your mind.*

Valerie closed her eyes, her face smooth and calm.

> *Your mind rests,*
> *The test now behind*
> *The past is present is future in your eyes.*

Dante continued, his words picking up speed and rhythm.

> *Your eyes clear,*
> *The fear now dies*
> *To return, to hurt—nevermore.*

Tears trickled from beneath Valerie's closed eyes, streaming down her cheeks.

> *Nevermore to be broken.*
> *Nevermore to be lost.*
> *This poem now spoken*
> *Forevermore pays the cost.*

Dante's voice faded into silence, but the echo of his words lingered in the space like smoke from a blown candle. I could still feel the rhythm of his words thrumming in my bones.

We all looked to Valerie, waiting, watching. She tilted her head down, her hair falling forward over her face.

I held my breath. The silence stretched out until it reached the corners of the room. I gnawed on my fingernail, chanting a one-word prayer in my mind: *Please.*

"Dante—" I whispered, but he held up his hand to hold my words. He kept his focus fixed on Valerie.

I glanced at Orlando, but he shrugged his shoulders and remained silent.

Valerie lifted her head. She looked first at Dante, then up to Orlando, then finally at me.

And I could see clearly in her blue eyes the shining light that I had been missing for months. The light of her old self.

"Abby?" she said, her voice trembling ever so slightly. Her tears continued to fall, and when she said my name, my tears spilled over as well.

With a wordless cry, I hugged her to me.

Dante rocked to his feet and stepped back to stand by his brother.

"Valerie!" I said her name over and over. "You're back. Are you better? You are, aren't you?"

Valerie nodded. "I missed you so much. It was like I was trapped behind a glass wall and no matter how much I yelled or screamed, no one could hear me or see me or reach me."

"How do you feel now, Valerie?" Dante asked.

In an instant, she had released me and wrapped Dante in a hug. "Thank you," she said. "I can't thank you enough. You are the best River Policeman ever."

A chill seized my tongue. Even Dante looked a little startled.

Valerie didn't seem to notice. "That's what I called you— *before*. Isn't it?"

"You remember that?" I asked carefully.

"I remember everything," she said.

"Everything?" Dante repeated. "I'm sorry. I didn't intend for you to."

"I did." Valerie patted Dante on the arm. "When you gave me that poem, I felt like there was a moment, there at the end, when I could choose. I could let everything go, start over clean, like none of this ever happened. Or I could remember everything—the good and the bad."

"There was something good about what happened to you?" I asked in amazement.

She tilted her head in thought. "My dreams were surprisingly vivid, which was kind of nice. And knowing my friends cared enough about me to try to save me—even when I felt like I was beyond saving—is worth remembering. And that moment when I was able to stand up to Zo—that felt really good." She smiled at me, a vintage, authentic, honest-to-goodness Valerie smile with all her spark and sass. "Given the circumstances, I think I made the right choice, don't you agree, darling?"

I laughed and wiped the tears from my eyes. "Yes, I agree completely."

CHAPTER
30

The courtroom was dark and empty. I shivered and rubbed at my arms. Valerie was the first one to enter the room, but that was because she didn't have the same kind of memories of this place that I had. Or that Dante and Orlando had, for that matter; they both hung back, hovering close to the walls, unwilling to draw too close to the black hourglass door that stood in the dead center of the room.

Dante's trial had been held earlier that day; his sentence had been carried out. His future had forever changed.

Domenico had let us into the courtroom, warning us to be quick. Before the door closed, I saw Dante pull Domenico aside, whisper a few words, and then hand off a small packet of letters, which the clerk stashed in his ever-present satchel.

I quickly lit a handful of candles, enough to see by, but not enough to be seen from outside the room.

"This is . . . amazing," Valerie murmured, her low voice carrying in the quiet room. She peered closer at the door, standing on her toes to examine every corner, every carving, every circle and crescent and star. She looked over her shoulder at Dante. "And you did this? By hand?"

"Didn't you see it before?" Orlando asked. "When you came through from the other side?"

Valerie shook her head, her fingers hovering over the swirls as though she could read the lines like Braille. "The other times I've been around the door, I wasn't quite myself. Plus, nothing beats the original. It looks brand-new."

"Careful," I warned, stepping up next to her. "Don't touch anything."

"I am being careful," she said, her mouth turning down in the slightest of pouts. "Honestly, Abby, I'm not crazy." Then she winked at me. "At least, not anymore."

Dante joined Valerie and me by the door. We stepped aside so he could face his creation one last time. His eyes roamed over the wood, and I saw his hands twitch as though remembering how it felt to touch the surface, to carve it and change it and make it his own. Then his fingers curled into a fist, the gold chains rippling, and I knew he remembered, too, how he had been honed and changed and claimed in turn.

"It's strange," he said quietly, awed and a little afraid. "I'm inside the machine. Even now, I can feel that connection—that echo of being in two places at once. I'm walking and counting and wondering what exactly it is that I'll see on the other side."

Orlando spoke up from behind us. "You'll see me. I'm waiting for you on the other side. That's what you said, right? That I found you there and saved you."

Dante turned his back to the door. Without a word, he reached out and pulled his brother into a crushing embrace.

"I won't say it enough then, so I will now. Thank you. Thank you, my brother, for being there for me—always."

Valerie walked all the way around the door, examining it from all sides. "Dante, seriously, this is a work of art. It's a masterpiece. It needs to be framed or something."

"It needs to be destroyed," Dante said firmly.

"What?" Valerie said, spinning on her heel. "But I thought this was the way home."

Dante shook his head. "This is not your door. This one is ours." He nodded to Orlando, who stood a pace away, his face pale in the candlelight. "This door won't work for you. I don't know what would happen to you if you tried to use it, and I don't dare find out."

"What about Orlando? Will it work for him?"

I didn't know what to say.

"Orlando *is* coming with us, right?" Valerie asked. "I mean, we can't leave him behind."

Orlando and Dante and I shared a look.

"We're leaving him behind?" Valerie said in shock.

"We have to," I said, though it broke my heart to hear the words come out of my mouth.

"No." Valerie folded her arms and frowned. "That's not fair."

"It doesn't have to be," Orlando said. "It only has to be what it is."

"But that doesn't make any sense," Valerie protested. "Why can't he come with us?"

"Because you and Abby are going back to the time where you belong. Orlando is already where he is supposed to be.

He only traveled a short distance through time." Dante hesitated. "And also because the door works in pairs. The other
half of *this* door was destroyed when I came through it from
the bank after Zo and Tony and V." Dante avoided Orlando's
gaze, keeping his attention on Valerie. "Once we destroy this
one, Orlando will have nowhere else to go."

"Then why are we here?"

"Like Dante said: to destroy the door," Orlando repeated,
a tone of finality in his voice. And relief.

Wiping away angry tears, Valerie aimed a kick at the door.
The thud of contact sounded like striking rocks. "Fine. So how
do we break this?"

Dante and I had talked about this moment, discussing
what our options could be, but no matter what solutions we
suggested for this impossible problem, there was clearly only
one choice.

I stepped toward the door and hesitantly touched the
gleaming brass hinge that bound the door to the frame. The
metal seemed to quiver under my fingers, shivering like a
struck chime. A trill of music sounded on the closed side of
the door. I listened to it fade away, wondering if the other
Dante walking in the darkness had heard it, and if so, if it had
brought him any comfort.

I felt for the small depression in the center of the middle
square and pushed. The hinge sprang free with a nearly silent
click. The notes from the chime grew louder, playing a melody that resonated through me. With swift and sure motions,
I collapsed the hinge down to its compact size. I could feel
Orlando's eyes on me, curious and cautious.

"Did you design it to do that?" he asked Dante. "It's ingenious."

"The door won't work without the hinge," Dante said as I cradled the mechanism against my chest.

"So, that's it?" Valerie asked, looking from me to the door. "We came all this way to do that?"

Dante shook his head. "This is only the first part."

"What's the rest?" Valerie asked.

In reply, Dante turned to me. I had said that I wanted to be the one to do this, but now that the moment was here, I wasn't sure if I could follow through.

I took a breath and crossed to Orlando. "You were there for me when I came through the door. You were there for me when my memory was stolen by Zo. You have been there for me every step of the way along this crazy, unpredictable journey. I would have been lost so many times over without you, Orlando." I looked down at the hinge, my reflection distorted by the flickering candlelight and the polished brass. "And I hope you can be there for me one last time."

Orlando's eyebrows drew close together. "What is it?"

"For this to work—for all the circles to be locked closed and for the river to stay clean and stable—we need someone to guard this hinge until . . ." I choked on the words. How could I ask the impossible of Orlando? Of Leo? He was my friend. But he was also the only one who could do it. "Until we meet again more than five hundred years from now."

I heard Valerie gasp. I felt Dante's hand touch my back lightly in quiet support. But my eyes were locked on Orlando, waiting to see his reaction.

He didn't move. Not to breathe, not to blink.

"That is . . . a long time," he said finally.

It was my turn to remain still. The hinge felt like a thousand pounds in my hands.

"If I say yes," he offered up his words carefully, "then we *will* meet again."

The way he said it made it sound less like a question and more like a wish. But I knew Orlando never made wishes; they were too painful.

I nodded. "Yes. We will meet again. We will actually become good friends."

Orlando's gaze flickered to Dante so fast, I would have missed it if I hadn't been watching for it.

I swallowed, watching as Orlando's decision moved across his face, the small lines of hope that had appeared around his mouth fading as his expression settled into a fixed determination.

He straightened his spine, tall and strong like a soldier preparing for battle or a lover fortunate to have been chosen. He placed his hand over his heart and bowed low. "I will help you however you need me to. I am yours to command, my lady."

"Thank you, Orlando," I said, touching his shoulder as relief and sadness flooded through me. "I will honor your vow."

He stood quickly, moving his fingers from his heart to his lips before holding his hand out to me, palm up.

I met Orlando's blue eyes, and I felt a spark of memory ignite inside me. We had stood like this once before, back among the scorched bones of the Dungeon, where he had—then, as now—sworn an unbreakable vow to me.

I knew what to do. I placed my free hand atop his, feeling the hard calluses on the pads of his fingers, the heel of his palm.

"There will come a time when I will need to ask you to honor this vow," I warned.

"Then I will wait for the day, my lady of light," he replied with dignity, "when I can fulfill my promise to you and make you proud of me."

"Oh, Orlando," I said, throwing my arms around his neck, the hinge still clutched in my hand.

He carefully folded his arms around me, hesitant at first, then tighter when he realized I wasn't going to let go right away.

"I will always be proud of you," I said in his ear. "Always."

Dante cleared his throat and Orlando let go of me, stepping back and taking the hinge from me in the same motion.

"Keep it safe," Dante said. "We're all counting on you."

"There's one more thing," Orlando said quietly, his gaze fixed on the hinge in his hands. "Before we destroy the rest of the door."

"What is it?" I asked. We had asked so much of Orlando; if there was something we could do to make his burden easier, I wanted to know about it.

"Valerie chose whether or not to remember," he said. "I want the same choice."

"You want to remember this?" I asked.

"No." Orlando looked up, not at me, but at Dante. "I want to forget. I don't want to remember this."

"Orlando—" Dante started, but his brother held up his hand.

"You said that in all those years to come, I'll help Zo survive his journey. Zo and Tony and V. But I've seen what he did. I know how much he hurt all of you." His eyes met Valerie's. "I know how this story ends. And if I remember all that, can you still be sure I'll help him? For this to work—for all the circles to be locked closed and for the river to be clean and stable"—he echoed my own words back to me—"I *can't* remember everything."

"He's right," I said. "His knowing his future could change it irrevocably. We can't risk it."

"But he can't forget everything," Dante countered. "He needs to know about the hinge—what it's for, why it's important."

"Then let me remember that, but take the rest." Orlando shook his head. "If I have that many years ahead of me, knowing the truth will kill me. You can't ask that of me." He swallowed. "Please don't ask that of me."

"You have to do it, Dante," Valerie said. "It would be a mercy."

Dante paused, looking to me for guidance. I nodded.

"All right," Dante said, though his gray eyes had turned dark with pain. "If that's what you wish."

My chest felt tight. Dante had worked so hard to reconnect with his brother, saying good-bye like this must be agony.

Dante tightened his mouth into a thin line, gathering the stillness that helped him transform his poetry into power.

Valerie hugged Orlando, long and tight. "I'll miss you. Be safe, okay?"

When she let go, I touched Orlando's arm. "It's going to be all right," I told him. "Do you trust me?"

His fingers curled around the prongs of the hinge. His eyes held mine. He nodded.

"Then don't look back," I whispered. Standing on my toes, I kissed him on the cheek, something soft and sweet. Something to remember me by—for as long as his memory would last.

Dante gestured for me to step back. Then he reached out to grip his brother's wrists, his strong hands covering the black chains. "Are you sure?" he asked one last time.

"I trust you," Orlando said, closing his eyes. "Do what must be done."

With a last look at me, Dante opened his mouth, and, to my surprise, the poem he offered to Orlando was one I knew. One I had heard in a long-ago dream. One I myself had recited on stage at the Dungeon.

> *In the darkness of night,*
> *demons strut, taunting, goading.*
> *In the light of day,*
> *angels sing glorious songs.*
> *In the time in between,*
> *We live our lives alone and searching.*
> *And sometimes, softly,*

You understand damnation.
All is forgotten, all is lost,
All but forgiveness
And the memory of her kiss.

As the last word trailed off into silence, Orlando collapsed to the floor.

I gasped and jumped back. Valerie grabbed my arm.

"Is he okay?" I whispered.

Dante nodded, looking down at his brother with both sorrow and pride on his face. "When he wakes up, he won't remember us being here. He'll know he needs to leave—and quickly—and he'll take the hinge with him. Domenico is waiting outside to help Orlando start his new life far away from here."

"Then we've done all we can do," I said.

"What about the door?" Valerie asked. "We can't leave it like this, can we?"

Dante roused himself from his thoughts and picked up a lit candle from the table. He held the flame close to the black wood until the fire caught the carvings, outlining them with light. I wouldn't have expected ordinary wood to catch so fast, but then again, this was no ordinary door. Before the door could entirely burn, however, Dante extinguished the fledgling fire. Smoke rose from the burn marks left behind. The markings that had once covered the center of the door—the point where the hourglass lines almost touched, the spiral nautilus shell, the hidden heart—had burned beyond recognition.

"Is it done?" I asked.

"It's enough," Dante answered, his words clipped. He blew out the candle and dropped it on the floor in front of the door that had been scorched black and stripped bare.

The time machine had been broken, and all that remained was a slab of wood in an empty room.

"Let's go home," I said. "It's time."

CHAPTER
31

The three of us stood in a row on the bank. The river looked like polished silver, a ribbon of light, smooth and sleek.

"Are you sure this is the way home?" Valerie asked.

"It's the only way," I said.

Dante inched the toe of his boot closer to the river, catching the reflection of time, which made him shine.

"And why are you doing this instead of him?" Valerie said to me but nodding toward Dante.

"Because she can speak the language of time," Dante answered for me. "And I can't."

"I wish I had gotten that gift," Valerie said. "It sounds way cooler than what I had."

"I don't know," I said. "You could see the connections between people and all the variations of their stories. That's pretty good, too."

Valerie shrugged. "I guess." She turned to Dante. "You're coming with us, right? I'm done with all this leaving-people-behind nonsense."

"Yes, I'm coming," Dante said. "But I can get where we're going myself."

"Oh, that's right. Big bad Master of Time can come and go as he pleases," Valerie teased.

Dante laughed. "I'm going wherever Abby is going."

"Where *are* we going?" Valerie asked.

"Back to the Dungeon. It's where we left from; it's where we'll return to." I looked across the river to the opposite side. I hadn't realized I had bitten my lip until Dante spoke quietly.

"The bridge isn't coming," he said quietly. "Neither is the door."

"I know. But I can't help wondering . . ." I sighed, my eyes scanning the empty bank one last time. "It's just that you're a Master of Time—and I'm not. And I won't be."

"Things will work out, Abby. You'll see." His small smile lit up his eyes.

"So, is there a magic word you have to say?" Valerie asked me. "Open sesame, or abracadabra?" She waved her hand in front of her with a flourish.

I laughed. "Nothing so grand, I'm afraid."

"Then what are we supposed to do?" she asked.

"This," I said. I took Valerie's hand in mine and spoke a single word: *home.*

And then we both stepped into the river of light.

✦

I noticed the smell first. A faint whiff of old smoke. The smell of something that had burned and long since fallen to ash.

"Abby?"

I turned around at the sound of Leo's voice.

Leo stood on the bottom step of the Dungeon, his face alight with joy.

Seeing him there gave me a sudden shift of déjà vu. It hadn't been that long ago that I had been in this very same Dungeon with Leo, saying good-bye to him before I walked through the door into the past. And it had been just a heartbeat ago when I had said good-bye to Orlando before I returned home to my future. And yet, after all the winding ways of the river, here he was, a little older, a little more worn, but still the same man. The same blue eyes, the same smile.

His eyes went immediately from me to Valerie to Dante. Without a word, he crossed the basement, heedless of the remaining debris that still littered the floor, and pulled his brother into an embrace.

I felt tears in my eyes, grateful that both men had survived their impossible journeys through the hourglass door.

They both carried scars—some visible, some invisible—but there were no more secrets between them. Now they were just two brothers, reunited after centuries apart, ready to face the future together as family.

Valerie sniffed a little as well, wiping away tears from her own eyes.

Leo turned to us, but he kept his arm slung around Dante's shoulders. "I'm glad to see that you are okay—both of you."

"It's good to be home," Valerie said. "And back to being myself. Though it will also be good to *actually* be home." She touched me on the arm and smiled. "Call me later? There's a hot shower and a long nap I've been neglecting for far too long." She lifted the hem of Caterina's green dress and headed for the stairs, pausing only long enough to give Dante a hug and kiss Leo on the cheek. "Dante, darling, can you give me a ride home?" she asked. "I'd rather not walk if I don't have to."

Dante glanced at me, and I nodded. "Bring back the plans, if you can. I'd like to take care of this as soon as possible."

"Of course," he said, gesturing for her to lead the way out of the basement.

As they disappeared up the stairs, I heard Valerie's voice singing back down, "What the Pirate King caught, isn't what the Pirate King thought, and we all have escaped from the Pirate King's plot." Her laughter was free and easy, and it made me smile to hear it.

"Is she going to be all right?" Leo asked.

"I think she will be just fine," I said.

Leo cleared away a space on the block of white-and-gold marble that remained beneath the high window. We sat down together; I kicked my heels against the stone, trying not to look at the door in the center of the room, but it was hard to ignore. The second time machine door. The one both Valerie and I had passed through—the only one still standing. The last of its kind.

"It's good to see you again, Abby," Leo said quietly. "It's been a long time."

"Not that long," I said. "Considering."

"It's been a long time since we've both been able to speak without secrets. Back then, you knew my future, but couldn't tell me about it. And, for a time here, I knew *your* future, but couldn't tell you about it."

"You knew I would go through the door? That when I went back in time, I would meet you on the bank? How?"

He nodded. "Because I remembered meeting you there."

"But you said you wanted to forget. And Dante's poem . . ." I furrowed my brow, thinking, and then understanding dawned. "Dante's poem was selective. Like you wanted."

"I remembered forgiveness," Leo said. "And you. I always remembered you."

"So, you've known all along what was waiting for me?"

"No, not everything. And not all at once." Leo looked down at his hands. "My memories came back slowly, over time. Usually, when important events happened—when I found Dante on the bank, when you asked me to fulfill my vow—I would remember other pieces of the puzzle. I couldn't always see how they fit together, or what kind of picture they would make, but I always knew that somehow, some way, you would be there on the bank when I needed you." He finally looked up at me, his blue eyes calm and steady. "Just as Dante needed to see you at the dungeon door, I needed to meet you on the bank. You have done more good than you know, Abby. For both of us."

A lump surfaced in my throat. "I'm sorry you had to wait so long before I could say thank you. For everything."

Leo's smile was a little crooked. "What's five hundred years or so between friends?"

I didn't want to ask it, but I had to. "What about Zo? I saw him be unraveled from time, but I still remember him."

Leo nodded as though he had expected to have this conversation with me. "I remember him too. That's because what happened with Zo once before still happened this time too. All of it. Zero Hour. The door. His efforts to destroy the river. It all happened."

"The good *and* the bad," I murmured.

"Exactly." Leo took my hand. "Zo may still be a part of your past, but he will no longer need to be part of your future. That is the good that came from closing the loop. Know that, whatever Zo did, it was his choices that led him to that final moment of destruction on the bank. He's gone. And you and Dante are not. Your future is your own again. And I consider that to be a happy ending to the story."

I agreed. I looked up as Dante descended the staircase into the basement.

"I'm sorry I wasn't back sooner. Your mom wasn't quite sure what to make of my request." Dante held up the scuffed binders containing the time machine blueprints. "I told her it was for a project we were working on."

My heart ached to see my family, but I needed to take care of this one thing first. I turned to Leo, answering the question on his face with a smile. "Then I think we're ready."

The three of us gathered around the blackened door frame. The time machine door hadn't changed, but I had. I ran my eyes over the frame, lingering over the markings that both V and Dante had made.

"Are you sure about this?" Dante asked me. "It's your door, after all."

"Positive. It has to go."

"Once it's destroyed, no one will be able to travel through time." I knew Dante wasn't advocating keeping the door; he only wanted to make sure I knew the ramifications of my actions. He didn't need to worry, though, because in this case, I knew *exactly* what I was doing.

For this to work, everything had to go.

"That's the plan," I said.

"And speaking of plans," Dante started. He set the binders against the door. Then he reached into his back pocket and pulled out a matchbook, which he handed to me.

I nodded and accepted the matches, and the responsibility. Dante was right: this was my door. Crouching down, I struck the first match and lit the edge of the papers. The flame caught immediately, the paper turning black and curling into hot ash.

The three of us stepped back as the entire set of blueprints burned red-gold.

The flames spread to the door, racing up the frame and along the front. Heat crackled out toward us in waves. I expected the room to fill with smoke, but the fire seemed to burn inward, consuming and claiming the wood.

I lifted my hand to shield my eyes from the light.

The fire flashed white-hot, then burned out into blackness.

I lowered my hand, blinking until my vision returned.

The markings on the door had been burned away. The air smelled charred, but also clean. I could hear the distant sound of chimes ringing softly, slowly, before they drifted away into silence.

I closed my eyes and listened to my heart. The sound was

even and regular. I took in a deep breath, feeling free from any lingering pressure in my lungs, my blood, my body. I could feel my hope turn to joy.

"Is that it?" Leo asked.

I touched his arm. "How do you feel?"

"Honestly? I'm relieved." He kicked at a lump of gray ash. "I'm glad it's dead."

"No." I increased the pressure on his arm. "How do you *feel?*"

"I don't understand," Leo said, glancing over at Dante.

"What are you driving at, Abby?" Dante's eyes were curious.

"When we were at the beginning of the river, you asked me to make a wish."

Dante nodded. "I thought it was so that you and Valerie could come home."

"It was a little more than that."

"Was it to close the loop?"

"That was part of it," I hedged.

"What *did* you wish for?" Leo asked, a tremor in his voice.

I turned to look at him, my eyes catching his and holding steady. "I wished that, once the doors were destroyed and the river was safe, those of us who were bound to the bank would be released. That we would be returned to the river."

All the blood drained from Leo's face, leaving his skin as white as his hair.

"Abby—" Dante started.

"The pressure, Leo. The pressure that tied you to the bank. It's gone. Can't you tell?"

Leo covered his eyes with his hands. His shoulders shook with his ragged breathing.

Dante went to his brother's side. "Leo?" he said, his voice low. Then he cleared his throat. "Orlando?"

At the sound of his true name, Orlando di Alessandro Casella looked up at me with tears in his eyes. He pressed his hand to his heart, then brushed his fingers to his lips and held out his hand to me, palm up. "I have done what you have asked. I waited and watched. I have honored my vow, my lady."

I stepped forward and placed my palm on his. "You have done all I have asked of you and more. Your vow is fulfilled."

Orlando drew in a shuddering breath, one that shook him all the way to his toes.

"No more needing to move between the river and the bank," I said. "No more needing to keep the balance. No more rules. Not for you or me or Valerie. No more endless years of being alone or saying good-bye. We are free from the bank. Free to live our lives like normal people again."

He couldn't speak. He simply swept me into his arms, his tears streaming down his cheek and onto mine.

"*Your* future is your own again too," I whispered in his ear. "You can live your life, Orlando. The way it was meant to be."

Dante looked at me, a little awed. "Thank you, Abby," he said, his voice thick with emotion. "Thank you for setting my brother free."

CHAPTER
32

The backyard was filled with the noise of joy. I closed my eyes and let the sounds wash over me: the wind through the trees, birds singing. A car driving past, the stereo thumping out the familiar bass notes of a Darwin Glass song. The high giggle of kids, followed by the rhythmic running of footsteps along the sidewalk. A sprinkler clicking on in the neighbor's yard and water hissing into the air.

I opened my eyes and slowly turned in a circle, taking in a sight that I had feared I would never see again. My family, together again, together forever.

Dad stood by the grill, tending to a row of hamburgers and a trio of hot dogs with a pair of silver tongs in one hand and a bottle of cream soda in the other. He was wearing his "Kiss the Cook" apron that made appearances only for backyard barbecues.

Mom and Cindy Kimball were relaxing together on a picnic bench, talking while a swarm of children—mostly from the Kimball clan—played a spirited game of hide-and-seek. Hannah and her friends Cori and McKenna were sitting back-to-back-to-back under a tree, swapping books and arguing about who was the best Brontë sister: Charlotte, Emily, or Anne.

Jason had brought Natalie to the party, but he seemed reluctant to leave her side for very long or even let go of her hand. She beamed under his constant attention, and it made me smile to see them so comfortable together. Valerie had gathered a lapful of flowers and was teaching Jason's younger sister, Bethany, how to make a daisy chain to wear in her hair.

Tears filled my eyes. I couldn't quite believe it. After all this time, I was back home. Back where I belonged.

The summer light felt so good on my face. I couldn't stop smiling.

"You look happy," Dante commented, coming up behind me and sliding his hands around my waist.

"I am happy," I said. "We started the party without you, though; you're late."

He pressed a kiss behind my ear. "Sorry."

I turned in Dante's arms and looked up into his face. His gray eyes were clear and bright. A smile tugged at his lips. He wore a pair of jeans and a crisp, new T-shirt with the word *CREW* written across the front. He looked surprisingly comfortable and casual. He looked like he belonged to this time and place now. Like he belonged with me.

"Fancy shirt. Where'd you get it?"

"This?" He looked down at his chest. "Oh, the community theater is staging *Hamlet* at the end of the summer and I signed up to help build the sets." He shrugged. "I do have some experience with building things."

"And with live theater," I reminded him. "Do they need any backstage help?"

"Maybe. I saw Valerie had signed up to audition for the role of Ophelia. Do you think she can handle it?"

"Probably better than anyone else I know," I said.

Dante surveyed the crowd with a smile. "Looks like everyone is here."

I looked around at the happy chaos. "They don't remember," I said softly. "It's been almost a whole week since we got back and no one knows that anything strange happened."

He traced a gentle finger across the thin scar that marked my cheek—a remnant of our final confrontation with Zo. "Of course not. Why would they? As far as anyone here knows, the river has always been flowing straight and true. Which is exactly how it should be."

I leaned into his embrace. "How can I ever thank you, Dante?"

He grinned and tightened his hold on me. "You can start by joining me for lunch. I'm starving."

That night I dreamed of the bank. It wasn't a traveling sort of dream; it was more like a memory, or maybe even a wish. In my dream, I stood in the center of a wide open plain. I could almost feel the sand beneath my bare feet. The sky still felt unnaturally close but less oppressive than usual. I felt oddly protected instead of threatened.

The light no longer carried the weird shade of all-time and

no-time. Now it reminded me of the moment just before the night decided to transform into dawn. I could almost feel the possibility of a sunrise on the horizon.

Almost. Almost.

I could hear the sound of the river roaring and crashing and hurling forward on its unstoppable journey. It sounded like the ocean, like blood, like breath.

It sounded like music.

A shadow rose in the corner of my eye. Turning, I saw a black door, freestanding in its frame, appear on the bank. It was the only spot of color for miles around. It looked like a hole cut into the world. Though I knew the door was closed, the blackness seemed to open wide, a yawning mouth of endless night waiting in this strange place of endless time to swallow the unwary traveler.

But whatever fear I had once had for the hourglass door was swept away in a rising tide of peace. Without its counterpart, the door was just a door. It no longer had the power to hurt me or the ones I loved. It would no longer rule my life.

An impossible breeze began blowing behind me, a push of warm air that tossed my hair over my shoulders, across my cheeks, into my eyes. The sand beneath me swirled up in golden spirals, miniature tornados that raced across the bank toward the door.

The river hummed and thrummed.

The bank hissed in the breeze.

The sand built up against the front of the door, mounding higher and higher like desert dunes.

The breeze turned into a gust into a wind into a storm.

The door trembled and shook.

An enormous clap of sound rang through the emptiness—a shot, a shout. Or a door slamming closed.

A crack bisected the door vertically, a clean slice that traveled straight through the hourglass carved on the front.

The two halves seemed to hang in the air for a moment, and then, with a rumbling sigh, the door dissolved into uncountable grains of sand.

And then the river washed them all away.

EPILOGUE

he Cathedral of the Angels was built during the fifteenth century and has remained a classic example of Italian Renaissance architecture to this day." Our tour guide gestured for the group of fifteen students wearing matching coats with the Emery College name and logo stitched across the breast to follow him deeper into the cathedral.

When Emery College announced that its winter study-abroad session would be held in none other than Florence, Italy, I was the first person to sign up—after Dante. An entire month of touring the finest museums, eating at the finest restaurants, and studying the classics? And doing it all with a gorgeous Italian man by my side? Sounded like a dream come true to me.

"Abby, Dante," my classmate Katie whispered. "Are you guys coming or what?" She motioned us closer, but Dante slowed his steps, lingering in front of the painted mural on the wall.

"We'll catch up," I said, waving her to go ahead and rejoin the group. We wore the same coats as the rest of our classmates, but Dante and I were the only two students who had been to the cathedral once before, though no one but us knew that. The cathedral was still as breathtakingly beautiful as the first time I'd seen it, but the building certainly showed its age. In my memory, the stones were perfectly cut and polished, not crumbling along the edges. I remembered the gold leaf gleaming, not flaking off and looking tarnished.

While Dante studied the mural, I wandered back to the alcoves where a row of statues stood. I was curious to see if what I remembered had remained.

The angel was still there.

His wings were still curved, but the tip of one had been broken off completely. Tears covered his cheeks, but now he also wept from a crack that cut across his eyes.

He had been through a lot and had suffered considerable damage at Zo's hands, but I was glad to see that he hadn't been broken beyond saving.

Dante came up behind me and read the small plaque that had been posted on the wall next to the angel. "St. Raphael. Patron saint of—among other things—apothecaries, blind people, happy meetings, travelers, and young people."

"Sounds like my kind of angel," I said. I bumped Dante's shoulder. "I think he looks a little like you."

He leaned close. "Then you should know that he is also the patron saint of lovers."

I turned and tilted my face up to meet his. "Is he, now? So, would he approve of us kissing in a church, do you think?"

"Absolutely." Dante cupped my head in his hands and kissed me with an intensity and a focus that he usually re-served for when he was working with time.

"Abby," he said, when he finally released my lips. "I have something for you. A present, a secret, and a promise."

My eyes fluttered open. "A present? What's the occasion?"

"The one-year anniversary of our first kiss."

I smiled. "Um, I hate to break it to you, but in that case, you're two weeks late."

"Would you believe me if I said that I had lost track of time?" Dante held me loosely around the waist and arched an eyebrow.

"Maybe," I granted. "It depends on the present."

He reached into the pocket of his Emery College coat and withdrew a small golden box, which he carefully placed in my palm.

I looked at him, then down at the box. I lifted the lid and gasped.

Nestled into the soft interior was a beautiful, golden oval locket. Like my long-lost, heart-shaped silver locket, this one had been carved and marked on the outside. But the markings on this locket clearly displayed the initials *D* and *A*, intertwined until it was impossible to see where one letter started and the other letter ended.

"Do you like it?" Dante asked quietly. "I made it especially for you. I've been working on it for a long time; it took me longer to finish than I thought. I'm not as good working with metal as I am with wood, but—"

"I love it," I interrupted, unable to take my eyes off the locket.

"Good," Dante said. "And now, the secret. I have been

meaning to tell you this for some time." He hesitated, then said carefully, "I'm no longer a Master of Time."

"What?" I looked up from the locket in surprise.

"I gave up being a Master of Time," he said again.

"What are you talking about? When?"

"The day you set Orlando free. I told you then that destroying the door would mean that no one would be able to travel through time again."

"I didn't think that included you," I said. "Otherwise—"

"Otherwise, what? You wouldn't have burned the door? You would have stayed a prisoner to the bank? You and Valerie and Orlando?"

I didn't answer; I didn't have to. I brushed my fingers over the initials on the locket. My thoughts whirled in confusion. How had I not known? I thought back over the last few months, searching for a clue or a hint that Dante had been changed. But there was nothing unusual. Dante was in all my memories, right by my side. And in all that time, I didn't remember him ever traveling to the bank or along the river. It hadn't seemed suspicious; I'd assumed he hadn't traveled through time because he didn't have to anymore. I hadn't suspected it was because he *couldn't* anymore.

Dante brushed his hand across my cheek. "Abby, it was my *choice*. Your wish may have set you free, but the power of it touched me as well. And the same way Valerie and Orlando had the choice to remember or to forget, I was given the choice whether or not to stay a Master of Time. It was a simple choice. Leo has seen five hundred years pass by, but we both know the toll it took. I didn't want that to be my future. I didn't want to live alone—*forever*. So when I had the chance, I took it. I chose to let it go."

I couldn't speak. Dante's sacrifice was too monumental; I couldn't wrap my mind around it.

"Why didn't you tell me when it happened? Why did you wait until now?"

"Because I wanted it to be here."

"In Italy?"

Dante shook his head. "Here, at the beginning of this new part of your life." He covered my hands with his. His gray eyes shone silver, endless and bright. "Because the truth is I chose *life*—with all its unpredictability and impossibilities and messiness, and with all its joy and beauty and love. I chose *you*, Abby. I want to be where you are. I want to be by your side as your life unfolds. Not as a Master of Time who will never age, never die. But as me—as Dante di Alessandro Casella." His voice dropped and his hands shook ever so slightly. "If you'll have me."

It wasn't even a question. It wasn't even a choice.

"Yes," I said, and when the word passed my lips, I felt like I was standing on the summer sun.

We both looked down at the locket in my hands. "Dante and Abby. Always and forever," he promised.

"Always and forever," I repeated.

"Until the end of time." Dante fastened the golden locket around my throat, his fingers lingering on the faint scars on my skin. He slid his hands along the curve of my neck, and I turned my face to his, finding his mouth, claiming it with my own.

It was a kiss that shook me to my very soul. Somewhere deep inside me, I felt like a door had been flung open, spilling out white light, welcoming me to my new life. A life where I could be with Dante and together we could follow our dreams wherever they took us. Together. Always and forever.

I couldn't wait to go through that door and see what waited for me beyond.

I knew I would never let go of this moment.

And I would never look back.

ACKNOWLEDGMENTS

Writing this trilogy has been a life-changing experience. I learned so much about myself, my craft, and my dreams that it would take another book to list them all. I also learned a lot about the people around me—namely that they are incredible, wonderful, devoted people who care about me more than I deserve and who love this story almost as much as I do.

Believe me when I say that the story of Abby and Dante *would not* have been possible without the help and support and encouragement of the following people:

The heroic team at Shadow Mountain, headed up by the Fantastic Four: Chris Schoebinger, Emily Watts, Richard Erickson, and Tonya Facemyer.

My stalwart writing group: Tony, Crystal, Annalisa, Pam, and Mary. And a special thanks to Heidi Taylor, who has read this book in more stages and more times than anyone else (maybe even me!) and who never failed to give me honest feedback when I needed it (and endless encouragement when I needed that, too).

My alpha and omega readers: Ally Condie, Becca Wilhite,

Josh Perkey, Karen Hoover, Cindi Cox, Valerie Hill, Anna Maxwell, and Jackie Benack. Every single one of them gave me amazing feedback, asked the best questions, and helped make this book soar.

My mom, who, during my darkest days, reminded me of the light inside of me and helped me remember what I needed to know.

My brother, Dennis, whose help included writing a draft of the ending of this book for me as a birthday present. After careful consideration, I ultimately didn't use his suggestions, though perhaps the story would have been more exciting with a zombie attack after all . . .

And I can't forget two men whose words of wisdom rang through my house night after night as I wrote and rewrote this story: Tim Gunn: "Make it work!" and Steve Holt: "Steve Holt!"

And finally, to the love of my life, Tracy. There are a million and one reasons why I dedicated all three books to him and he knows all of them. This time, though, it's for encouraging me to blow up the Buy More. For making me lose Lucky Strikes. And for knowing when to catch me when I fall, and when to let me fly. This victory is for you, Tracy. I love you— always and forever.

READING GUIDE

1. Zo uses music to strip away Abby's memories, while Dante uses poetry to bring them back. Are there songs, poems, or other works of art that have changed the way you thought or felt?

2. Orlando struggles in the story with wanting to be a hero but feeling like he has failed. What does it mean to be a hero? Which characters demonstrated heroic qualities in the story?

3. The characters all have different gifts and talents that work on the bank: Dante can see the future; Abby can speak the language of time. What are some of your gifts and talents? How can you use them to help other people?

4. Trust is an important element of the story. What is the relationship between trust and love? Can you trust someone you don't love? Can you love someone you don't trust?

5. The idea of not looking back is repeated through the book. Are there dangers to looking back too much? What about not looking back enough?

6. When Orlando says that he doesn't like to make wishes and be reminded of what he doesn't have, Abby says that he has missed the whole point of wishing. What is the point of wishing? What wishes have you made? Have any of them come true?

7. Dante writes letters to his parents to help reassure them that he will be all right and to tell them the good parts of his story. If you wrote a letter to your parents, what would you say?

8. Zo says that "a promise is a promise, no matter who makes it." Is he right? Are there some promises that should be broken?

9. Dante tells Abby that forever is a blank canvas and a place where creation happens. What do you think forever looks like? If you could live forever, what would you do?

10. Dante asks Abby, "What did we come here for if not to change things?" Is there anything about your past you would like to change? If given the choice, would you choose to accept the good *and* the bad? Would you choose to remember, like Valerie? Or choose to forget, like Orlando?